The Close of the Age

An End Time Novel

Dr. Lily Corsello

Contents

THE CLOSE OF THE AGE

Night came on with gathering gloom,
For a world now death silent as a tomb.
The bright stars, this night, had hidden themselves from view;
Can these all be portentous signs of something new?

Earth's armies had marched forth from the ages,
With her philosophers, poets, dreamers, and sages.
Her people had built empires of old,
And now, alas, earth—left in the cold!

Widespread, famine, illness, and disease,
Had now deprived and replaced her ease,
That even Nature revolted with earthquake, fire, and tempest,
What had been her pure, grand, and ideal bequest.

The world is approaching the darkest hour of the night,
As visions of paradise are burst upon man's sight.
O mystic, glorious night, what do you hold?
I detect in the air—a great event shall man behold.

Strike of the clock—the twelfth hour!
A shout is heard with a blaze of power.
A heavenly trumpet sounds to glory,
As a choir of angels sing a new story.

O men of little faith—you are asleep;
Remember you have an appointment to keep.
Ah, but look, those faithful are ready and awake

With glory, blessing, and heaven to make.

Then were they drawn away from earth's crust,
In the twinkling of an eye by a Great Magnetic Gust.
The graves were opened, and the dead stirred;
Yet all this took place without one word.

And so, the history of the earth had turned the final page,
For this event was the Close of the Age.

by Lily Corsello

Chapter 1
The Dawn of a New Day

Elira leapt from her light beige couch. A flash of the brightest light she had ever seen lit up her entire living room. *What was that? A huge bolt of lightning? Hmmm…but no thunder. Never seen light like that before! Such a piercing bright white. Different. What could that have been? Interesting, and yet…* She caught herself speaking out loud, "Strange!"

Elira stroked back her bright auburn hair. "I've got to see what's going on here!" she mumbled to herself as she looked up at the sky outside her window. She shrugged her shoulders. *The sky doesn't look any different.* She glanced downward at the street and sidewalk. A few of her neighbors had come out, pointing upward and talking to one another.

Elira grabbed her phone and texted Ben. "Did you see that?!"

Her boyfriend, Ben, shot a quick text back. "Yeah! That huge flash in the sky just now? Freaky!!! What was it?"

"It doesn't feel right! What do you think it was?"

"Dunno!" Ben answered by text, "I did hear some cars crashing in the street and some screams happening at the same time. It kinda sounded like a bomb went off not far from here. Maybe at the airport?"

"A bomb? Really?! This is creeping me out!" Elira texted quickly as she glanced out her window again and exhaled. More neighbors outside now, all looking shocked and some crying. She typed a final text. "I'm going downstairs to see what's up. I'll keep you posted if I hear anything." She rushed out the door with her phone in hand.

"OK. me, too! Love you!"

The elevators were jammed packed. Everyone had the same idea. Elira stood by nervously for an elevator, but then headed for the stairwell. A few more residents were already headed down the stairs, anxiously talking about the strange light and the chaotic noises of things colliding either in the sky or on the streets.

When Elira opened the door onto the sidewalk in front of her apartment building, she heard a neighbor say to others around her, "I hear there's been some wild event where several people in our area are missing! It seems to have happened at the same time the very bright light flashed."

"Yeah!" said another. "There's also lots of bad car accidents that have occurred on some surrounding streets! Did you hear all those crashes?"

Another lady sighed. "This can't be happening! Are we under an attack of some kind?!"

"Lemme look," Elira spoke up. "I haven't seen any notifications pop up on my phone yet." Just as she turned her phone upright to look, it buzzed. *What??? This is insane!* She read out loud to the others around her, "Major plane crashes have been reported from multiple cities around the world."

"Is this another 9/11?!" one man asked, shouting out for all the group to hear.

Some nearby neighbors came running up to ask for help for

victims in crashed cars over on the next street. Elira heard sirens and saw the chaos of first responders trying to make their way to people who were injured or killed. As she scanned the pandemonium around her, she looked in disbelief at a helicopter tail sticking vertically up behind a home close by. Apparently, it had taken a nosedive into a yard. *Absolutely insane...what's going on?*

Elira texted another short message to Ben, but it didn't go through. She tried again. No go. *I'm just going to get into my jeep and drive to him. I need to be with Ben,* she thought.

BACK AT HIS APARTMENT, Ben grabbed his car keys. No doubt Elira must be freaking out. He texted, "I'm on my way to you." The text couldn't get through. "What the heck?" He tried again. "Ugh! How ridiculous!"

Suddenly, Ben heard a loud knock at his front door. He opened it to find Elira, tears dropping out from her blue-green eyes and running down the soft blush of her cheeks. She hugged Ben tightly and kissed him, his sandy-colored hair brushing across her face.

"Hey, I was about to speed off to your apartment to check on you!" Ben said. "I knew you'd be scared to death."

"That's exactly why I'm here. I wanted to check on you! What's happened? Heard anything new or official?" Elira asked.

"First, I want you to know that I love you, and I'm so glad you were not one of the ones who disappeared," Ben said as his caramel-colored eyes also started to tear up.

"I love you, too, Ben! And I'm so happy you're here!" Elira plopped onto Ben's blue-gray sofa, her eyes filling again with tears of joy—this time for the fact they were spared from any of the mayhem that was happening. "I've only received one notification about plane crashes that have been reported around the world, and I think my phone service is dead!"

"Me, too! Ben replied. But I'm so concerned for Mom right now! I was able to reach Dad by phone for just a few minutes before we got cut off, and he was beside himself with deep concern over the whereabouts of Mom. He couldn't find her anywhere in the house. All he found were her clothes, watch, and wedding band on the floor of the bathroom."

"What? Only her clothes and jewelry? That's cr-a-a-azy! I heard my neighbors reporting there were missing people there, too, but I didn't hear about their clothes or jewelry. Has he asked his neighbors and friends what they've seen?"

"He did ask a few, but no one could tell him anything about Mom. None of her church friends could be reached. No one near their home knows what happened, and they are fearing the worst for all those missing!"

"From what I remember, your mom is a staunch Messianic Jewish believer, isn't she? And didn't she have some rather fantastic beliefs about the end of the world?" Elira asked as she rolled her eyes.

"Yeah, she did, and she'd speak about it often to Dad and me. She said that all believers in Jesus would be gathered up one day to meet Him and they would turn up missing all over the world. I'm pretty sure she called this event the Rapture, but even speaking about this now makes me wonder whether this is not just some hairbrained scheme perpetrated by a bunch of Christian believers!"

"Well, you don't have to worry about that. You and I know there can only be a scientific or political explanation for all this —nothing more! After all, being in engineering technology with the DOD has made me believe in facts only."

Elira got up and walked toward Ben's TV to pick up the remote. *How could anybody take this whole affair to such a crazy level as Ben's mom believed? What everyone needs now is to keep their heads on straight.*

"Ben, I think it will soon come out that a mass disappearance of people was caused by some planet's orbital pull or some vortex like a black hole. I also suspect that such an extraordinary phenomenon like this could've only been caused by self-serving foreign governments seeking distraction, control, and power over our world."

Elira tightened her grip on the remote and thought again. *Things always have a rational, scientific explanation, or it would be absolute absurdity and there is enough of that going around! We need to keep our heads on straight!*

Ben sat up in his chair and nervously rubbed his forehead as he listened carefully to everything Elira was saying. "What you're saying makes sense. Not only are you beautiful; you're so intelligent and knowledgeable about world events, especially working for the Department of Defense. You're right! I cannot sink into Mom's wild beliefs, but somehow, I have an eerie feeling about all this. What if she were right?"

"Well, Ben, clearly your mom is not the only one gone, and she loves you and your dad very much," Elira soothed. "I'm sure our U.S. government will get to the bottom of this, and all the missing people will be able to be returned to their countries and families once again. I can't imagine a so-called Messiah that would separate families like this and allow for such emotional pain and heartache. Your mother's beliefs were extreme and deranged. You can't believe that this is what has happened!"

"I don't really know what happened, but Mom definitely warned this day would come! She said this event would be followed closely by the 'Great Tribulation,' where there'd be a lot of suffering and persecution like never experienced before. But...okay, Elira, I'll try to stay rational and push all this stuff out of my mind and wait to hear and see what happens in the next few days."

Could Ben possibly be entertaining what his mother believed as fact? Could this be the Ben she knew and loved, the successful self-made businessman, who's always analytical and an incredible entrepreneur? This is crazy talk!

Elira placed the remote down. "Well, staying rational is key! I'm sure a thorough investigation is under way; so, let's go check on your dad."

Chapter 2
The New Normal

Elira quickly got into Ben's car without thinking about how she looked, whether her clothes matched, or her hair was brushed. No time for that. Ben was already in his car and had waved at her to hurry in. Together, they drove to the other side of town to Ben's dad's home where they found neighbors gathered outside in wide-eyed wonder and confusion.

Ben's dad stood clearly bewildered with hands to his head among his neighbors who milled about as if dazed. Several spoke at once, describing what they had seen. There was very little to tell except for the blinding, radiant white light that came in a flash and then the aftermath of overwhelming darkness and loss. It had happened in the blink of an eye.

"Are you okay, Dad?" Ben asked.

"Son, fifteen people have disappeared in this neighborhood alone and one of them is your mother!" His body twitched as he ran a hand through his disheveled, short, salt-and-pepper colored hair. "She is vulnerable and easily influenced. I can't imagine what has happened to her or where she is. I'm so worried! What can I do? What will I do without her?"

"All is not lost, Simon." Elira patted him on the back. "We will eventually hear an explanation from the authorities, and these people will be found."

"I hope they'll be found alive and well," Simon said, "but I'm scared that the worst has happened, and I will never see Esther again!"

Just then, some neighbors walked up.

"Hey, there, Bill!" Simon called out. "I've lost Esther!" He shook as he spoke. "I wonder where she is, if she's all right, and if I'll ever see her again."

"Simon, Mary and I lost our niece. My sister-in-law said that she was driving her car back home from a night class when she disappeared. The car was found crashed into a tree by the side of the road, but she was gone without a trace except for her clothing, jewelry, and some other things she had with her. We're concerned about who might have abducted her, but we understand that many others, both young and old are missing, too! What's this all about?"

"My daughter disappeared, and she's only seventeen years old!" another of Simon's neighbors, Gail, said as she walked up. "She's a senior in high school. She had so much ambition, and my husband and I had so many dreams for her life. How can she be gone without a trace? She was in her bedroom asleep last night, but we found her missing this morning with only her pajamas left behind on the bed!" Gail gripped opposite elbows with her hands wrenching each one. "The news reports are just trying to keep everyone calm. They said that countries are each conducting their own investigations! Why, even the President said that this is a time for calm and patience as the US government does all it can to help. Are they kidding?" She threw her hands up into the air. "That's impossible with so many family members missing all at the same time! It's so strange. Horrific, unthinkable!"

Ben looked around at his dad's neighbors in utter wonder. *So, Dad and I are not the only ones this has happened to, and these neighbors know nothing more than we do. I guess we're victims of something far beyond ourselves! Where could all these people have gone? This has got to be what Mom warned us about. This must be the end of the world!*

"What do you think, Mike?" Simon asked another neighbor.

"Yeah! There has never been such a freaky world event like this one! This worldwide disappearance must be the dark, foreboding omen of a sinister force whose aim is instilling fear over us all. Masses of people have been kidnapped for what? To put us in a helpless and hopeless position. What if this is a plan for a new world government where all nations will be controlled and regulated as one?"

"This is exactly what those who have perpetrated this want-- to ruin us!" shouted another neighbor named Betty. "We'll all become lunatics speculating on this event and its outcome. That's exactly how we'll be laughed at, for our weakness and fear!" She raised her hand to her forehead and shook her head.

"Do you really think so, Betty?" Simon asked. "I feel this disaster has already unbalanced all of us! We are all experiencing something totally unknown. I know people have sporadically come up missing, but not to this extent before."

Out of the corner of his eye, Simon saw another neighbor come up and push Betty from behind.

"Who do you think you are? Talking about weakness and fear! None of us have that or will get it! We are stronger than that!" Duncan screamed at Betty defiantly.

Soon, a fight broke out as neighbors verbally and physically attacked each other. Fists flew between men, and women shoved and kicked each other, pulling each other's hair. Ben pulled his dad away and motioned for Elira to follow them into his dad's home. Ben pushed his back against the inside of their front door and instantly locked it behind them.

Simon sank into his plush brown easy chair and broke down and wept, head in his hands. "I hate how everything seems to have changed in my life in just a few hours. I hate that my kind, beautiful Esther is gone! Who took her? Is she safe? Will I see her again?"

Elira turned on Simon's small living room television. Right before their eyes, the chaos unfolded. Scenes from all over the world showed people desperately looking for answers and recounting their own experiences of the event. World leaders spoke to their nations about what they could gather as evidence and what the next steps might be in discerning the future. The Congress of the United States was even now in an emergency session to determine what would be done to assist in the investigation efforts to find those who were lost.

The Russian president felt that it was counterterrorism from unspoken and unknown enemies. An Arabic leader felt it was sabotage by certain governments, including Israel, to create fear and panic. European Union and UK leaders implored people to stay calm and considered whether this event might even signal the entry of extraterrestrial beings.

"To determine our way of life," one newscaster said, an astonished look in her blue eyes, "it is being speculated that extraterrestrials took masses of people away by night and might be doing experiments and studies on them at another planet!"

Was there no sane, credible evidence for what everyone was now referring to as 'The Disappearance'? Ben rubbed his dad's shoulders. *Maybe he could wake up from this bad dream. Couldn't happen soon enough for all of us.*

A few Christian believers who appeared visibly shaken and upset spoke to TV news personnel and claimed what happened was called "the Rapture of the Church" in The Bible. To their utter sadness and disappointment, they were left behind because they had not been spiritually prepared for it.

Simon teared up again. "Esther always told me that this day would come, and I needed to be ready, but I didn't believe in her 'Yeshua HaMashiah.'"

"That sounds like Hebrew. What does that mean?" Elira quickly asked.

"Yes, it's Hebrew. It means 'Jesus, the Anointed One!'" Simon took a deep breath. "Now what she predicted has happened, and she was right!"

Ben could almost read Elira's thoughts by the emotions painted on her face. "I don't trust these left-behind believers," she said, squeezing her left hand that rested on her lap into a fist. "They hold on to the belief that this is the only true, real explanation; and for me, faith is only a myth."

"Mom talked about it," Ben said again, shaking his head, "but I never bought into it. In the context of religion and faith, though, it makes sense." *Why hadn't he listened to her?* "Now I feel like those left-behind Christian believers we saw on TV. I knew Mom's faith changed her life. I didn't understand and didn't want to be a part of it. Now I regret it!" He wept bitterly as he dropped into a brown suede chair beside his dad.

"I am not convinced," Elira said, "that any of this is really what happened. Sure, it looks like the most plausible explanation to justify and confirm Christian belief, but there must be a scientific, military, or political explanation. Nothing more." She kept her face turned toward the TV.

Jessica Owens, a prominent reporter from CBS, stated that just within a few hours of the event, they were discovering that most people who had disappeared had been involved in either the Christian community or in Christian ministry. Evangelists, pastors, lay leaders and their families, and many parishioners all seemed to be missing. Missionaries in foreign countries and many of their converts all over the world were gone.

How is this possible? Ben wondered.

Several pilots and copilots who were in their cockpits suddenly disappeared, causing their fellow pilots, if they were not also gone, to land the planes on their own. Many planes simply crashed worldwide. Drivers of cars, buses, and trains disappeared, and these vehicles also crashed, derailed, or drifted to the side of the road into ditches.

Many people reported to news correspondents of persons who disappeared in front of their eyes: schoolteachers in their classrooms, corporate executives holding company meetings, investors on Wall Street making trades, and even members of Congress were instantaneously gone before the eyes of their colleagues.

Ben squirmed nervously in his chair with his eyes glued to the TV. "What an unparalleled occurrence in world history! Nothing has ever eclipsed this, not even the COVID-19 global pandemic that rocked the second decade of our century, Elira! This catastrophic event has now become the world's newest focus and threat."

"Don't be fooled, Ben, we will all overcome this, too!" Elira confidently responded.

Right at that moment, Jessica Owens reported, "There is mass anxiety, fear, panic, and hysteria in all affected populations of the world, and the military and National Guard of most countries have been mobilized to maintain law and order."

"And rightfully so," the news anchor added, "this unconventional period calls for calm amidst chaos."

Calm amidst chaos! How can that ever happen? "Dad, do you feel like we can achieve calm amidst this chaos soon?" Ben asked.

"I can't imagine it, Son! I think those days are permanently behind us!"

Ben gripped at the sudden nauseous feeling in his stomach. *Could we be about to enter a time of great distress? Will life as we know it disappear? Will our personalities change forever; or worse yet, will we be destroyed and die? Is this the Great Tribulation?*

Ben looked helplessly at his dad and Elira, and then dropped his head into the open palms of both his hands.

Chapter 3
Unfolding Developments

Elira turned off the TV. Enough for now. She meandered into the kitchen.

"Simon, would you like something to eat?" she asked.

"Thanks for asking, but I can't imagine eating a thing right now, dear." Simon picked up his phone and saw numerous voicemails and texts that finally were able to come in from family and friends, but returning their calls and texts was impossible with so many mobile phone towers overwhelmed and crashed by so many customers on such a dark day.

"Ben, honey, could I fix you something to eat?"

"Like Dad, I can hardly eat anything right now, honey, but thanks for thinking about us."

Hearing their responses, Elira also decided she had no appetite and left the kitchen to sit on Simon's brown leather sofa. All she could do was look at Ben and Simon. Her tears joined theirs.

"This is certainly going to make our world an angrier and more distrustful place!" she said as she moved over closer to

Ben and Simon. "That's the fallout from all this because even when these people are found, life won't be lived in the same way again. There will be more safety measures and protocols than ever before." Ben and Simon barely nodded. Elira sighed deeply. *Should I burden them with what I think since they are in the throes of grief over Esther and everyone else right now? I should be the one to stay positive and rational.*

Elira couldn't help herself. She had to get up and turn on the TV again. This time, a Middle Eastern leader and spokesman talked about establishing world peace to end these horrible events. Elira was vaguely familiar with this man, Ibrahim Mizrah, a Palestinian of Jewish descent on his father's side. His mother was a Palestinian who came from another Middle Eastern country, possibly Saudi Arabia, although the origin was not clear. He was a spokesman for the Arab-Israeli world and the impasse between the two of them.

"Peace is possible not only between Israel and its neighbors, but also for the entire world!" Mizrah declared.

"How can you assume that with all that's occurred?" asked the TV news anchor, Ms. Owens.

"I assure you that appropriate dialogue and working with one another is the answer! Putting down weapons and coming together for discussion can help us all to unify, especially now! With The Disappearance, we all need cooperation rather than dissension to focus our attention against any outside forces who have attempted to sabotage our world."

"That may be easier said than done, Mr. Mizrah!" Ms. Owens said staring into the TV cameras.

"Brokering peace is the absolute goal and focus, and I promise that it will be accomplished!"

Elira looked at Ben and nodded. *How soothing and reassuring. What eloquence, intelligence, charisma, and charm! Could this be the "man of the hour" for this chaotic world?* She drew Ben closer to her and peered into his sad eyes. "I think things will get better from all the hardships we have endured. We need strong leadership, and I see it coming, Ben, don't you?"

Elira glanced at Simon. "Do you feel the same way as I do, Simon?"

"I feel good, of course, that the world can inherit some peace right now, but I can't help but think that this tragic event could've been averted if a leader of peace had been involved to begin with. I hope this man can turn it around like he's saying he can."

"What do you mean?" Elira said as she leaned over and wiped some dust off the coffee table with her finger.

"Breaking News!" A different news anchor's loud voice suddenly comes on. "What appeared to be a vicious rumor has now been proven true by U.S. and foreign investigators. Cemeteries all over the United States and the world have found graves and crypts robbed of bodies with no evidence of where they have gone! Additionally, both the U.S. and the world continue to study and assess the full aftermath of this unprecedented historical event.

Even cremated remains in some homes have been reported as missing! Many scientists, politicians, intelligence personnel, and leaders are weighing in on the possibility that someone or something has decided to not only bring live, but also dead, specimens of humans back with them to their location."

Ben grimaced. "It seems like a plot of such proportion never before been seen in our world, and those responsible have been so clever as to not leave any trace of who or what they are or represent!"

Elira noted the devastated look in Ben's eyes. "You know, Ben, there are always conspiracy theorists. I'm sure they fantastically think all these living and dead people have been moved into bunkers below the earth's crust or some orbiting station around the planet that can't be detected in space. Isn't this how it's always been? They have many ways to explain away strife between nations which can result in world dominance, extraterrestrial or not."

Now the news anchor on television broke to a waiting correspondent on the scene with several religious leaders.

"This was nothing more than a cause-and-effect relationship because the world has been going terribly awry," one clergyman declared.

"Yes, but you are not telling the full truth," another said. "The graves were opened because of a resurrection of dead believers before living believers would be 'raptured' or caught up in our earth's atmosphere to meet the Lord Jesus Christ."

Elira shook her head. "You must admit this seems so very far-fetched, Ben! You certainly don't believe this, do you?"

Ben and Simon stared at the TV. "I don't think this is far-fetched. Do you, Dad?"

"From what your mother always told us, this doesn't seem coincidental!"

"I think Mom was right," Ben affirmed. "She said this would happen, and I don't see a better explanation for the unearthed graves. Do you, Elira? If this is not a resurrection, then what an unparalleled sacrilege to all the humans who had been resting in those graves across the world, and what for? It seems impossible to be able to desecrate all those graves at once! Elira, if you are a person of education and looking for a scientific explanation, that would be far-fetched!"

Elira clawed at the back of her neck. *He can't be thinking this way! What's going on?* "Look, Ben, we can't continue to stay here at home and wonder what is happening in the outside world just by watching the news. Let's look for ourselves. How about it? There's one cemetery at the outskirts of our town. It will give us a chance to get out of here for a while. This constant news is making me feel jittery anyway."

Ben didn't immediately respond, but simply glanced over at his dad for the answer.

"I think that would be a good thing for us to do, Son. Let's just drive around and see what's happening for ourselves!" Simon said.

Elira stepped outside the front door with Ben and Simon only to find that neighbors were still violently clashing.

"What's happening?" Elira cried, "This is preposterous! Why are they shouting names and cursing at one another? Can't we stick together during this frightening and uncertain time? I don't understand what has happened to all of us!"

The three quickly got into Ben's car and headed toward the only cemetery outside of town. On their way there, they drove through different neighborhoods only to find similar scenes of pandemonium and havoc. When they finally arrived at the cemetery, Ben parked his car off the side of the street. Elira slid out of the car and looked out over the graves from a distance. Drawing closer, she saw some unearthed graves with old, decrepit, and rusted caskets opened, but abandoned, with nothing but empty space inside. Some of the caskets were corroded and in fragments, but there was no trace of any human remains inside. Each casket seemed to have erupted out of the ground with tremendous force and was lying open for all to see. As Ben bent to examine an empty casket, Elira surveyed the rest of the cemetery. There weren't a lot of graves like this. Most in this cemetery were intact and had not been obviously pillaged at all.

A creepy, dark feeling came over Elira. *There is no real scientific or political explanation for all this, especially since it happened all over the world at once, with no thought to any country's ideology. Perhaps humanity was not alone, and a greater force had invaded it? If so, was this force evil or good?* Elira felt sick and wished she could turn back the clock by just a few hours to the point before all this horror in the world began.

Ben came to her side and put his arm around her. Looking into her eyes for the first time since all this took place, he saw the fright and horror in them.

Chapter 4
Growing Animosity

As Ben, Elira, and Simon returned home, Simon looked out the windows of Ben's car to find another car and its driver careening recklessly down the streets with no thought to pedestrians, pets, or other drivers. Soon a huge boom was heard, and screams and curses flew out everywhere.

"Oh mmm...yyy...!" Simon stammered. "Just look at the injured people and dog lying on the sidewalk. The driver is laughing and speeding away. Where has plain human decency, empathy, or affection gone? Obedience to laws and rules of society has thoroughly evaporated!"

Upon arriving at his home, Simon made a dash out of Ben's car not wanting to be too close to what he had just witnessed.

The surly neighbor who had earlier pushed the other neighbor, Betty, walked up to Simon with an arrogant attitude. "Just where were you now?" Duncan shouted, his face hot, sweaty, and ruddy as his hair, his chestnut brown eyes bulging with fierce rage.

"Why?" Simon asked. "My family and I drove through the

town to see just what had happened around us. Is that a problem for you?"

"Oh, not at all!" Duncan retorted sarcastically. "You know that your wife predicted this fiasco, and it seems that some people like her have made all the chaos of this so-called 'The Disappearance' possible and are driving us all mad so they can prove their foolish theory of the end of the world!"

"Leave my wife out of this!" Simon said standing to his full five feet ten inches. "I am already torn up by her disappearance, and I don't believe this is about her and her beliefs!"

"You are a fool!" Duncan sneered. "You will soon see that these Christians have perpetrated a huge hoax and have put the world in bedlam to prove their hairbrained myths. They will soon be found where they are hiding and be brought to justice! As if it weren't enough that every natural disaster and even global pandemics have happened to us, these foolish jokesters have had to bring this about, too! This world has endured enough destructive events and anyone who would cause more destruction and distress needs to be damned to hell, if there is one!"

The veins in Simon's neck bulged as his blood pressure rose in obstinance to Duncan's accusations. "Why you loathsome worm! I want nothing more than to flatten you to the ground. You have always been belligerent, crass, and mouthy, but now you've gone too far!" Simon grabbed a rake lying by his hedge on the ground nearby. "I'll teach you civility and respect for me and my wife once and for all."

Ben quickly jumped between them and interjected in a calm voice. "Dad, why let this fool get you into trouble because you know that's what he wants? Just let it go and move on into the house. He never thinks about what he says anyway and always makes little to no sense."

Simon's anger somewhat de-escalated as he heard his son

speak. "I have no use for a confrontation with you, Duncan!" Simon uncurled his fisted hand from the rake and dropped it to the ground. "Nothing would be accomplished anyway, except for a brawl. Just look at our other neighbors! They would love to see that happen, but I'm going home now."

"Coward!" Duncan cried out, "You are afraid to fight because you know you are wrong, and I would win! The whole lot of you be damned!"

With great difficulty, Simon kept his cool and gestured for Ben and Elira to head inside with him.

Once inside his living room, Simon drew back a curtain across the front window that exposed the front lawn where neighbors were still standing. *What a rowdy night! How dangerous to see neighbors roaming the streets in agitation and restlessness. There are sure to be more conflicts in town.*

Simon gasped. "What's going on? I see some neighbors piling into cars, Ben. With their intense and irrational anger, I can only guess that they might be headed to possibly loot and destroy some businesses and government centers."

Ben frowned. "They just need time to absorb and adjust to what has happened instead of acting out!"

Simon rapidly locked and bolted the doors and windows. *The world has gone mad!*

"I'm so glad that we made it inside the home, and we are safe for now," Elira clutched at her shirt sleeve as she spoke. "How horrific for us to have to lock and bolt the door! It wasn't too long ago we could leave our front doors unlocked and not have to worry about any uninvited guests or neighbors."

Ben let out a sigh. "You're right!"

Simon took a seat at his walnut dining room table and exhaled loudly. "I hate this current world and what has happened. I hope that wherever Esther is, she has been spared all this!"

Elira shot a surprised glance at Ben and strode softly past Simon to turn on the TV. "Look! It's CNN with some more breaking news!"

Simon turned his face toward the TV. "There is a panel of scientists. Let's listen."

"This is undoubtedly the work of an extraterrestrial race! It is obvious that all these people could not be missing at once except for some entity outside of our own planet," reported one of the scientists.

"I know you are a renowned NASA scientist," the news anchor responded, "however, this seems a bit too unrealistic to believe. What would be their motive?"

"Experimentation and ultimate takeover of our planet and way of life, possibly to assimilate us into their own existence," said the scientist.

Simon drew near the TV to read the name of the scientist as Elira spoke it out loud. "It's Dr. Arthur Bennett. He's not a slouch when it comes to knowledge of extraterrestrial life. Although I have never bought into his views, I'm well-acquainted with his articles."

"Although we never found conclusive evidence of intelligent life on any planets in our own solar system, we do believe that there are other solar systems in our galaxy that could possibly carry intelligent life. NASA has been looking for, and studying the possibility of, extraterrestrial life on other planets for several years now. Planets in other solar systems and galaxies could have life forms more intelligent than we humans and who have now decided to actively pursue studies on us," Dr. Bennett said and coughed as he adjusted his eyeglasses.

Elira and Ben winced at each other, while Simon gasped. "I can't believe that!"

Is this really what has occurred to my beloved wife? It can't be possible that Esther has been kidnapped and held for observation and experimen-

tation on another planet! If so, why her? How ironic she believed in a "Rapture" of Christian believers, but what took place was an extraterrestrial kidnapping?! Will I ever get her back; and, if so, will she be the woman I knew?

Simon gazed forward in wide-eyed bewilderment at Elira and Ben who stared back at him in absolute silence.

Chapter 5
A Different Time

A month passed with no further answers. Elira was perturbed and agitated. She picked up her phone to get to the bottom of The Disappearance. *What could be going on and where could all these people be anyway? There had to be a scientific explanation beyond the sudden appearance from nowhere of an alien race such as Dr. Bennett had suggested to the world on CNN. What foolishness! Can world governments, including our own U.S., be hiding something from all of us?* Elira continued to muse and think.

She tried reaching her contacts at NASA whom she knew through her work at the U.S. DOD and couldn't reach anyone. She slammed her phone defiantly on the ground. *How ridiculous! The world has changed so much and so soon! Not for better!*

Elira looked up at Ben and Simon who jolted from their seats with the slam of her phone to the floor. "I'm sorry to have startled you both, but I'm enraged! I am thoroughly unconvinced that we have an extraterrestrial presence that suddenly appeared out of nowhere to kidnap a third of the world's population. That's asinine! Who can believe that? I just tried calling my NASA contacts, but no one is available."

Ben gingerly sat back down. "Elira, you know that government agencies all over the world must be so slammed with phone calls and questions right now regarding all this. I am sure NASA will be unreachable for some time. They are busy searching for answers."

"Yes, I know you're right, but I want answers, and I felt I could use a direct line to my contacts to get them! Like me, I'm sure that many of the regular employees have not returned to work yet because the world is still reeling from all this. Those in executive positions are at the forefront of finding answers, and, of course, will be for some time. As for me, I've not received word to return to my position at the office yet or to work from home, but I expect they will need me soon enough, and maybe I can then get some answers."

Simon got up from his chair and walked to the kitchen to look for snacks. "I am a bit hungry and think that we should all get a small bite of food. We haven't been eating much of anything lately."

"Simon, I will be glad to fix something light for all of us. What do you have available?" Elira walked into the kitchen to see.

"I have some leftover chicken and fresh salad."

"Good! I will make us small bowls of salad with sliced chicken on top. Where are your salad dressings?"

"Right inside the fridge door."

Elira grabbed all the ingredients she needed from the refrigerator and began making the salads. "Grab your own fork, napkin, and bowl," she said as she placed the salad and sliced chicken into each bowl. Suddenly a disturbing thought crossed her mind. *How long will our food supply last and will we be able to get more?*

Ben got up to retrieve his bowl after his dad got his and added salad dressing to both of their bowls. Elira grabbed hers and quickly added her salad dressing. All three returned to the living room.

"I'm going to turn the TV back on as we eat," Elira said.

Ben put down his fork. "I don't think that's a good idea, Elira. It'll just cause us anxiety and indigestion."

Elira abruptly put down the remote and picked up her phone instead. As she looked at her phone, deep concern spread rapidly over her face. "Whoa, yikes! Ben, do you know what I just read on my phone?" Ben was annoyed, but shrugged his shoulders.

"Curfews have been set all over the country for 8:00 P.M! It sounds like when we endured COVID-19 or when there was violence and destruction in cities from racial and ethnic protests of injustice! Do you remember the chaos, violence, and looting? Well, due to that, it has now been declared that each citizen throughout the United States will be answerable to their own local authorities and police."

"I can't say that I'm surprised," Ben answered as he took another bite of salad. "After all, it isn't a bad idea during such an unstable time as this."

Elira shifted in her seat. "Yeah, but there's more. Every citizen's whereabouts will be monitored! As I begin to work from home, my daily report to my superiors would have to be checked out by local police and government authorities who also report to their higher government officials."

"Wow!" Simon interjected. "Talk about almost totalitarian control!"

"Yes, Simon, but it gets 'better' than that! No longer will churches, synagogues, or any other religious organizations be allowed to meet. They will be closed to mitigate any end-time beliefs that could fuel mass hysteria. I realize that fact alone would have been hard for Esther to accept because any faith perspective seems to be unpopular now. It would be hard to deal with banks, businesses, workplaces, and government agencies if one's beliefs are suspect. It might be hard to keep a job or to hold onto any financial wealth or deal with the legal process for any religious people."

Ben and Simon glimpsed at each other skeptically. Ben shook his head. "Can this be true? What will they accomplish by this? They are adding insult to injury for us."

"Although I miss my dear Esther with all my heart, I know this would have crippled her! She loved the freedom to attend synagogue."

Ben and Simon looked with dismay at each other as Elira pitifully glanced at each of them. *How hard it must be for anyone with any religion or faith right now,* she pondered sadly.

Chapter 6
The New World Order

Elira sat quietly on her powered-blue, queen-sized bed staring at the empty spaces of her tiny apartment and musing about all that had happened in the world since she was last here.

"I still can't imagine how much the world has changed in just six months, Ben. It is uncanny! I am glad that we have decided to live with Simon to conserve money and to be together as a family!"

Ben came to Elira's side with another empty box in his hand. "I'm sure glad that I left my apartment quickly by giving up a lot of my things. It seems like we are still at the start of packing yours! Here, I brought you this box to pack up the things you want to keep from your bedroom."

"Ben, you're not listening. I'm still in awe about the time period in which we have been destined to live and I'm just glad we'll be together with Simon. I can't believe there is talk of a one-world government and a one-world currency now. Everything's happening so fast."

"I know, Elira, it makes me sad and mad all at once about

this time in our lives, but can I spend the rest of my life dwelling on it? I'm especially upset about not seeing Mom for half a year already; and, as you know, Dad has decided to have a funeral for her without the evidence of her death. It's all we can do to honor her memory and bring closure to her loss. We just hope it will be attended by family and friends that are left since we believe her rabbi and all her Messianic congregation friends may no longer be here either." Ben swallowed hard. "It's so difficult for us to accept and to say goodbye when we don't have clear evidence that she is dead. She is simply gone with no clue that she is returning any time soon."

"Well, I'm positive, Ben, that the memorial will be attended by enough of us who knew and loved her, and I'm also glad to see that we will host it at Simon's home. After all, that is where the three of us live now that life has utterly changed for us. It's so much better to live in the completely paid-off home Simon has, than to live separately during the upheaval of this time."

"Yes, I am happy to be a 'family' during this turbulent time."

"It's still so odd that after all the investigations that have taken place throughout the world, The Disappearance has affected only evangelical believers both living and dead! I can't wrap my head around that! Think about it, Ben. Can it possibly be a religious plot as some have speculated? I'm beginning to suspect it for myself."

"Elira, you know very well The Disappearance is either what Mom talked about, which is not a religious plot or scheme, or it's what investigators have ultimately concluded: The Disappearance was advanced by an unknown, intergalactic civilization far superior to Earth's own and who still need to make themselves known to the humans of Earth. Nothing more! And I am tired of rehashing this with you. You can't imagine the fear I feel either way."

Elira fell silent reaching out to tenderly stroke Ben's arm. "I know it must adversely affect you in so many ways. You have lost your mom with no closure as to how this happened; and, if it is as she predicted, you feel the fear of having been left behind. But if it is an extraterrestrial civilization that has perpetrated this, then we're all their targets, too. Of course, you feel that fear also. Either way, I have come to grips with the most likely fact that we have become victims of something or someone greater than ourselves, and it's just been extremely hard for me to go along with either of these two far-fetched options."

Ben placed the box down on the floor and sat next to Elira putting his arm around her, "You don't have to worry about that. The new one-world government has plans to take possession of funds from different space administrations and continue to comb space for more clues. Maybe they will come up with something of more substance than a kidnapping for experimental or nefarious purposes from an outside civilization."

"If they do, I can't figure out why the victims were devout Christian believers. It makes the Rapture option sound like a true option, and that is ridiculous," Elira said. "Ben, you know that individual world governments investigated the Rapture 'theory,' which is what it should be called, and they could not confirm with absolute certainty that all who disappeared were devout Christian believers. This makes the Rapture option not as realistic as that of a kidnapping by extraterrestrials. During one of my online work meetings, the DOD established that the religious option of a Rapture was completely fake anyway."

Elira rose from her seated position on the bed and began placing items she wanted into the box Ben gave her. "Despite this talk of options for The Disappearance, I am so glad that you and Simon have finally accepted the fact that your mom is permanently gone and possibly deceased."

A FEW DAYS later the memorial that Ben arranged for his mom was attended by a small group of neighbors, friends, and family in Simon's home.

Elira, Ben, and Simon walked into the living room where a small group of chairs were set up for the few mourners already gathered there. All three greeted the others and sat down.

Simon got up to speak.

"It is an honor to welcome each of you to this simple memorial for my wife, Esther. She is, and was, the love of my life. She gave my life joy and increased that joy when she gave birth to our son, Ben. We so enjoyed life together and had the opportunity to do many exciting and adventurous things, such as white water rafting and climbing the highest peak we could in the Rocky Mountains. We always had a love of the outdoors, of family, and of just being together.

Somehow, at one point in her life, she became acquainted with Messianic Judaism. She converted to being a believer in Jesus Christ as her Messiah. She began to spend a lot of time attending and serving at our local Messianic Jewish temple. Many times, I found myself feeling jealous of the time she spent there, but I saw that it gave her a new purpose for living and a joy for the afterlife, which she called heaven. I can't help but feel that she might have become entangled with a cult of some type and that is why she and most of her congregation are missing. But Esther was always a committed woman: to family, her ideals, and her precious faith.

My hope is that she has found heaven and that she is in the place of peace, love, and joy that she believed in. I miss her so very much and feel cheated of her existence with us, but I have resigned myself to be at peace and happiness for her sake. I will continue to love and miss you, Esther, until the day I die."

Simon shed tears that he wiped away with his handkerchief and sat down. The silence in the room was deafening.

Ben now got up and spoke with a quivering voice. "I can't help to feel that Mom was stolen from us. She had so much to live for and never would have left her family like this. I just hope that wherever she is, she's safe. She was the best Mom a child could ever have. She was always concerned with me and my needs. She taught me all she knew about life and relating to others. She would have given her life for mine.

She also shared her faith with me—a faith she felt was the answer to life. She loved her Lord Jesus Christ and wanted Dad and I to embrace Him too. She never put pressure on us, but I know she prayed for us always. The last time I saw Mom, she was sitting with her arm around Dad in this very same living room and they were laughing together. I miss her all the time and wonder if I will ever see her again. I hold out hope that she will return, but I must allow her to go on and keep her memory close to my heart. Mom," Ben cried out, "you're always in my heart!" The tears streamed down Ben's face, and he sat down.

Elira got up. "I want to thank everyone for coming, I would like to direct all of you to a memory book where you could each write down a memory of Esther that the family could keep. There are refreshments to enjoy in the kitchen. Once again, thanks for coming and supporting Simon and Ben by honoring Esther's memory." After she spoke, people stood up and came to offer Simon and Ben their condolences.

Chapter 7
A Changing Way of Life

Three months later, Elira entered her bank by appointment only, to exchange all the spare dollars that she, Ben, and Simon possessed into the New World currency. She didn't have to be concerned about the monies held in their separate bank accounts and investment vehicles because they would automatically turn over. The new one-world government had promised a renewed prosperity and ability to utilize the same currency over the entire globe.

Elira nostalgically looked down at the dollars she slid toward the teller. *What an end to a long, historic era. I'll never see or use the American dollar again!*

Elira quickly got back home to Ben and Simon where, after coming in, she planted herself on Simon's sofa. "One thing I like about what has happened in our world now is that we are unified against any extraterrestrial threats, and my money will hold the same value no matter where I travel. It'll be wonderful to have a uniform economy and government where no conflict can exist anymore because we are all part of the same world system!"

"I don't think you realize, Elira, how badly things can go if those at the helm of this New World government become corrupt." Simon said. "Do you remember Germany and Hitler during World War Two? My wife's parents were killed in the Holocaust because an egomaniac dictator thought it best to exterminate all Jews!" Simon leaned back in his armchair, and added, "My only hope is that this Ibrahim Mizrah, who is part Jewish and part Palestinian, can continue to be a bridge for the countries of the Middle East to peacefully coexist and that he will not turn out to be a psychopathic leader of this New World government!"

"I agree," Ben said from the other end of the sofa. "I'm afraid only time will tell."

At that, Simon's face posed a faraway look as he shuddered at the thought of an incomprehensibly worse scenario for the Jews.

Elira got up off the sofa and grabbed her car keys once again. "Now that I have the New World currency in hand, I think I should go to our local grocery store to see if I can find some food to cover us for the remainder of this week. After all, we had chaotic and unsafe communities across the world following The Disappearance. I hope that, armed with this new currency, I will have a better chance now to buy needed items, but I hear that the anger and aggression at grocery stores has grown formidable due to the limited supplies and high demand." Elira took a deep breath.

"Let me come with you," Ben said, as he followed Elira outside. "Two are better than one where there may be conflict."

"All right," Elira said, "but I hope your father is safe here, without us. You know his neighbors can be judgmental of him."

Ben took hold of his black leather jacket from the back seat of Elira's car and sat down in the car seat beside her. "All we can do is try to take it a day at a time. He'll be okay. We won't be gone long."

Simon stepped onto his front porch to wave goodbye to the couple. Unfortunately, his resentful neighbor, Duncan, was out doing some yard work. He caught a glimpse of Simon at the door.

"What is my Jewish neighbor up to today?" Duncan lashed out. "The nations of the world would be better off without you Jews! Why should Ibrahim make a peace covenant with Israel anyway?" He stabbed his shovel into the ground. "The Middle East has always been a hotbed because of Israel. Maybe Hitler had the right idea, huh?" Duncan was clearly itching for a fight with Simon.

From her car, Elira could sense Simon's blood boiling at Duncan's anti-Semitic rant. She knew Simon was aware of the thin line Israel held with all its enemies in the world, and he'd already expressed grave concerns about this "man of peace," named Ibrahim Mizrah. Elira wondered why Duncan had such hatred for the Jews and Simon. Maybe Duncan didn't believe in any religion at all, let alone Judaism, from which Christianity developed.

"You know, you might be right, but we will let Ibrahim and the New World Government figure this one out!" Simon slammed and bolted the front door with a loud click.

Whew! Another altercation avoided, Elira thought. It's so sad prejudice still seemingly could not be conquered by a one-world philosophy.

"I think Simon can clearly handle himself," Elira said to Ben. "We need food, so let's brave the store and see if our new currency actually gets us anything."

Elira and Ben drove to the supermarket. They saw long lines of people waiting to enter because there was a run on grocery store supplies. Apparently, others had received their new currency too.

Once inside the grocery store, Elira stopped at the meat counter. No beef available. At least there was some chicken left. As she stepped back to place the package of chicken in the shopping cart, she accidently bumped a lady beside her.

"Hey! What do you think you're doing? Stay in your own place! We all want to get in for the poultry that's left, too!" the woman snapped.

"What do you mean?" Elira asked. "Everyone is crowded into this store. I didn't intentionally bump you. Why can't you just understand that and live with it?"

Ben sensed an argument ensuing and pulled Elira out of the way. "Let's go get toilet paper, honey!" He grabbed Elira's hand and the cart and walked to another aisle. The woman glared at them as they left.

"What ever happened with people being courteous to one another?"

"I don't know, Elira. We live in a very different time!"

After picking up the items they could find, Elira and Ben made it to the cash register.

"Get out of my way!" yelled a man just behind them. "You cut in front of me!"

"I don't know what you mean," Ben shot back. "I didn't even notice you in line."

"Why you little liar!" He took a swing at Ben. Ben ducked and pulled Elira and the cart back behind the maniac.

"Please be my guest!" Ben motioned for the man to go ahead of them.

As the man went ahead of them in line, he bumped their cart off to the side. It took everything in Ben and Elira's power to not retaliate.

Finally, Ben and Elira made their way in line to the cashier. She glanced at them with disdain. "I hope you're prepared to pay with New World currency. I do not accept dollars or any other currency."

Elira opened her purse to pull out the money. "There's no problem. We have it!"

The cashier proceeded to scan each item and Elira handed her the total amount. "Ben, please take these to the car. I am waiting for our change."

"There's no change!" The cashier snapped back. "We just round up the total with this new currency! Get with the program!"

Elira was shocked at the rudeness and impudence of the cashier. "You don't have to bark at me!" Elira said. The cashier lunged at Elira who swiftly moved out of the way and ran to her car. When she got to the car, Ben was already sitting inside and saw the shocked expression on Elira's face. He scratched his head. "You look like you've seen a ghost, honey! What happened?"

"The sheer rudeness and deference of the cashier! Why so much anger?"

"Welcome to the new normal with our One-World Government! I think people are so mistrusting, angry, and belligerent anymore! How horrible!"

Elira shrugged her shoulders and turned on the car radio. "Speaking of the New World, I wonder what's been happening today."

"You don't quit listening to the news, which I believe is depressing and anxiety-producing each time we listen to it!" Ben placed his right hand over his mouth to choke down a cough.

Driving home, Elira heard what transpired during the day on the car radio. A newscaster's booming voice came over the radio. "Ibrahim Mizrah, the charismatic peacemaker and New World leader, who had been given the nod for his major world leadership position by all the countries united in our One-World Government, has just announced the terms of a final peace agreement between Israel and its Arab neighbors."

A short statement in Ibrahim's voice came over the radio, "Today, I announce a historic breakthrough in Arab-Israeli relations going forward. A new, improved peace plan will reestablish the original Palestinian state to coexist with Israel. In turn, the Israelis will have the right to rebuild the ancient Jewish temple at Jerusalem. Israel and Palestine will share Jerusalem as the capital of their respective nations. This historic treaty is part of the New World Government that I promised would usher in one-world peace. Never again will we be vulnerable to threats from outside our planet. The Disappearance, or anything like it, will not occur again. We have also established and mobilized a one-world military, made up of the militaries of various countries, and whose might is incomparable to any other individual country's military of the past. Welcome to the amazing, new opportunities of our New World Government! Also, with the advent of our New World economy, I guarantee prosperity will soon take root all over the world. Please be patient as we grow this new economy and until everyone has opportunity to convert to our new currency."

"And with that, our New World leader's announcement has ended!" The newscaster's voice piped in.

Elira glanced at Ben and lowered the volume on the radio. "Things continue to happen so quickly," Elira said as she reached over to hold Ben's hand in hers. "Suddenly, we are living in a new and different era just short of a year since The Disappearance. Wow! And this new leader isn't wasting any time to change more as quickly as possible."

"Maybe he's afraid that we'll all be caught short of world-wide defense and economic power should something like The Disappearance occur again," Ben replied, "And next time, perhaps even a worse event might happen, for which he wants to be prepared." Elira nodded and pulled into Simon's driveway with their meager groceries.

"Hello, Simon!" Elira called out as she entered the front door. "I think Ben and I were able to get some groceries for another day. The supplies are slim, but we got what we could; and while everyone is adapting to the New World currency, we must pay more because the smaller change is not available. Did you hear what happened today?"

Simon straightened himself up from having taken a nap on his sofa. "No, what happened?"

"Why, Simon, this new leader, Ibrahim Mizrah, has announced a final peace agreement between Israel and its Arab neighbors. The Palestinians and Jews alike will share Jerusalem as the same capital city; and, of all things, he's reassuring the Jews that a new Jewish temple will be built in Jerusalem!"

"Well, this is quite a change from what we have seen for hundreds of years!" Simon said, throwing his hands up into the air. "Can it really be? I'll have to see it to believe it!"

"I think this man is a new type of leader that is ushering in the peace that was greatly needed for many centuries. The Disappearance has certainly helped bring Mizrah and his new ways of thinking into being," Elira spoke as she took out the groceries and began to put dinner together. "I believe you and Ben will be pleased to see the changes!"

Simon stretched his legs out. "I hope you're right!"

Ben looked concerned as he walked over to Simon and sat down next to him. "I hope you're right, too, Elira. It seems so impossible to achieve, but how welcome it would be if it could really materialize."

Chapter 8
Escalating Occurrences

B en yawned widely as he walked to the kitchen in his navy-blue pajamas and black flip flops. He desperately needed to fix a pot of coffee. It had certainly been a long night of tossing and turning for rest or sleep. He brushed his hand through his scruffy hair and turned on the very small kitchen TV. It seemed like the world was bombarded daily with breaking news of more changes to those already made. *Would anything remain stable for a while?*

A news anchor, a woman dressed in red, declared "There are new developments with Israel today. We just received word that Ibrahim Mizrah, who has declared himself Master of the New World Order and who had successfully brokered a peace treaty between Israel and its Arab neighbors, is denouncing Russia's unilateral escalation of aggression toward Israel!

Russia has not been pleased with Arab allies at peace with Israel. Historically, it has dominated Arab attitudes against Israel to counter the United States and its support of Israel. But now, it is reported that Russia has declared an all-out war with Israel and is advancing toward the country.

Additionally, the countries of Iran, Libya, and Turkey have also made the decision to ally themselves with Russia and advance toward Israel. Despite international world peace being proclaimed by Master Mizrah, war has broken out," the news anchor declared.

"When will peace come to Jerusalem and favor to Israel?" Dad asked as he came in from the living room. "Look who dropped by early this morning and was waiting for you to get up?" Ben looked up to see his friend, Bernard, or Bernie, as he was affectionately called.

"What are you doing here this morning, Bernie?" Ben asked.

"It looks like this New World Order has become a sham!" Bernie declared. "Why, we have been suffering with food shortages, increased military and police presence and control, financial impoverishment and job loss, increasing mental-emotional duress and physical illnesses. Now we hear of wars and rumors of even more wars breaking out! This is such a miserable time."

"Things have changed for the worse since Esther left!" Dad said.

A loud banging sounded at the door. As Dad opened the door, Duncan flew in like a bat out of hell.

"Now Jewish vermin," he shouted at the top of his lungs, "Israel and the Jews will be defeated in this New World. It's about time, and we'll all have peace!"

Ben and Bernie jumped into action to hold Duncan back. "Get out of here!" Ben shouted. Duncan advanced toward Ben with a closed fist.

"No, you don't!" Ben's dad stepped in to save Ben. The fist meant for Ben hit Ben's dad straight on his temple, and he fell to the floor.

"Nooooo!" Ben screamed, as he and Bernie jumped on Duncan. The fist fight continued until Duncan got loose and stumbled toward the front door.

Ben glared at Duncan while pointing to Dad. "Look at what you've done! He's elderly and he's not getting up at all!"

Duncan shrugged his shoulders in defiance. "What do I care! He got in the middle, and he got what was coming to him!"

Bernie rushed to open the front door and gave Duncan a swift kick out. "Stay out of our lives and homes, you anti-Semitic pig!" Bernie screamed at Duncan, quickly shutting and locking the door behind him.

"You will regret this!" Duncan was heard threatening as he lurched forward in a daze toward his home.

Bernie turned back around to find Ben on the floor next to his dad with some furniture and lamps around them overturned, broken, or shattered.

"Dad's head is bleeding and he's unconscious! Bernie, please call 911 right now!"

Bernie rushed to his phone and called. He heard a voice respond. "What's your emergency?" the dispatcher asked.

"We have an elderly man who has received a blow to the head in a physical assault. He's down on the floor, bleeding from the head, and is unresponsive. Please send an ambulance immediately!"

"Is he breathing?"

"Yes!"

"Okay, we'll send an ambulance immediately!"

"By the way, can you also dispatch the police to apprehend the man who dealt him the blow to his head?" Bernie asked.

"What is the name of the elderly, unresponsive man?'

"Simon Goldberg!"

"Okay, and what is the name of the man who hit him and where does he live?"

"His name is Duncan Abbott, and he lives right next door!"

"Can you give a description of Mr. Abbott?"

"He has fiery red hair and brown eyes. He stands about five-feet, eight-inches tall and is extremely overweight."

"Okay, we'll also dispatch a police officer right now! Is he armed?"

"Not that I know of. He was not armed when he was here."

"Do you feel he is an imminent threat to Simon again?"

"Yes, I do. He says that Simon deserved what he got, and we will all regret what happened."

"Is the ambulance there now?"

Bernie motioned for Ben to check. Ben got up to look out the window and gave a nod back to Bernie. "Yes, they are," Bernie replied.

"Okay, please open the door for them, and the police are on their way."

"Thank you!"

Bernie unlocked and opened the front door. In rushed the paramedics with a stretcher and their equipment. A tall, lanky paramedic with a rather thin nose, black hair, and beady dark eyes knelt by Simon to check his vitals and look at his head injury.

"We'll transport him to the hospital, but how did this happen?"

Ben quickly responded. "His next-door neighbor rushed at us when we opened the front door for him. My dad moved between us to help, but he received a punch to the head."

"Well, I don't know what you have going on with that neighbor, but your dad should never have involved himself." Ben recoiled at the paramedic's judgment of Dad. He wondered why he didn't have any compassion for what had happened to him.

At that moment, the police arrived and two officers walked in. Ben noticed one of them coming up to him and Bernie.

"So, what's happened here?" the police officer asked Ben and

Bernie as he placed one hand in his back pocket to grab a recording device to capture the details.

"Our neighbor banged on my dad's door. When we let him in, he bounded toward me with vicious, derogatory, and anti-Semitic accusations. He took a swing at me, but my dad stepped in and got a blow to the head instead."

The police officer smirked. "I don't understand why the neighbor would do that if there wasn't some sort of previous provocation. What has been going on between your dad and his neighbor?"

Ben looked in disbelief at what he heard from the officer and shot a cursory glance at both officers, and then looked seriously into the eyes of the first officer. "Sir, with all due respect, Dad has done nothing except to live next door to this bigoted ingrate. Dad has always tried to be a kind and a thoughtful neighbor to him. Instead, Dad's neighbor consistently derides us for Mom's Christian beliefs. You see, she was a Messianic Jew, and has not been seen or heard of since The Disappearance."

The police officers looked askance at each other. "I don't think there is any need for us to question your dad's neighbor, Duncan Abbott."

"Yes," the other officer disdainfully agreed, "This obviously is a personal quarrel between the two of them and doesn't warrant criminal apprehension or detention of Mr. Abbott."

"What? Dad is lying here in a puddle of blood that is profusely flowing from his head injury. Isn't that enough physical assault to be considered criminal?"

"Once again," the first officer said patronizingly, "this is a personal matter between two neighbors which unfortunately resulted in an injury that took place due to your dad's interference. This is a lesson for both you and your dad to never engage in what you assume is self-defense."

Now Bernie became enraged. "If Ben's dad had not come

between them, then Ben would've been hurt. Duncan's intention was to assault, no matter who was going to receive it."

"That's a moot point," argued the first officer, as he turned to the other officer and said, "Our work is finished here. We can file a report, but there is no reason to bother Mr. Abbott."

Without another word, the two officers casually walked out the front door to go about the rest of their day.

Ben stared in astonishment at Bernie and the paramedics who were still attempting to wrap gauze around his dad's head.

"Things seem skewed in favor of evil, Bernie! I don't like that!"

"I can't help but agree," Bernie voiced to Ben as he caught one of the paramedics out of the corner of his eye acting obviously offended by what Ben had just said. Bernie stopped speaking as the paramedic stood up.

"We got your dad's head wound wrapped and confined at this time. We will now place him on the gurney and take him to the hospital."

"Okay," Ben nodded. "I will be there shortly."

Both paramedics got on their feet to lift Simon onto a gurney and then wheeled him out of the home. Ben hastily picked up his car keys, and he and Bernie exited the front door to get into the car for the drive to the hospital.

"This drive will be one of the longest of my life, Bernie! I hope and pray that Dad will be okay. It concerns me that he lost consciousness and is continuing to bleed. He must have received a bad blow."

"Just hang on until you speak to a doctor! You don't know what's going on and it might be more positive than you're thinking right now, Ben."

At the hospital, Ben and Bernie asked to speak to the doctor in charge. After a while, the doctor came out to meet them wearing green scrubs, a light blue face mask, and light blue gloves. The doctor's eyes reflected a serious look as he spoke.

"Your dad has suffered a concussion and traumatic brain injury. He received twelve stitches; and due to his age, we've admitted him for observation and bed rest."

"May I go in to see him?" Ben asked.

"You may go in, but he's still unconscious and needs rest. Please just go in for a minute or two."

Ben and Bernie walked down the corridor to Simon's room. Ben looked in on his dad's still form on the bed. There were tubes and machines hooked up to him. Ben cried. "I love you, Dad! You will be much better soon. Mom would want you to fight and come back. You and I need to be together." He bent over his dad's face to give him a kiss, and Bernie reached out to hug Ben.

"He's in good hands now, Ben. Don't worry!" Bernie said in a consoling voice.

"I don't know about that, Bernie. Things are getting darker for us and everyone around the world. This world has always held prejudice for religious, racial, and ethnic minorities, but now it's no longer a place for anyone ostracized and condemned by the New World Order. That's what's happening to us, Bernie! Duncan is just a glimpse into that! Dad, and we ourselves, may be at risk for more bias and intimidation. Just think of the Jewish Holocaust in World War II. Since that time in history, it looked like the world realized the atrocities of anti-Semitism, but now society's attitudes have become dangerous again. Those who've had family members vanish due to The Disappearance are looked on suspiciously. And if Jews are involved in problems with their Arab neighbors, then special requirements are placed on them unlike others."

"Well, I hadn't thought of it in that way, but you might be

right! I can see what you are saying. This world has gotten scarier," Bernie said.

"Not to change the subject, Bernie, but I think we need to head home. Elira must be beside herself wondering what has happened."

"Sure thing! Let's go!"

Ben and Bernie sat in silence on the way home. When they both arrived back to Simon's house, Bernie got out of Ben's car and into his own.

"Bye, Ben! Keep me posted on your dad. I will be thinking about him. Say 'hello' to Elira."

"Bye, Bernie! Will do!" Ben said as he turned and unlocked the door to Dad's home.

As Ben walked in, Elira ran to him, her face visible with deep concern.

"Oh, honey, I'm so glad you're safe! I was worried sick about what had happened to you. I tried over and over again to call your cell phone, but I always got your voicemail until I got home and saw that you had left your phone here. But what really troubled me the most was the blood I saw on the floor! I was so afraid for you, and I realized your dad was gone. The chaos of all this broken furniture and glass terrified me that either one or both of you had been injured or worse yet, killed! All I could think of was a home invasion had happened. I was ready to call the police when you walked in."

"Oh, Elira, I wish it were a home invasion! It would be better to accept that than what it turned out to be!" Ben said.

Elira set her phone down on the coffee table as her eyes widened. "What really happened?"

"Elira," Ben cried, tucking her in for a hug. "Dad was assaulted by Duncan and taken to the hospital. He's in critical condition due to a brain injury. He received twelve stitches on the left side of his head. They're keeping him sedated and will continue to evaluate his condition."

"Oh no! Will he be all right?" Elira squeezed Ben close.

"I don't know right now; but Elira, promise me that in the future, you will not dare call the police! They're not for us! They sided with Duncan and let him go."

"No way! How? What did they think?"

"They felt Dad was the instigator. Somehow, we're being targeted because of The Disappearance. I feel like we're in danger."

"What do you mean?" Elira asked.

"People having family members in The Disappearance are believed to be part of a global hoax and considered troublemakers. Don't you see that's exactly why the New World Order has ordered synagogues and all places of worship closed to lessen any frenzy for what they fear as false end time beliefs?"

"Oh, Ben, that can't be! You're just overreacting because the police made a wrong decision that was not in favor of you and your dad."

"No, Elira, I think law and justice no longer exist and haven't for a while. Instead, lawlessness and evil have become the norm even with the authorities and police."

Ben slid the armchair back to its proper place, and Elira helped clean up. They brought the debris from the fight to the curb when suddenly Ben glanced up to see Duncan contemptuously watching them through his open window.

"Jewish scum!" Duncan hollered. "The Arabs have it right! I hope the war against Israel will destroy your sorry nation forever!"

Ben took a deep breath and tightly gripped a broken dining room chair—a substitute for rushing at Duncan and throwing the chair toward him at his open window. *I can't fathom the severe hatred he has for me and Dad. What have we done to him?* Ben thought, and then shook his head. *Love and compassion have turned cold and are getting colder with each passing day.* Ben ignored Duncan and wandered inside. He turned on the TV while Elira made two egg salad sandwiches.

"Breaking news!" the news anchor declared, "Israel is at war! Russia and its allies have now invaded Israel!" Ben watched missile strikes into Israel and the advancement of tanks and military personnel. "It appears popularity for Israeli support is waning in the U.S.," the anchor said. "Since Russia and Iran have allied themselves against Israel, the U.S. President Marlene Rothschild, along with Congress, believes it would be in the United States' best interest to avoid a major conflict with these two nations."

The news anchor continued to speak. "Also, what we are hearing out of Africa this evening is that there is major famine there. People are so desperate for food that they are killing one another in an unsuccessful attempt to get it. We also have reports from our U.S. news correspondents of widespread wild-fires all over the West and major flooding and mudslides in the Midwest in what is decidedly the greatest threat to the populations of many states. As if that isn't enough, a large earthquake —8.0 on the Richter Scale—has been detected in India and another one in Mexico registering 7.5."

Ben shut off the TV as Elira entered the living room with their sandwiches.

Ben lifted his plate and took a bite of his sandwich. "Every news report is so negative and devastating anymore. I don't even want to expose myself to the news."

"I agree, but we can't bury our heads in the sand." Elira reached for her sandwich and took a bite. "Boy, this is a good sandwich, but I wonder how long we'll have food. Supplies are getting scarcer each time we go to the grocery store. More shortages are coming."

"You know, Elira, these things are not new to us. So much began in the last century and the first half of this century as a preview of what was to come. If you remember, there were floods, wildfires, and destruction of our water and air. Even the polar ice caps melted and now the polar bears and penguins are extinct species! The sea levels rose, and many islands of the world flooded and disappeared. Some of the beautiful Greek and Caribbean islands were lost and all of the Florida Keys. Gone with them is the great, cosmopolitan city of Miami. What's left are homes built on stilts in the ocean shoreline attainable by boat only. Food sources became scarcer with such monumental climate change. Scientists warned we were destroying the ozone layer of the atmosphere and heating up our planet. I think from now on you should just look at the headlines on your computer and keep me posted on the main stories. I don't want to look at TV for myself anymore."

"I agree!" Elira dropped into the other armchair, which now had a large tear in the rolled arm. "Perhaps we should just not turn on the news at all, but so many changes occur from day to day, I feel like we need to be in the know."

"Maybe we should listen in every other day," Ben countered. "Like I said, listen and give me the major rundown of events." He was done with the news. He was about done with this whole New World Order. Newer wasn't better. The empty, anxious feeling in the pit of his stomach was there again.

Chapter 9
A Time of Transition

Elira poured herself a cup of coffee. Only two cups left from the stash they had pooled together! What would they do now? Ben loves his coffee but supplies of it are so low in the stores. Elira knew she could deal with it, but what about Ben?

Ben stepped into the kitchen. "Hey, Elira, want to come with me to see Dad this morning?" He looked over from her to the kitchen counter. "Oh good, there's coffee!"

Elira couldn't tell Ben this was his last cup. Maybe it was best to save that announcement for tomorrow, especially with what was going on with Simon.

"Sure! I hope he gets to come home today." Elira shoved Ben's favorite mug along the countertop toward him and shifted over to fill it with coffee.

"Hey, anything new going on I need to hear about?"

"I need to get dressed, but I'll check the computer."

"Okay, sweetheart!"

Elira turned on her computer, pivoted to her closet, and pulled out a print blouse and blue jeans. *This always looks good on me! Hmmm…what will the news headlines be about today?* She squinted at her computer from her closet to check.

"Ben," she suddenly yelled, "apparently Israel has been attacked by Russia and its allies, and another major earthquake has happened!"

"Wow! No surprise about Israel!" Ben yelled from the kitchen.

"Yes, but while people lay sleeping overnight, a massive earthquake, recorded at 9.5 on the Richter Scale, occurred in the mountains of Israel where the war with Russia and its allies broke out at its thickest. The aftershocks continued for several hours. Eighty-three percent of the armies allied against Israel were killed in an avalanche that occurred when the mountains shook, caved, and crumbled," Elira added. She pondered what this meant. *How odd. How could this have happened?* "Ben, that means Israel has likely been spared! What's that all about?"

"Don't you see, Elira? It's got to be a miracle. Mom once told me that some nations would gather themselves against Israel, but God would spare the nation and hide some Israelis for a time."

"Take a look here," Elira continued. "It says that several tsunamis were launched from the Mediterranean Sea by the high magnitude earthquake and have affected many Middle Eastern nations, including Israel."

"More and more, Elira, I think Mom had the right faith, and I feel so miserable." Ben's mug struck the computer desktop as he set it down.

"Ben, I wouldn't go that far! You keep harping on this. Like I've always said and I'm tired of repeating myself: It may look like all this fits into the Christian worldview, but I feel it's all coincidental."

Ben looked down at his watch. "Let's get going."

"Yeah, I'm ready!"

At the hospital, Simon didn't remember a lot of what had happened to him, and he appeared unable to recognize Ben or Elira.

Ben asked a nurse if they could speak to Simon's doctor. They waited for a long while, when finally, the doctor came out to see them.

"Hello, my name is Dr. Ellen Shephard, the neurologist treating your dad. I don't really have a good prognosis for Simon. Because of his age and the place where the blow occurred, I think he will suffer effects from this for the rest of his life. First, we are continuing to monitor him for any brain bleed. A brain bleed can be lethal. However, if he survives that, he will possibly have some cognitive deficits that will remain. Depending on the severity of the damage to his head, his memory and mood may change considerably, and he may have difficulty talking and walking. I wish I could give you a better prognosis, but for a man over the age of sixty-five, a severe blow to the head is a life-changing injury, if not a life-threatening one! I'm sorry. We are doing all we can, and we'll keep you posted on his day-to-day progress. We'll release him from the hospital when we deem it safe for him to return home. Any questions?"

Poor Ben, Elira thought.

Ben stumbled backward. "This can't be happening. No! I've lost Mom and now Dad, too! It's unthinkable! Where did my 'normal' life go?" His knees buckled on the edge of Simon's bed. Ben bent over Dad's bed whimpering.

"Have you done any preliminary tests yet for the brain bleed you're now monitoring?" Elira asked.

"Yes, we performed a CT scan right away, and the good news is that, so far, we could not see a bleed, but we need to give it more time."

"Thanks for all you're doing to help." Elira responded.

"You're welcome! I must go now." The doctor stepped back

toward the door. "Thanks for coming in to see him. Many times, older folks can be forgotten by family. Have a good day!" Dr. Shephard exited the room and disappeared down the long corridor.

Ben turned to Elira. "It's not fair that the police didn't apprehend Duncan in light of all this! I wonder if the police are in his pocket and there's some major corruption going on. Dad may never be the same again and doesn't even recognize me."

Ben sobbed uncontrollably while Elira patted him on the back and hugged him. "Come on. Let's go home. We can't do any good here right now. Your dad needs the rest, and he's sleeping again."

They returned to the car. On the way home, Elira needed to stop for groceries again. *Money is growing scarce, but I hope I can come home with some protein and a vegetable for dinner.*

"Ben, I need to stop for groceries again. They run out fast."

"I wish I could help you pay for them, but my business hasn't turned around since completely tanking after The Disappearance. I know you aren't working full-time either. I just don't know how long this will last. Fear, hunger, and depression seem to be increasing everywhere."

"Money and jobs aren't a focus any longer, Ben. Survival is and thankfully, we live in Simon's paid-off home and have his share of any income to add to our own. That helps us."

Ben's heart began to beat out of his chest, and he felt faint. "It never occurred to me before, but I now worry what would happen if Dad died. It would not only be an emotional blow, but a financial one, too! Three are better than two." Ben suddenly looked pale as his hands shook on the steering wheel.

"Pull off to the side of the road now, Ben!" Elira rushed to grab the steering wheel. "I think you're having a panic attack!" Ben complied and got off the road while Elira tossed her left leg over Ben's legs to press on the brakes and then used her right hand to put the car in park. "Wow! That was close!" Elira exclaimed as she got out of the car. She opened the door on Ben's side. "Come on, can you get out of the car and stand?" she asked.

"Dunno...I'll try!" Ben swung his body around and struggled to place his wobbly legs and feet on the ground. "I don't think I can stand up without falling down, Elira."

"Okay, Ben, take several deep, long breaths. Watch me do it." Ben looked at her, but things seemed fuzzy. "Ben!" Elira shouted, "just lie across the bucket seats and continue your deep breathing. You're fine. Simon's not dead. We'll be able to survive as much as anyone else in this economy."

Ben listened and continued with deeper breaths, holding in a breath, and releasing it slowly. "I'm feeling better now. I think the panic is passing."

"Good! Do you think that you can sit up?"

"I'll try to lift myself up and sit first and then try to stand outside the car."

"Okay, honey, take your time." Elira said.

Ben sat up first and waited a minute. Soon he put some weight on his legs to stand and then to exit the driver seat of his car.

"Can you put weight on those feet with no problem?"

"Yes, Elira, it looks like I can!" Ben stretched his arms over-head. He let out a deep sigh. "I didn't know that worry about the loss of Dad, and any repercussions from it, would affect me like this!"

"Of course, it would!" Elira responded. Elira gave Ben a quick hug and walked him to the other side of the car. Ben sat on the passenger side while Elira returned to the driver's side. "Now, I'm going to get us out of here and home."

"Thank you, honey," Ben sheepishly replied, feeling like a weak coward for experiencing such panic.

"Although our money is not where it used to be, and we don't have access to the food or other social pleasures we once enjoyed, we're surviving. Don't worry! Just take it one day at a time," Elira said.

"It's funny you should say, 'Just take it one day at a time.' Mom always used that expression and told me that Messiah Jesus declared it in His Sermon on the Mount. It seems like there're some sound principles to live by in the Bible which meant so much to her."

"You know, I think there's a lot of common sense in the Bible, but religion can lull a lot of people from life's realities. In fact, Karl Marx described religion as 'the opium of the people,'" Elira replied.

Ben remained quiet until they reached home. Ben went to lie down, and Elira couldn't find much food to put together for lunch.

"Ben, I'll still need to go to the grocery store where we headed before you had your panic attack. I dread going, but I must! We have nothing much left."

Ben nodded. "I just don't know how much will be left at the grocery store, too! Will you be okay going on your own? It's combative out there!"

"You need to rest and take your mind off of things. I think I'll be able to handle it."

"Okay." Ben sat up to give Elira a kiss, but instead she bent down to kiss him and left.

At the grocery store, the shelves were bare, much more than Elira had ever seen before. She gathered what few items she could—some pasta, a can of tuna, lettuce, and powdered milk. Not much, but she would be able to make a meal or two. She took her place in line.

It wasn't long before one lady claimed that another lady had slyly come up ahead of her in line behind Elira. The lady who supposedly cut into the line shouted expletives at the other lady and pushed her back. The two broke into a physical fight. Elira ignored them, but soon a security guard, with the name "Harry" embroidered on his uniform, came up to stop the fight. Elira decided to get out of the way and leapt behind the cash register next to the cashier. The woman who had pushed back the other woman then attacked Harry.

"What are you doing?" Harry demanded as he pulled out his gun and cursed at her. "Are you a lunatic? Stand still!" The woman tried to wrestle the gun out of his hand. A shot went off. Those around that area jolted at its sound. The woman fell to the ground with no further visible movement.

Elira screamed. Some others in line shouted curses. Others rose in anger at Harry, but he warned them to hold back any aggression toward him or he would shoot them, too.

"All of you stay standing right where you are now or I'll shoot!" Harry shouted. People heeded his voice and froze.

Before long, an ambulance came, and the paramedics rushed into the store, checking the motionless woman for a pulse. Elira could see they listened for breathing and used a stethoscope to try and find a heartbeat. Finding none, they loaded the woman's body into the ambulance without a further attempt to save her life. The crowd stood shocked and silent.

Harry brushed himself off. "She deserved what happened to her, the insane fool! And the rest of you will, too, if you don't mind your place!" He walked away scowling. More sirens sounded, and police rushed in to apprehend the other woman involved in the fight and take eyewitness testimony from bystanders and Harry.

In a frenzy to get away from the store as fast as she could, Elira threw money on the counter for the cashier, took all her groceries, and raced to her car to return home. What a world to live in anymore! Such violence! What a risk to leave home. She felt sick to her stomach. *Lives are expendable,* she thought.

When home, she recounted everything to Ben, who put his arms around her and squeezed her into his chest.

"Elira, I'm glad you're safe, and I should go for groceries myself or go with you from now on! I know I had asked you to look at headlines on the computer to let me know what's happening in the world, but let's turn on the TV today to hear what's going on, especially in the war with Israel."

Elira turned the TV on and sat beside Ben on the sofa.

A news anchor came on screen. "Master Ibrahim Mizrah, now more fondly called Master Ibrahim, by his title and first name only, has announced that there is a famine over a third of the world, and it's getting worse. Wars have broken out in various countries. The war between Israel and Russia and its allies is escalating and costing more lives and money daily. Master Ibrahim is now stating the New World currency is becoming scarce, and more needs to be made and distributed."

Elira shot a nervous glance at Ben. "With famine on the rise, it'll be even harder for us to buy food. We need to hoard what we can to serve us for the near future until this hopefully passes, but I don't want to go buy food any longer in this hostile environment. Perhaps we can just plant a garden of vegetables and beans! What do you think?"

"Not a bad idea at all! Let's see if we can get some seeds, maybe from the vegetables we do buy! We can also buy dried beans and plant them." Ben replied.

Elira's phone rang. It was her longtime friend, Jane, from high school. They had always kept in touch. Elira stepped away from the sofa next to Ben and walked into her bedroom.

"Elira, how've you and Ben been holding up these past several months since The Disappearance?"

"Oh, Jane, things have worsened. Ben and I are not working

much anymore. Of course, Ben's business failed during the aftermath of The Disappearance, and he doesn't have the resources to get back on his feet. As you know, borrowing money is not possible at the banks right now. I'm not working steadily in my function as an engineering technologist until my position is reassigned to the New World Order. Simon is in the hospital because he was attacked by his next-door neighbor, Duncan. Duncan has been nasty to Ben, too, when he sees him. We fear that he is ratcheting up his fury and rage to bully us into possibly selling Simon's home to him and leaving the neighborhood." Elira sat up against one of the pink pillows on her bed. It was good to hear Jane's voice again.

"There's so much backlash against the Jewish people right now. You should probably not stay with Ben and Simon at their home!" Jane said.

"Whatta you mean by that?" Elira asked drumming her index finger on the end table next to her bed.

"I'm sure you heard that as much as eighty-three percent of the Russian allied army has been wiped out in the mountains of Israel by an earthquake and fire that seemed to come up out of nowhere. Now more of the world has aligned with the cause of Russia, and the Arab nations are seething with rage, vowing more revenge toward Israel. Even Master Ibrahim is no longer enforcing the peace treaty with Israel!" Jane said.

"I know! My head spins with all the new daily developments, but I love Ben and eventually want to marry him. I can't leave him and his poor dad," Elira replied.

"You might be endangered with them, Elira."

"I'll have to consider my options and take my chances. How about you? How are you doing?"

"We're barely holding a roof over our heads, and we go hungry a lot, with only one good meal a day. I wish our lives were back where they were when we were children," Jane's voiced cracked.

"I do too! I wish I could turn back time or that I could wake up and find this is all a nightmare," Elira replied.

"With all of this going on, I know that God can't exist, and I'm glad I have not foolishly believed in Him like some," Jane said.

"Me too, Jane, and I always say that to Ben, but he has received too much of his mother's influence."

"He would be a fool to believe like she did; and by the way, where is she now after all these many months?"

"I know and I agree, but I have to get back to Ben now and hopefully find a little something for lunch."

"Good luck, Elira. Please do take care of yourself with Ben and Simon. Don't become a target! You're not even Jewish."

With that, Jane ended the call, and Elira walked from her bedroom to the fridge. She found one apple and some peanut butter. Not too long ago, this was just a tiny snack for her. Looking pitifully at the two meager items, she sighed. *How much life has changed!*

Chapter 10
Increasing Persecution

The Russian-Israeli War did end with the defeat of Russia and its Arab allies. As a result, Israel was hated now more than ever before and only after natural, or possibly supernatural forces, such as the earthquake and fires, had helped them to win.

Ben nervously paced back and forth listening to Elira's recounting of the most recent news. "Elira, are you saying that 144,000 Israelis are gone with no trace of where they are?"

"Yes, Ben, that's what I'm saying! The news is reporting that Master Ibrahim and his sources believe that these Israelis have fled and taken cover somewhere, but the location has not yet been discovered despite an active search by military personnel and satellite image."

"Wow! It is as if this is The Disappearance all over again, except that no one witnessed any disappearance before their very eyes! I told you, Elira, Mom said God would hide some Israelis from the destruction that would come upon Israel during the time she called 'the Great Tribulation.'"

"Well, Ben, remember what I've been saying all along about

myths and fantastic beliefs! It may look like a fulfillment of what your mom told you, but it makes practical sense that some Israelis would go into hiding because of the war with Russia and the tremendous damage done by the earthquake."

"Elira, don't you get it? It's inevitable! Jews will be more despised and shunned now because it's hard for the world to believe Israel got the upper hand with Russia and that a large number of Israelis have had the ability to hide away. I'm sure the New World Order is wondering what Israel is up to and is not happy with what happened."

"How do you know that? Master Ibrahim tried to broker peace for Israel with its Middle Eastern neighbors. I am sure he is glad for the fact that the Israelis made it through this latest aggression by Russia and its Middle Eastern allies," Elira replied.

"Okay, Elira, we'll soon see what happens," Ben said.

"Oh, Ben, you're thinking with your mom's beliefs again! I think you fear her predictions are fact!"

Ben, repulsed at Elira's response, marched out of her bedroom into the living room. He dropped onto the sofa with a huge sigh. *Elira thinks I'm crazy, but what if Mom's faith was right after all? It may be crazy, but it doesn't look like coincidence.*

WHEN BEN OPENED the door of his dad's home to throw out trash, Duncan came running up with four other neighbors in tow.

"Well, has the despicable Simon disappeared now too?" he taunted him, referring to the recent disappearance of 144,000 Israelis. Ben's blood pressure rose. He could feel his heart beats pounding in the veins that bulged from his neck.

Elira heard Duncan's insulting remark and came running to the door beside Ben.

A neighbor named Sheryl spoke up. "We were so tired of hearing Esther and her foolhardy beliefs about a Rapture of Christian believers. She also mentioned that a number of Jews would be removed and kept safe by God, too, from what she called 'the Great Tribulation,' whatever that means!"

"Yes," said Lauren, another neighbor. "Why haven't you disappeared yourself?" She glared at Elira. "You're not a Jew, and yet you stay with them. What's your problem? Wars always seem to be fought because of them! Now where are those 144,000 people? Where are they hiding? They had help from earthquakes and fires to win the war, and now like cowards, some of them are hiding!"

Ben found that his hands were clenching into fists.

"This whole Christian-Jewish disappearing act has to go!" said another neighbor, Tom. "What foolishness these extreme beliefs and acts have become while the rest of us are suffering in a world with many challenges right now! It is unconscionable that all this is being made into a circus. What a nasty, cruel joke."

"Yep!" Wimberly, yet another neighbor, exclaimed. "And how both Christians and Jews have obviously planned this hoax for a long time and finally succeeded in pulling it off! It shows belief in God is a sham! Shame on you both for associating with it!"

Ben was going to explode. Elira felt threatened for their safety as neighbors got up close to them to ask more questions.

"You hateful, anti-Semitic cowards! Why don't you return to your 'dog shelters,' you low-lifes, picking on me and my girl-friend! We have about as much to do with these events as you do! Get out of our faces right now!" Ben raged.

The neighbors also rebuffed with rage, ready for a physical

fight. Elira acted quickly to diffuse the situation. "Ben, you go inside. I'll place the garbage in the trash can for us, no problem."

Ben was breathing heavily. Not moving an inch, he glared long and hard at the group. *I must go inside, or I'll kill them.* With all his might, Ben turned and walked into the living room while Elira addressed them.

"Look, I didn't fall in love with Ben because he believes in these farfetched lies! Ben and Simon do not believe in any of this. That is why they are both still here and not part of any play-acting plot." Elira stepped over to place the bag of garbage in its can next to the garage.

"Well, you will endure a lot of adversity, you fool!" Duncan sneered. "It seems like the nations of the New World Order have not taken a liking to this new disappearance, this time by Jews, and they are meeting to determine sanctions and repercussions for those Jews who are still around. Simon may lose everything after all, the scoundrel!"

Elira could not understand Duncan's hate. If she were to believe in a hell, she felt this hate for Jews and Christians had come right out of there. "Whatever happens, happens!" Elira replied. "As for me, I'm not leaving Ben for something that neither he nor Simon believe in just because they are Jews by birth!"

Elira backed away slowly up the front step, all the while watching the neighbors intently, as she slammed the front door behind her and locked it.

Ben gazed at her with shock in his eyes. "It's happening already!"

Elira studied Ben's face. "What are you talking about?"

"The persecution of Jews," Ben replied.

"Don't be silly. This is only one hateful, anti-Semitic

neighbor who has collected other neighbors who are filled with fears and anxieties. This world is more unstable with all that has happened. Don't jump to conclusions, Ben! Let's check in for any further news."

"Okay but remember to be careful about a steady diet of news."

"Ben, we can't keep our heads buried, right?"

Elira grabbed the remote to turn on the TV. A news correspondent on the ground in Jerusalem was reporting: "With the latest disappearance of 144,000 Israelis who cannot be found, Master Ibrahim has imposed stiff regulations and sanctions on all Israelis and Jews throughout the world. Additionally, he has announced that the peace treaty with Israel has been broken because these 144,000 Israelis have suspiciously hidden themselves from the New World Government."

"What does that mean for all Israelis and Jews?" the news anchor asked.

"Well, at this time, it is unknown what all the regulations and sanctions will entail, but there are a couple of them effective immediately. Master Ibrahim has ordered the seizure of all monies, property, and assets of those already indicated as Jews, Israelis, or of Israeli origin on the New World's data base. Additionally, they are required to register with their local authorities to confirm their ethnicity and to become a separate part of the New World data base," the news correspondent replied.

"Wow! Isn't this a huge form of discrimination?" the news anchor asked.

"Well, if you wish to call it 'discrimination,' you must keep in mind monitoring of these people is of utmost importance given the events that have unfolded in the last several days. Jewish and Israeli bank accounts must be frozen, and their assets seized for ultimate review by the New World Government."

"What will they do in the meantime to exist?" the news anchor asked.

"It seems like it will be up to them to rely on other family and friends who have the New World currency to help them subsist until their money can be returned to them. However, going forward, their money and other assets will remain the possession of the New World Order always. They will only be managers, but not owners of their assets any longer. This is to keep them from any further suspicious activity. Master Ibrahim takes the disappearance of the 144,000 Israelis very seriously," the correspondent added.

"I'm thinking that some of those that might not be listed of Jewish or Israeli origin yet may be tempted to remove their money and transfer their assets before they can be discovered. What happens to them when and if they are discovered?" The news anchor asked.

"Any who have not registered and are eventually discovered and caught by the authorities will be imprisoned and any of their money or property seized permanently. They will be stripped of everything," the news correspondent replied.

This time Ben grabbed the remote, shut off the TV, and collapsed into his easy chair, head in hands. "This is what I was afraid of, Elira. It's becoming ugly now for all us Jews!" Ben wailed from the depths of his being. Elira rushed to his side. Wrapping her arms around him, she cradled him.

"Honey, don't worry. We've got each other. We've already tapped into my savings, and we'll continue to use it until you can manage your dad's money again. I know he's got the old Medicare system paying for his medical bills, and you can pay what's owed after that from his own funds."

"Elira, you don't understand. Even Dad's house will be seized from us. Yes, maybe we can manage it for ourselves for a while; but someday, the New World Order may just command us to leave Dad's home. After all, it belongs to them now. Whether I register or not, they can discover this home and us." Ben cried uncontrollably.

Elira's phone dinged with a news notification. She feared looking at it, but Ben motioned at her to check. "What does it say, Elira?" Ben asked.

Elira quickly read it. "Well, it's saying what we've already heard on TV, but there is one more bit of news." She dreaded to tell him.

"What's that?"

Elira hesitated. "Master Ibrahim will be going to the new temple he authorized the Jews to build at Jerusalem and he will take possession of it."

Ben couldn't believe what he heard. "Didn't I just tell you, Elira? Our possessions are no longer ours and can be taken at will!" Once again, the feeling of nausea overtook him. He felt faint and started to shake. *Mom was right. This is the end of the world, and I was left behind. We're all doomed!*

"Ben…Ben?" Elira noticed his panic. "Here, lie down! Take some deep breaths. You'll be fine." She eased him onto the sofa and placed a pillow behind his head. Ben felt like the room was closing in on him. Thoughts were racing so fast through his mind that his head spun. "Elira, honey, things are looking fuzzy. My arms and hands are tingling."

"Ben, you just need to focus on your breathing and on us right now…here…in the present. Whatever you fear for the future may not happen. Stop it, please!"

"Why is this happening to Jews when the number of Christians who disappeared was a whole lot more?"

"Ben, it's the same for the family members of those in The Disappearance. All churches have been closed to ensure that nothing like The Disappearance or worse ever happens again. Faith and religion are suspect in general. And, as I've often told you, faith and religion are an opiate for people. They're myths that keep people bound."

"What will we do to survive? I've lost hope for survival." Ben sobbed.

Elira patted his chest. "Let's look for what money your dad may still have here at the house, and let's use it until we can get your bank accounts unfrozen!" Elira wrapped her arms around his waist. "It sounds like we should register first anyway. We may be able to take some money out before we register. We'll just have to see what we can do."

"I don't know, Elira. They may have already frozen my dad's and my accounts."

"We'll see about that. Until then, no worries, honey."

Ben felt comforted by her words, but then thought of his mom. His mom was wise to escape all of this. *I need to learn what she believed. I've got to experience what she had.* Ben felt better and sat up.

Elira got up from the sofa. "I'll head to my room to get my purse and then we can go."

Ben walked down the hallway behind her and went straight to his parents' bedroom. It was still there on the nightstand! Ben picked up his mom's Bible and pressed it hard to his chest and heart. *I've got to read this.* He glanced up to notice Elira in the doorway pausing to look at what he was doing. She abruptly turned away.

I bet she hates what I just did. She's afraid I'm going to become like Mom, and she'll lose me, too.

"Come on," Elira spoke up from her bedroom. "Let's check for any leftover money in the house, and then let's head to the bank. Didn't Simon say he'd stashed some money away? Do you know where? After that, we should pay him a visit and see how he's doing."

"Yes, indeed!" Ben agreed, but not without first putting

Mom's Bible near his bed where he could read it later that night. *How good to be able to read Mom's Bible,* he thought.

Chapter 11
A Devastating Turn of Events

Elira counted the money she and Ben found deep in Simon's closet. She looked up at Ben with disappointment, "Honey, it only amounts to about $500—pocket change!"

"Didn't Dad have some more stashed away?"

"No, Ben, no more after you found the $100 bill he had inserted in your mom's Bible. That makes the total of $500." Ben glanced at the cash in Elira's hand with dismay as Elira summed up their financial situation.

"Unfortunately, this won't go far. It takes a day's wages just to buy a loaf of bread anymore, and just imagine buying meat! I'm wondering if it's even available anymore. Perhaps high government officials and the extremely wealthy might be able to find and purchase it, but not us. I so miss the days when we went to dinner at exquisite restaurants and enjoyed a meal and wine together!" Elira sighed.

"We are still the lucky ones, Elira. One-fourth of the world's population have died, many from malnourishment and starvation—if tornadoes, floods, wildfires, earthquakes, and worldwide pandemics have not taken them," Ben replied.

"What a miserable time to be alive!" Elira exclaimed. "Sometimes I think that we might also die as victims of the crime and lawlessness that has dramatically increased across our world. Murder and homicide are out of bounds. At least buying a loaf of bread will help us to survive another day or two. I know that you and I, along with other people, are looking underweight these days. I recently took in a few of our clothes for us to better fit in. Enough of that! Come now. Let's go visit your dad and stop in at the bank to see if we can get more money out before that opportunity is gone," Elira said.

"Okay," Ben said and walked as if in a trance toward the door. Elira quietly tucked the $500 into her purse and headed out with him.

"HERE WE ARE!" Ben said. They both got out of the car and walked into the bank. One of the tellers signaled for them to approach.

"How may I help you?" the teller asked.

Ben pulled up his bank identification. "I need to get some cash." The teller looked at his ID and scanned it into her own bank computer terminal. "I'm sorry," she said, "but that account has already been frozen by the New World Order until further notice."

Elira shot a quick glance at Ben. Ben fidgeted nervously and hung his head. The teller returned his ID to him. *Unbelievable! So quickly! What am I going to do now?* Ben thought.

Elira took out her ID. "Here's mine. I'd like to withdraw some cash." The teller scanned Elira's ID.

"How much would you like?" the teller asked.

"I'd like three thousand New World dollars; and, I also have an additional $500 in cash that never got converted into the New World currency. Please convert it and add it to the total amount being withdrawn." The teller sniffled and complied with her request, eyeing both Ben and Elira silently.

"Here you are!" she said as she gave Elira the cash and receipt. "The equivalent in New World currency is $3250. She counted it out for Elira and said, "Of course, this total amount includes the conversion of the old $500 minus the conversion fees we also take out."

Elira looked stunned at the amount left over from the original $500 Simon had. Only half of it! Nonetheless, she said, "Thank you!" Elira placed the money in her purse and took Ben's hand. She calmly walked to the door and left the bank.

Ben stood at his car still in disbelief. "I can't believe it, Elira! Just like that. I now have nothing!" He wept.

"Ben, remember it's frozen, but not forever! You'll get it back soon."

"Yes, but it will never be mine to possess again! I'm no longer the owner of it or any of what Dad, Mom, or I had. I'm now just a 'manager.' It's...it's such a violation of my personhood and independence! You can't even imagine!" Elira got him into the car and climbed in herself.

"Honey, I know it is such a violation and affront to you, your personhood, and what you worked for! No, I can't imagine it because I'm not in your place. I feel sorry for you, but it will be okay. The earth went through an unprecedented time with The Disappearance; and now, precautions are being quickly taken to avoid further trouble, and I guess the government felt the announcement from Master Ibrahim was sufficient notification to all those affected. Some may not be discovered yet until they register or are caught first."

"I didn't even bother to ask, but I'm sure that Dad's money is frozen, too."

"You both have the same last name; and undoubtedly, if yours is frozen, I'm sure Simon's is also."

"Now what are we going to do?" Ben asked again.

"We've been over this, Ben. Like I said, we'll survive until your accounts are reopened. We have my money to depend on. That's better than nothing." *Wow! Poor Ben!* Elira thought. *So good to be Gentile right now. I can't tell Ben that. It shouldn't matter, but it does!*

"We also need to register you and your dad in that separate database that Master Ibrahim was talking about. The sooner we do that, the sooner you can get to your money. You don't want to be discovered as not having registered."

"That's a good idea. I will drive there before we visit Dad," Ben said.

"Okay, great!"

They arrived at the county office set up for registration of any persons of partial or full Jewish and/or Israeli descent. Ben went up to a window and showed his ID to a county official. The official looked at Ben's ID with a cold, blank expression on his face and motioned silently with his index finger to computers set up for digital registration.

Elira and Ben walked over to one of the computers. Elira peered over Ben's shoulder as he filled out information detailing his parents' names, dates of birth, and their primary residence address online. The online form also asked about his family's countries of origin. He input all the information requested. At the end of the registration, a notice came up online to tell Ben that any of his or his family's assets would be released for supervised management under the auspices of the New World government in about ten to fifteen business days.

Elira grabbed Ben's arm in hers. "Come on. You're done now. Let's go."

"Yeah, you're right!" Ben stood up from the computer desk and walked with Elira to the exit.

As they were leaving, Elira caught a contemptible glance out of the corner of her eye from the official who had initially motioned them to the computers. *Why is he looking at me that way? That's creepy! What's he thinking?*

"Ben, I don't feel comfortable here at all."

"Sure, Elira, we're leaving," Ben said and picked up his pace.

The man who had given Elira the contemptible look suddenly shouted to her. "Just wait a minute! Are you with him?"

Sizing him up as trouble, Elira rebuffed at his question. "Why, yes! Is there a problem?"

"Oh, yes, there is! You are a Gentile, and here's fair warning: If you plan on marrying him, you will also have to register here and have your assets turned over to the New World Order."

The realization hit Elira like a ton of bricks. *Yes, this is going to be trouble.! I never thought of it. Calm is what I need now!* She gave him a condescending glance. "There's no problem at all with that!"

"Okay, Miss, that's fine…it's your problem, not mine!" he snickered. Elira felt a cold chill run down her back. This evil was beyond bounds. *I've become a victim, too.* She hesitated for a moment while Ben took her hand and walked out of the building. Elira was now the one to have an empty, anxious feeling in the pit of her stomach.

"Are you okay, honey?" Ben asked.

"Ben, I know you feel like a second-class citizen, but now I feel that way, too!"

"I can see that! He was a bully trying to instill fear into you, a Gentile, ironically just for being with me."

"I know, Ben! This is getting horrifying. It looks like they would prefer us not to be together. Let's just go see your dad now. I don't know how much gas we have left in the car to make it anywhere else."

ELIRA AND BEN pulled up to Whispering Pines Convalescent and Rehabilitation Center.

"Ben, this is such a massive facility with a beautiful view from its all-glass front of its well-manicured gardens.

"Elira, let's go in and register at the front desk.

The receptionist, whose lapel tag read "Wanda," didn't look up from her desk at all.

Ben cleared his throat. "Ummm....Do we need to sign in?"

"Of course, everyone is required to," Wanda snapped and continued with her work at the desk. After Ben signed in, she curtly handed him a pass and without another word, pointed down the hallway to her right.

Ben and Elira quietly walked down the hallway hand in hand. Ben entered his dad's room first and was shocked at what he saw. Simon was lying in his hospital bed, looking tired and thin. He had lost a lot of weight and was in a deep sleep.

Elira's eyes slowly scanned the room. She reacted with alarm. "The room smells like urine and is awfully dirty. Ben, I honestly don't believe your dad is receiving much physical therapy or rehabilitation at all—or even eating enough food! I'm concerned. How do you feel about it?"

"I agree. Dad is only a specter of what he was when he entered here! What's this about?" Ben came to his dad's side. Simon slowly opened his eyes to look up at his son.

"How are you, Dad?" Ben asked.

Simon's response was delayed; but finally, he moved his lips and whispered, "I am so tired! Who are you?"

"Dad, it's Ben…your only child. Don't you recognize me?"

"Oh, okay, Son," Simon replied. "Am I going somewhere with you? What do you want?" Ben turned to look at Elira with complete astonishment. She read the concern all over Ben's face.

Simon has lost his sense of reality. He's deteriorating. Not now! Not for Ben! Elira thought.

"Dad, Elira and I came to see you. You are in a rehab center to get stronger and better, but it looks like you're not doing well here. You've lost weight. Do they get you out of bed to exercise at all?"

"Exercise? What do you mean? I'm very tired."

"Listen, Dad, I will try to get you out of here and home with me as soon as possible. Do you understand what I'm saying?"

"This is my home, isn't it? Where are you going to take me? I don't know who you are! Please leave me alone!"

Ben was stunned. "Dad doesn't even know I'm his son, Elira! Let's get him out of here before he dies!"

He grabbed Elira's hand and left the room. He marched to the reception desk. "I demand to see the director!" Ben exclaimed.

"She's not available," Wanda said.

"I'm taking Dad out of this facility right now!"

"That would be against medical advice," Wanda retorted.

"I'll sign all the documents I need to. Just get them," Ben snapped back.

Wanda picked up the phone, pressed a button on it, and a moment later a woman came running down the hallway to where Ben and Elira were standing.

"I'm Marianna Haywood, the assistant clinical director. What can I do to help you?" she asked.

"I want to remove my father from this horrific center NOW!" Ben shouted.

"You can't do that, sir! There is protocol that must be followed, and you can't remove him on a personal whim."

"Are you crazy? Yes, I can! I am his son, and I have the right to remove my dad if I feel his treatment here is not satisfactory. It doesn't even seem ethical how you treat the patients here!"

"I hear your concerns. First, your father is a competent adult who signed his own papers to be placed in rehabilitation. Unless you have power of attorney or health surrogacy on behalf of your father, or if he is declared legally incompetent, you cannot do anything. Let me also remind you that this center takes money to operate, and there is an accumulated balance owed us for Simon's care that must be paid before his release. Perhaps you're unaware that his bank account is frozen, evidenced by the fact that we have been unable to receive our auto-payments from it for the portion the old Medicare system does not cover. We cannot receive any further payments until it is reopened. Do I make myself clear, Mr. Goldberg?"

Ben was even more furious but knew calling the police would yield him nothing. They clearly had the upper hand, and he couldn't alienate them further by his actions and behavior. He also worried about worse repercussions for his dad.

"I will contact an attorney and take this up in a few days. My father needs exercise and mental stimulation. I found him sedated, sleepy, and much thinner. I bet he doesn't eat the meals he's given because he sleeps too much of the time and the food is removed before he can eat some of it by the time he wakes up. He is regressing, not only physically, but mentally."

"Your father is a senior adult with a brain injury. He is coping the best he can with the help we give him. We're not miracle workers! And he is very resistant to any type of therapy offered. Severe irritability and anger are part of the fallout of his brain injury. I think you will find that you and your dad are receiving the best that can be offered here. Wanda will be glad to see you out now!"

Before Ben could speak another word in reply, security guards came up, took each of them by the arms and escorted them speedily outside the facility. "Unbelievable," exclaimed Ben. "That was so fast it made my head spin!"

"Yes," Elira replied. "I'm with you on that! All we can do is head for the car."

"Dad is doomed in this facility unless I can get him out! I will have to see what I can do!"

"For sure!" Elira said. "It seems hopeless for him here! What's more is that payment can only come through when the New World Government is well-pleased to release it! What a terrifying time! Such control."

"Elira, I feel so bad that you are experiencing this with me."

"Nonsense!" Elira pulled him in for a kiss.

"I love you dearly," Ben said to her. "I think it's time that I find any Messianic Jewish believers who may be left here on earth. Mom believed so much in Yeshua HaMashiach and I need to discover her faith. I need some peace."

Elira took a step back. "Ben, you know that's hocus-pocus! You are pulling at straws to get answers. Be careful. You could suffer death for such outlandish beliefs, and to no avail. The New World Government does not take kindly to Jews or Messianic Jews, and people who call themselves 'born-again' Christians either."

"Honestly, right now, I believe that Mom's faith will buoy me up above the mire of this unbelievable mess. It did for her. She always felt uplifted when she connected to God. I have been thinking for some time now that she had the correct faith that I lacked."

Once home, Ben tried to look online for the phone number

of his mom's rabbi. When he found it, he called, but no response. He found other numbers of people he felt were part of her Messianic congregation. He got through to one of the women in the congregation.

"Hello, who is this?" the voice on the phone asked.

"Hi, my name is Ben Goldberg. I'm Esther Goldberg's son. My mother was lost during The Disappearance. Is Rhoda Newman available?"

"No, Rhoda Newman also left in The Disappearance. I'm her daughter, Ruth Newman. What do you need?"

"I want to speak to someone about the Bible and the Messianic Jewish tradition. Is the rabbi of the Messianic congregation still around?"

"No, he isn't! He also left during The Disappearance. What do you want from the rabbi or any of his congregation who went with him?"

"I want to know their beliefs. My mom so wholeheartedly gave her life for those beliefs."

"I can help you a bit with that. As you probably know, they believed in Jesus as their Messiah. They spoke of the Rapture, the time when Christ would come in the clouds and draw them heavenward to escape the Great Tribulation. I believe we were left behind because we did not believe, nor receive, Messiah Jesus as our Savior," Ruth said.

"Yes, I agree. I'm sad about it. My mom never wanted this to happen," Ben said.

"All we can do now is receive Messiah Jesus as they did. It may be that we will go through major persecution and death to be joined with Him, because the others were raptured and escaped ahead of time," Ruth responded.

"I don't even know how to receive Messiah Jesus!" Ben exclaimed, "And I know nothing of the Bible. My mom tried to share it with me, but I wouldn't listen, and whatever she tried to tell me, didn't stick."

Ruth exhaled and continued speaking, "Among my mom's papers, I found a prayer she left for me. The prayer is called a 'Sinner's Prayer,' which asks Jesus to come into my heart and forgive me of my sins. She instructed me to pray that prayer, or anything like it, and Jesus would come into my heart and life. I would become a new person in Jesus Christ, saved from my sin and the darkness of the time we're living in. I have prayed that prayer and have begun to read the Bible. I now believe as my mother did, and I know that Messiah Jesus has come to live in my heart. I am different, changed, and I desire to be like Jesus—full of love and light. I don't want to do the old things I was involved in that led to emptiness and hurt in my life."

Hearing this from Ruth, Ben was filled with hope. *Maybe… just maybe…it's not too late to make a connection to God and to Mom's legacy.*

"Is there any possibility that we could meet, and you could bring me your mother's prayer with her instructions and anything else she left you that explains her deeply personal faith?" Ben asked and then added, "I would like to look at what she left you and review all of it. I still have my mom's Bible, and I will start to read it, but I don't have any clue where to begin. It seems tedious and unintelligible to me," Ben said.

"It did to me at first too," Ruth responded, "but after I received Jesus into my heart and life, I started reading my mom's Bible, beginning with the New Testament, and it began to make perfect sense to me." Ruth paused and continued, "In fact, one of the apostle Paul's letters describes the Bible, or the Word of God, as not making any sense to an unbeliever. The apostle Paul was a chief apostle of Messiah Jesus. Paul had also been a Jewish rabbi and member of the elite Jewish body of elders known as the Sanhedrin."

"Interesting! Was he persecuted in his day for being a believer in Jesus, too?" Ben asked.

"Yes, he was! He died a Christian martyr, but not before he taught about Jesus to all the known world of his day. He began as a persecutor of Christians himself before he was converted to Christ. I read about it in the Acts of the Apostles in the New Testament."

"Wow! My girlfriend, Elira, and I need to meet you in person. You are an answer for all that I've been wanting to know since The Disappearance. When can we meet?" Ben asked.

"Right now, I cannot drive my car anywhere. I'm limited on gasoline, and I don't know about city transportation."

"Where do you live?" Ben asked.

"I live in Beacon Light Estates, just off the main highway exiting the city, but I try not to leave my home much anymore. Too dangerous!"

"Well, we definitely could come see you, but you are right about not leaving home unless it's necessary these days. Let's just plan on meeting by phone. It would be easier for both of us. I could set a time and day with you where Elira can also join us."

"Sounds good to me! Sooner rather than later is best because we don't know how much longer we can share and talk about faith, especially since the closure of churches and synagogues. I hope our phones will not be tapped!"

"Yes, I agree. Let me talk with Elira, and I think we can speak together within the next two days, if that's all right with you."

"Yes. Just call me back with the exact day and time," Ruth said.

"Yes, I will, and thank you so much for what you have explained to me today! It has been such an encouragement to hear what you had to say and to get to know you. Mom spoke of your mother so very much, and apparently, they were rather close friends."

"Yes, I think they were, but I know your mother couldn't always associate with mine in the presence of your father and many of their Jewish friends who were not believers like our mothers were," Ruth added.

"That must have been so difficult and awkward for them. I wish I had Mom here again and could speak to her about her faith and tell her that I understand her more now," Ben said.

"Yes, I know my mother would be so proud of the decision I made to receive Messiah Jesus—she wanted that for me so much! But it's better late, than never."

"You're right! Nice to talk with you, and I'll call you back soon. Bye for now," Ben said.

"Bye!"

Ben set the phone down and went to find Elira. *Would she continue to scoff at his search for faith?"*

Chapter 12
An Impending Doom

Ben entered the kitchen and found Elira at the table with her laptop open as she scrolled through news headlines that were getting grislier by the day. He looked over her shoulder and paused at one headline. "What? There's an increase of shark and whale attacks on boats and ships in the ocean? Really? And on land, too, wild animals like bears, coyotes, and cougars are targeting more human beings than ever before?"

"Yeah, Ben, isn't that just odd?"

"I'd say it is! But probably not a coincidence. Even the animal kingdom is in revolt. Elira, we need to go to talk to Ruth."

Elira turned to Ben. "Who? What…? What's going on?"

"I called a church friend of Mom's. Mom's friend is gone too, but her daughter, Ruth, answered. I want to meet Ruth—she is left behind like us. I suggested a further phone call with the three of us, but I really need to be there to get a look at items she received from her mom."

"Really, Ben, is that necessary? You spoke to her by phone,

and we must conserve what money we have. Gas prices have increased five times. Things are hard to come by all over the world."

"I know, but she doesn't live far. Like I said, it would be good for me to review what she's got."

"I am not interested in the beliefs and philosophies of your mom and her friend. This is just a time when horrific things are happening, but not any different from some of the atrocities, pandemics, and natural phenomena that have taken place all throughout human history as I've said before. So, what's the big deal? If you want to go, go on your own, but be careful. It's not an inviting atmosphere out there, especially for you."

"Okay. If it's fine with you, I'll go right now."

"Why the hurry?"

"I don't know. I just feel things happen every day, and I don't want to miss out on this opportunity."

"Okay, suit yourself."

"Thanks for your understanding. I'll call her now."

Ben went back to the living room and phoned Ruth again. "Ruth," Ben said, "I talked with Elira, but she's not interested in a phone call to review the items your mom left behind. If it's okay with you, I'd like to come see them for myself today."

"I really have nothing else planned. So, yes, it's fine for you to come over today."

"Okay. I'll be right over," Ben said.

"Oh, okay. Then I'll see you soon."

Ben took the car keys, kissed Elira, and said 'goodbye' as he walked out the front door. He slipped into his car and backed onto the street. As he did so, he noticed Duncan next door glaring at him from over the hedges that separated their two properties. Such seething hate. *What a freak!*

Ruth's home was a modest house in a subdivision of middle-class homes where families lived, and children grew up. The neighborhood had a little park with a walking path and a jungle gym. The park was deserted and unkempt now.

As he exited his car, the front door to the home opened, and Ruth stepped out with a big smile. She had golden blonde hair that glowed in the afternoon sun and bright blue eyes. She was dressed in jeans and an orange T-shirt, with brown flip-flops on her feet.

"You must be Ben, Esther's son!" Ruth shouted out to Ben as he walked up.

"Indeed, and it's so nice to meet you in person, Ruth! You have your mother's hair and blue eyes!"

"People have always told me how much I look like my mother, and oh, how I miss her these days! Come on into my living room."

Ben stepped into the cozy home. It had a good-sized living and dining room combo with an open kitchen and barstools at a counter facing the living room.

Ruth motioned for Ben to sit at the dining room table, and she brought out her mother's articles. "Let me show you my mother's Bible," Ruth said. "You can see so many pages have been underlined. She also wrote in the margins, undoubtedly during sermons that the rabbi gave. I also see tear stains on certain pages where what she read must have moved her."

Ben took up the Bible with trembling hands and opened it. The pages fell to a place where apparently Rhoda had read many times about the love of God through Messiah Jesus. The verse that stuck out was John 3:16, with heavy highlights and notes all around it. In fact, there were several paper announcements from her congregation placed within that page.

Ben read the verse. "'For God so loved the world that He gave His one and only Son that whoever believes in Him shall not perish but have eternal life.'" Ben looked at Ruth, his eyes filling with tears.

"This must be what our mothers discovered!"

"Why yes!" Ruth exclaimed. "Yes, it is, and that's why they've not had to endure what we are now experiencing. They were literally taken out of the Great Tribulation we're experiencing today—the time when the world will pass through such a time of trouble and evil that has never, ever been endured in all human history."

"But how does this happen? Just by simply believing?"

"Okay, let me show you another passage of Scripture," Ruth said. "This states that Jesus is the Way to God, the Father. It is located a few chapters away in the same gospel of John, in John 14:6. Jesus says here, 'I am the Way, the Truth, and the Life; no one comes to the Father except through Me.'"

"Ruth, how do I get this Messiah to be my Way to God?"

"Here's the 'Sinner's Prayer' my mother left me. It's a rather simple prayer and doesn't have to be prayed word-for-word as it is here. Its meaning can be expressed in your own words."

Ben stared at the prayer. He yearned to find peace, to see Mom again, and to know the Messiah she knew. He also knew Dad and their Jewish traditions did not accept Jesus as the true Messiah, but he had no struggle with fulfilling the greatest longing of his heart: to know the transforming power his mom had come to know that changed the trajectory of her life and how she behaved.

"I want to pray this prayer, Ruth! You have prayed it too, right? Will you pray it with me?" Ben asked.

"I have prayed it, and it has meant everything to me! Yes, let's pray it together if you are ready and mean it."

"Yes, I'm ready!" Ben exclaimed.

Together they prayed, "Jesus, I know that You came to die for my sins on the cross so that I may live in right-standing before God, our heavenly Father. I ask you to forgive my sins and to come into my life. Be my Savior and Lord and help me to live for You. Thank you. Amen."

After they finished praying, Ben shed some more tears. This time, he cried with joy for the freedom he now felt in his heart. The struggle within him was over and he experienced genuine peace for the first time.

"Mom would have loved to see this day. Oh, how I wish she were here to witness it now! But somehow, I strangely feel her presence and joy just the same, as if she were here. I believe she knows," Ben said.

"I believe she does too, and she will be waiting in heaven for you to join her there!"

"I wish Dad and Elira could know the peace I feel right now. Elira is completely closed off to it. That's why she isn't here with us, and Dad is so far gone cognitively that I wouldn't know if he could comprehend what he'd be praying," Ben said.

"There is a time and place for everything. Just pray for them," Ruth answered. "God has their lives and situations in His hand. Now you'll need to grow in your new faith. I think reading the gospel of John in the New Testament is a good place to begin. When you've completed that, you can go back to the gospel of Matthew and read the other two gospels, Mark and Luke, and then the rest of the New Testament. Finally, you can go to the first book of the Old Testament, Genesis, and read through the entire Old Testament. That should help you to understand everything from creation to now. You'll also understand from Jewish history and prophecy how Messiah Jesus was ordained to come from God for the salvation of all people. Wait...all that said, do you have a Bible?" Ruth asked.

"Yes, I have Mom's Bible. I'll begin to read it, especially now. I truly feel light as a feather and full of joy. I desire to learn more about Him and His Word," Ben replied.

"Great! I guess you'll need to get back to Elira now. What are you going to do about your dad?"

"I don't know. I feel like I have very little power to help him. I'm going to seek out an attorney and see if I can bring him home," Ben said.

"I know a good attorney of our own heritage. He visited our mothers' Messianic synagogue once. I think he was curious about Messianic Judaism. He never returned to the synagogue after his first visit, though, and of course he was not part of The Disappearance—or, as you'll learn, the Bible calls it, 'the Rapture.'"

"What's his name?" Ben asked.

"His name is Michael Bachman. You'll find him on Center Street. The street number is 1112, and he's in suite four."

"Fine. I'll look him up and give him a call. I must be going, Ruth. I enjoyed the time we shared about Jesus. I believe it's been a turning point for me. God richly bless you!"

"And you, too!" Ruth replied as they made their way to her front door.

"I will never forget this moment!" Ben said, as he walked over the front door threshold toward his car.

"Shalom aleichem!" Ruth said.

"Aleichem shalom!" Ben replied. "Unto you, peace!"

As Ben drove home, so many thoughts were swirling in his head. What would Elira think or say if she knew he was now a Christian believer? What would happen to their relationship? Also, what would happen if Dad could understand his conversion, and how would that impact their father-son relationship? He thought of his mom, also, and how proud and joyous she must be now.

Soon he rounded the bend toward home and made his way onto the doorstep. This time Duncan was nowhere around, and Ben was relieved. Perhaps Duncan was sleeping off one of his many drunken stupors. It was no secret that Duncan drank a lot, and Ben wondered if that added to his maniacal rages. But as Ben slid the key into the door, he heard the voice of another neighbor, Sheila, from two doors down, who was walking her dog.

"What makes you so happy right now?" Sheila shouted. Somehow, she could see a difference in his demeanor. "You've always looked sad and anxious."

Not wanting to share his new experience, Ben only said, "That doesn't mean I have to be sad and anxious all the time, does it? I can choose to feel differently."

"Okay then! Sorry I asked." Sheila flippantly shouted back.

Ben wished she would just mind her own business and leave him alone. He didn't trust people in the neighborhood, or in this new world for that matter.

Ben stepped into his home and locked the front door behind him. He looked around the room for Elira but he didn't see her. He walked toward the bedroom, where he found her on her computer again.

"Hi, Elira, I'm home," Ben said. He noticed she was heavily involved in listening to more developing news.

She finally spoke, "Hi honey, I'm so scared! There are new developments in the New World government! Instead of an international database of every living person on earth and the use of a world currency, Master Ibrahim has now announced the use of an implanted chip inside every person which will be used to identify the person and their medical, social, family, and career history and also to be used for buying and selling anything. The implanted chip will have a number for each person, just like a Social Security number. The only difference is that every chip will also have the three digits—666, which is the code of the New World Order. But that's not all! Master Ibrahim now states that any Christian believers, like those who were part of The Disappearance, along with the 144,000 Jews who disappeared, will no longer be able to participate in the New World Order but remain on a separate list. They remain suspect to the New World Order unless the same requirements are met by them: Take the implanted chip."

Elira looked him straight in the eye. "I hope this will encourage you not to foolishly accept the beliefs your mother held and that you will break ties with Ruth, who apparently has bought into her mother's beliefs."

Ben's face flushed and he looked away. He didn't know what to do with this newest development. What would he say to Elira? She doesn't know anything about what has happened, but no way was he getting that implant. He'd die first.

"Ben don't tell me that you bought into Ruth's rhetoric. I should've not let you go alone, and I should've monitored what went on. I hope she hasn't brainwashed you."

"Elira, I prayed tonight to receive Messiah Jesus into my heart. I wanted to experience the same encounter with God through Jesus Christ that Mom had. I'm sorry if you find that offensive; but when I spoke with Ruth and saw what her mother had left her, it all came together for me."

"Noooo!" Elira jumped out of her chair and screamed at him. "You didn't! How could you? You know better than that!" She pounded his chest with her fists. "You are educated and enlightened! Why would you buy into voodoo and a hocus-pocus philosophy that cost your mother and Ruth's mother their lives? Now it will cost you your life, too, unless you accept the standards and requirements of the New World Order!"

Ben stepped back and braced himself from Elira's rage. "My life belongs to Messiah Jesus now. I have experienced a peace and joy that nothing in this world can replace. I can't conform to standards that would defy my faith."

"You're such a fool!" Elira screeched. "I love you, but how

can I keep loving someone who would throw an opportunity to live life, and live life with me, for a myth and a mythical person! Unbelievable! Foolhardy and stupid!"

Elira ran out of the kitchen toward her bedroom, tears streaming down her face. Ben quickly grabbed her arm. She spun around.

"Elira, I love you with all my heart. I will always love you, and I want to marry you. I know that my newfound faith is hard for you to understand, but I have no problem staying with you if you have no problem staying with me—until we may have to go in different directions. Who knows what will be imposed by this New World Order?"

Elira cried inconsolably.

She hates Christianity and what it's doing to her, and what it did to my mom and my dad, Ben mused. *Poor thing! What can I do?"*

"Ben, don't you see our relationship is doomed?" Elira asked. "We're already going in different directions. We may marry, but you may suffer and die for your faith, and I will be alone. We are on two separate paths, and our relationship will inevitably end."

"I totally understand; but if you're willing, I am willing to go further together until we can no longer continue," Ben said.

"I'll have to think about that. I'm not willing to suffer any harm due to your foolishness. I will let you know of my decision. In the meantime, I'll have to say good night. I'm so tired." She kissed him lightly on the cheek and made her way into her bedroom as she continued to weep.

Ben wondered about their future. He prayed out loud, "Dear Lord Jesus, Your will be done in this relationship and in all my life." He picked up his mom's Bible, sat on the couch in the living room, turned to the gospel of John, and began reading it.

Chapter 13
A Faith to Survive

Elira paced back and forth in her bedroom after a night of restless sleep. She was conflicted about her future with Ben and indecisive about what to do. *If I stay with Ben, he could suffer punishment and death for not complying to this recent edict of the New World Order. I could also be hurt because I am with him. I can't pay for his foolishness! I love him, though, and I don't want to leave him. What do I do?* Elira whimpered and left her room to find Ben.

She found Ben asleep on the sofa with his mom's Bible in his hands. He looked so handsome and innocent as a child as he slept peacefully. She cursed the move he made to take on his mom's religion. She sat beside him and saw that the Bible was opened to John. She had never even looked at a Bible. She read a few verses of the page. *What a bunch of hogwash! Here is the story of a Jewish carpenter who spurred a worldwide religion that to this day threatens reality and science and bamboozles certain weak-minded persons to follow it!*

Soon, Ben stirred. He reached out to hug her tightly.

"I love you, Elira! Please don't think of leaving me!" Ben pleaded.

"How can I think of staying with you when it would mean death for you and for me?" Elira asked. "That's completely foolish!"

"Where will you go? What will you do? At least we can stay together and weather life's storms together," Ben urged.

It did make sense to Elira that she could just wait and see, although she knew it would not work in their favor with such a strict and controlling world government.

Elira sighed. "I will have to stay here for now. I don't really want to leave because I don't have anywhere to go anyway, but your decision may leave me no other choice in the face of persecution and death from the authorities. I'm hoping you will come to your senses in time and renounce this foolish religion."

"Okay, let's stay together a little longer until we know for sure what happens next."

She hugged Ben tight. *How is he going to survive? How will we survive?* Elira saw Ben's lips moving. *Was he praying?*

After a few minutes, Ben pulled back and looked at Elira. "I have a lead on an attorney to help Dad. I'll call him in the morning," Ben said.

Elira shifted back. "Well, then, let's figure out how to divide up his care. I want to do my part—he's been so gracious to allow me to stay here."

EARLY AFTERNOON SUNSHINE broke through the living room window as Ben awoke after having fallen asleep again on the couch for a few hours. Elira's head was on his shoulder as she also slept after a mainly sleepless night. He gently tilted her head back against the sofa and left her asleep while he made a call to attorney Michael Bachman.

"Good afternoon. Michael Bachman's office."

"Good afternoon. My name is Ben Goldberg, and I am interested in having Mr. Bachman help me with getting my father released from a rehabilitation center where he has been held for several weeks now. His condition has progressively deteriorated from a TBI he suffered when he was physically assaulted by a neighbor. He is cognitively incapacitated to voice his own desire to leave, and he is not getting any better with the treatment there. I was referred to your office by Ruth Newman."

"I see," said the female voice on the other end. "Let me check if he is available." She put Ben on hold.

Not long after, a deeper voice came on the phone. "Hello, this is Michael Bachman. I understand you were referred by Ruth Newman to help with your dad's situation."

"Yes," Ben said. "I need legal help to get my dad declared incompetent, and I need to be appointed his guardian so that I can get him out of a physical rehab facility where he has not made any progress. I want to take him to his home where I can care for him."

"I will be glad to take your case. Right now, you know that Jews are suspect after the disappearance of 144,000 of us. You did well to reach out to me, but I hope that as we go to court, it will not be a problem to get incompetency proven and your appointment as guardian solidified. We need a favorable judge, but medical records will also help. What is the name of the rehabilitation center?"

"Whispering Pines Convalescence and Rehabilitation Center," Ben said.

The attorney said, "I will send them a letter to release all his medical records to this office and will give them a deadline of ten business days to produce these records for us. When we receive the records, I will review them with a nonpartial doctor and explore whether he needs to be declared incompetent. I will get back with you after that. In the meantime, please make an appointment with our receptionist, Shelley, to come in and fill out some initial paperwork, and we will also need to get a retainer of $1500 if you can give that to us when you come in."

"As you're probably aware, my bank account is currently frozen due to the New World Order's decree for all Jews. I'll need to check on whether funds are now available for use," Ben said.

"Yes, of course I am aware of it. I have also been affected by that but have learned to keep cash in a safe at home for such a time when it might be necessary. That has helped me in the interim while we all must wait. If you are not able to have the retainer by your first visit to us, don't worry about it. I will proceed with the case until you can make a payment. I visited the Messianic temple of your friend's mother, Rhoda Newman. I went only once but was impressed with the faith of these fellow Jews. I was not ready to buy into it for myself, but it was so eye-opening to see how they were so committed to, and transformed by, their faith."

"Both Ruth and I have discovered that we, too, wish that we had become committed when our mothers shared their faith with us, but we didn't, and we both have been left behind to confront what they each told us would happen," Ben said.

"Yes, I suspect that it's hard to accept that you made a mistake by not following in your mother's faith, and I also wonder if I have been left behind because of my own unwillingness to accept the Christian faith," Michael Bachman replied.

"We will have to see what happens next. In the meantime, thank you for speaking with me and taking on my dad's case. I'll be glad to make an appointment to come in as soon as possible," Ben said.

"Okay. it was a pleasure speaking with you, and I'll transfer you back to Shelley right now."

Shelley's friendly voice soon came on, and she helped Ben set an appointment for later in the afternoon. Ben ended the call and rejoined Elira, who was just waking up on the couch.

"Hey there, Sunshine!" Ben called out.

"Hey!" Elira responded, but then her facial expression soured as she suddenly became aware of her predicament with Ben. "Oh, Ben, what will become of us! I'm so sad!"

"We agreed to take it a day at a time and enjoy each moment we can together," Ben reminded her.

"I know, but it's hard to do that because I don't see a future for us."

"Elira, that's true for any of us right now, and it will only worsen."

"Ben, that's nonsense. As I've noted repeatedly, these times have occurred throughout human history. Look at the Holocaust and the horrible reign of Hitler and his Nazi Party. Your dad even referred to it in light of today's world developments, but it passed, and Hitler and his Nazis were defeated. The world went on."

Ben changed the subject to tell Elira about his phone call to Mr. Bachman. Elira listened intently. "That's excellent news! I'm glad to hear that you might be able to rescue Simon from Whispering Pines."

She had to have some caffeine now to keep going. She got up to get them tea. She was disgusted with tea. *How I miss coffee! This New World Order will have to stabilize the economy and get us living like we used to again! I can't take this much longer.* She exhaled and walked over to Ben with tea for them both and turned on the TV news.

"Elira, why must we listen to the news so much? It's depressing. It's not healthy for us anymore. Look at what it's done to us with the most recent news of the implanted chip requirement."

"Ben, what are you thinking? I've told you before: we just can't bury our heads in the sand!" *He's getting crazier,* she thought.

The anchorwoman from CBS News was reporting. "Master Ibrahim has now set a deadline for the entire world population to receive their government-ordered implants. They must be received within the next six months from the original decree. It has also been determined by the New World government that the implant will be inserted in either one of two places: the wrist or the forehead. This will simplify the ability for the authorities to scan the implant." Elira's eyes began tearing up again.

Ben shut the TV off and pulled Elira to himself, hugging her with both his arms completely around her.

"Elira," Ben whispered, "don't worry about what happens in six months. There's a lot of time beforehand for us, and we don't know what God will allow before that time comes."

"It doesn't give us much time. Don't you see that this faith of yours has already come between us, because I have no qualms about the implant—but you do, and it's all because of your newfound beliefs. I'll get the implant. I have to!" Elira laid her head on his shoulder.

"Well, I also have to follow my conscience and my heart. I love you, but I love God and His commandments more. I don't want to suffer persecution or death, but this horrible decree is coming down to us from an evil entity that is seeking worldwide control." Ben looked at Elira's downtrodden face. "Would you want to come with me to see Mr. Bachman?" Ben asked.

"Definitely, I want to make sure that all is in place to release Simon from the captivity of the rehabilitation center!" Elira retorted.

"Let's plan on leaving about 2:30 P.M. I have a 3:00 P.M. appointment."

"Okay, I will make sure everything we need to do will be completed by then," Elira said.

WHEN BEN and Elira exited their front door, Duncan jumped out in front of them and sneered at them, like a spry demonic spirit.

"This is a hell of a time for you both, isn't it?" Duncan snarled. "You two lovebirds are doomed now! You, the Jew with a Messianic heritage, and you, the Gentile who wants to go down with him like the *Titanic*! Duncan let out a wicked laugh. Perfect that you both can finally be destroyed! You fools!"

Duncan was so close to Ben that Ben could feel the heat and stench of Duncan's breath. It was almost like he was exhaling sulfur-like smoke.

Ben widened his eyes and took a swing at Duncan to get out of his way, but Duncan still stood there, as if he had devilish power and resistance. Ben had already read enough of Mom's Bible last night to see how Jesus had dealt with demonic powers who tried to inhibit and defeat Him. Recognizing that this battle now was not with a mere human being, but an obvious demonic spirit within Duncan, Ben used what he knew of God's power through Jesus Christ, and said, "I rebuke you, Satan, in Jesus's name!"

Duncan fell back, as if paralyzed. Ben grabbed Elira's hand, and they walked around Duncan without incident. As Ben started the car, Elira gazed with shock at Duncan. Duncan had still not attempted to move.

Then she looked at Ben. "What just happened there?" Elira asked.

"There are very real spiritual powers in the universe—one is the power of God and the other is the power of Satan. I simply called on God's power, which is mightier than Satan's," Ben said, as he shrugged and added, "As you've just clearly seen!"

Elira's face looked stunned and doubtful.

∾

WHEN THEY WALKED into Mr. Bachman's office later, Shelley greeted them, and Ben introduced Elira to her.

"Mr. Bachman will be right with you," Shelley said. "You can just have a seat here in the reception area for a few minutes."

Ben led Elira to a comfortable orange suede couch where they sat to wait. "Elira, I found some more cash money in Dad's safe in the closet. I am going to use that money to pay the attorney while we wait on Dad's and my bank accounts to be unfrozen."

"I'm glad you found some more money because what I have is for us to live on until you are able to use some of your own money again. I think that will be soon enough now. It has been a couple of weeks. Maybe we should check with the bank today."

As Elira was speaking, Michael Bachman entered the reception area. "Hello, Ben."

"Hello, Mr. Bachman. Let me introduce you to Elira." Mr. Bachman stuck his hand out to shake hers as Elira smiled broadly. "Nice to meet you!" she said, and all three of them proceeded into Michael Bachman's office.

"Well, now that you are here, I just want to tell you that I have contacted the facility, and they're aware that you have retained me as your attorney. I told them that a demand letter would be forthcoming regarding the medical records for Simon Goldberg. They seemed unfazed, but we will go to court to determine his competency."

"Thanks, Mr. Bachman," Ben said. "I have also brought some cash as a deposit. I have $500 with me today."

"Fine. I have some affidavits for you to sign on the cognitive ability of your dad to make his own decisions. Also, are you his only next of kin?"

"Yes, I am his only child," Ben responded.

"Okay, then, do you also have any will or testament that shows that he has left his earthly assets to you upon his death?"

"Yes, I already thought of bringing his last will and testament in so that it can show that I'm his heir and obviously the executor of his will, and that I was entrusted by Dad to manage his estate and affairs."

"Okay, please give me that, and I will have Shelley scan a copy of it."

Ben signed the affidavits at the areas that were marked for his signature. He put the $500 on Michael Bachman's desk and received a written receipt in return. Shelley returned with his dad's original last will and testament and handed it to Ben.

"At this point, we have done all that is necessary. I will send the letter for your dad's medical records to his rehabilitation center. In the interim, you should go see your dad again and try to take a video of his condition if you can. That would be helpful for our case."

"Okay, Mr. Bachman, and thanks," Ben replied.

"It was certainly a pleasure to meet you, Elira," Michael Bachman added, and then he escorted them both out of his office.

As Ben and Elira exited the premises, they said goodbye to Shelley, who flashed a broad smile at them, and then they got back into their car.

"I think you have a good attorney to take your case," Elira said.

"I think so too. I am grateful Ruth gave me his name. I think we need to go see Dad now. Are you up to it?"

"Well, I am up to it, but it hurts to see you so distraught when you see your dad's condition. I also don't want us to be mistreated for looking after your dad."

"Elira, I can't help if my relationship to Dad as his son threatens anyone at the facility. I just need to do what I have to do."

"Of course; of course. Let's go now," Elira replied.

Ben wondered how his dad would look today. He couldn't wait for the legal case to resolve itself in favor of his dad returning home.

When they arrived at the center, everything looked just as it had each time they had been there before. In the lobby was Wanda, who was always there to greet guests. They signed in without a word to her.

Wanda spoke to them in a surly manner. "I will have to check if Mr. Goldberg can be seen right now. He had his nurse and the physical therapist working with him earlier."

"No problem. I can wait a few minutes. Let me know when he can see visitors," Ben said.

Wanda stood with a scowl and walked down the corridor to Simon's room. She disappeared inside the room. Soon she came out with the nurse. They frowned at Ben and Elira being there.

"Mr. Goldberg," the nurse said, "your father has just thrown up and needs a change of bedding. We've been attempting to work with his legs and feet to get him more mobile. He has fought us and is very weak. He needs his rest. You will have to wait until we clean him up, but he is extremely agitated right now."

With that communication from the nurse, Ben's displeasure with the facility and its staff grew even more.

"I will head to his room as soon as you are done cleaning

him—or I can even help you with that myself—but I am here to see him, and I won't leave until I do." Ben declared as he stood up, widened his stance, and crossed his arms defiantly.

The nurse's face contorted into a look of disdain, and without saying another word, she strode away in the opposite direction of Simon's room. Ben and Elira continued to wait while Wanda resumed her position behind the counter. Several minutes went by, but Ben never saw the nurse return, and he finally had enough.

When Wanda wasn't looking, he flew down the hallway and into his dad's room. Wanda came running after him, but it was too late. Ben saw that his dad was on the floor obviously having some sort of seizure, his dad's arms spread straight out with wrists flexed, shaking, and he was foaming at the mouth. Ben screamed. "Dad! Dad!" He knelt beside him and tried holding his dad's head off the ground as his dad thrashed around.

"You don't belong in here right now!" Wanda yelled, "Get out!" Wanda pushed an emergency button that resounded all through the center. Ben remembered what the lawyer said about taking a video and immediately began recording on his phone as other staff rushed in.

"Grab him!" Wanda ordered. They took Ben by his arms and shoulders and dragged him all the way back down the corridor to the lobby.

Elira froze at the sight of the center personnel dragging Ben, his clothes stained with some of his dad's fluids. "Hey! What's going on here? Why are you forcing him out of his dad's room?" she demanded.

"He was told not to be in there until we were ready for him! He has violated our protocol for visitors," Wanda countered with rage.

"Yes, definitely!" another member of the staff yelled out.

"And we'll call the police to keep him from stirring up trouble until we can finish our work."

"What work?" Elira cried out. "There has been no one attending to Simon the whole time we waited here in the lobby."

The staff personnel who had a hold of Ben shoved him toward Elira and left without another word. Elira grabbed a hold of Ben in utter amazement before he fell to the floor. *This is all getting scarier. What's going to happen to us...to me?*

"Elira, this is all becoming out of hand. We are targets of a vicious evil! Let's get out of here now!"

Chapter 14
A Miracle of Faith

B en skidded into Michael Bachman's parking lot and jumped out of the car. He needed to get to him as soon as possible to save his dad's life because he didn't trust sending any pictures or videos to the attorney electronically. Everything now was being monitored by the government, and Ben mistrusted digital transmission. Besides, he wanted Mr. Bachman to see his dad's condition in person to realize its urgency.

He shoved the foyer door open and abruptly spoke to Shelley. "It's extremely critical for Mr. Bachman to get an immediate injunction to get my father out of his care center NOW!" Ben declared. "I have a video here of his further deterioration to near death. Please, I must see Mr. Bachman, if only for a moment."

Shelley glanced up to look at Ben. Startled by his demeanor, she immediately ran into Michael Bachman's office, returning with the attorney in short order. Michael Bachman saw the amazed look on Ben's face and his disheveled appearance. "What is it, Ben?" Mr. Bachman asked calmly.

Ben showed him the videos. "I just came back now from

Whispering Pines. Look at Dad lying on the floor with foam coming out of his mouth! No one attended to him in the fifteen or so minutes that Elira and I were waiting for them to let us in his room. You must do something right away or Dad will die! We can't wait!"

"I will prepare papers right now for an immediate injunction to have you obtain guardianship of your father and for him to cease to receive any further care at the facility."

Ben groaned with relief. "Thanks so much for your prompt response to this, Mr. Bachman! I will await the disposition of the injunction. Unfortunately, I don't think I can remove him by calling the ambulance unless I have a judge to order his removal, right?"

"That's right," Mr. Bachman replied.

Ben returned to the car with Elira. Looking at his gas gauge, he realized his gas tank was low.

Ben punched his steering wheel with his fist. "Elira, of all times to need gas! But if we get the injunction, I need to meet the ambulance and I need gas to do that. How I hate the sky-rocketing prices and long lines of this New World Order's oil supply shortage. It doesn't work for me, and it likely doesn't work for anyone else!" He let out a loud sigh.

"You gonna be okay?" Elira asked.

"As best as I can be. I am confident that Mr. Bachman is doing his best for us, and everything will work out! I just hate hunting for gas. I thought our world had planned to move past dependence on oil a decade or two ago. Hasn't happened!"

"I know. I get frustrated, too," Elira said.

They drove by two gas stations that were closed, and Ben wondered if the car would make it if they had to go home to wait for the immediate injunction. Finally, they saw a gas station with a line of cars. Ben steered into the line and hoped his car would be one of the lucky ones to get some gas before it ran out.

They slowly inched their way up to the pump. It wasn't surprising to see some drivers trying to jump the line. Arguments ensued. Ben looked at Elira, shaking his head, and said, "What an utterly competitive and selfish world we live in!" Ben prayed they could get to the pump without a negative incident. They soon became the second car in line when Ben heard one man shouting to another.

"Hey, man, are you an idiot or something? Are you still using the old monetary method of New World currency for the pump? Why don't you get with it? I received the chip on my wrist this week, and all I do is place my wrist on the pump's scanner and I'm done—no problem."

"Don't push me. I am not YOU!" the other man shouted. "I'll be on board with it, but when is none of your business."

Ben shuddered, then gasped when he saw the first man walk up and take a swing at the second man, bloodying his face.

"Learn to speak with respect!" said the first man as he scanned his wrist, jumped into his car, and sped away.

Elira looked bewildered. "What just happened?"

"Having a chip doesn't help people with growing anger and strife," Ben said shaking his head.

"I know, Ben, but this is the world we live in. You need to realize this. Sooner or later, everyone has to comply with the economic system set up by Master Ibrahim and the New World Order."

Tears welled up in Ben's eyes as he heard the woman he loved say this, and he feared for her eternal destination apart from God and apart from the love they shared.

Ben made it to the pump, and Elira used her money to pay. "Ben, we can only get five gallons per car. It's not much, but it's better than an empty tank. We'll probably have to stop again in another day or two."

They made it home into their driveway just as Ben's phone

rang.

"Michael Bachman here. I was able to get a sympathetic judge who saw the videos and gave an immediate injunction for guardianship of your father along with a stay of further treatment by the care facility. You need to pick your dad up immediately, as the center has already received the judge's order by email followed up by a phone call from the judge himself."

"Wow! Great! Thank you, Mr. Bachman! I am headed there right now. Bye!"

Ben turned to Elira. "Thank God we were able to get some gas for the car. The judge ordered an immediate injunction for my guardianship of Dad, and I need to pick him up as soon as I can. Will you come with me?"

"Of course. As I've told you, I plan on being with you and helping you all the way through this process." Elira backed the car out of the driveway and drove them toward Whispering Pines.

"I hope that everything with Dad's discharge from this facility will go well," Ben said. "I'm worried about how weak he has become and about taking him home. I feel they'll not help him or me for anything."

"I agree. I wonder what condition he'll be in and whether we should even try to bring him back by car. I doubt they'll give you any further instructions to help in his recovery at home," Elira answered.

"I won't depend on any friendly cooperation from them; but now that the court is involved, they should mind their actions and what they do with Dad's discharge from their facility."

Once at the center, the director rushed out of the facility to meet Ben and Elira as though she had been standing by for their arrival.

"Hello, my name is Dr. Karen Fetzer. I am the executive director of Whispering Pines. I know you wished to see me last time you sought discharge for your father, but I'm here now to facilitate it. However, I have some bad news for you. Your father is in an advanced deteriorated condition. I suspect he has an underlying brain bleed which presents with seizures. Taking him home would not be to his advantage or yours. I would personally advise you to have an ambulance take him directly to the hospital."

Ben reeled in sheer unbelief. *They succeeded in killing him!* Then rage he could not contain bubbled up from his core. He exploded. "Your wretched facility has succeeded in bringing my father to death! Rehab for a TBI should not result in decreased health and death. You've targeted an innocent man for your own obvious hate and bias. This is MURDER!"

"Mr. Goldberg, believe all the outrageous assumptions you want to about us, but your father never did improve from his head injury, but rather got worse, and we have been trying to give him all the care we could with what we had to work with."

As he looked at her, Ben noticed Dr. Fetzer's forehead, where it seemed she had a stitch or two. As he stared more closely, he realized she had already become a recipient of the infamous digital chip of the New World Order, with its first numbers no doubt being 666. He turned away in disgust and realized he could not fight the evil force that now existed in her. Within his heart, he reached out in silent prayer for the Holy Spirit to help him know what to do next to keep his father alive longer.

"Okay, then, call an ambulance to take him to the hospital immediately, and I will follow it there," Ben replied.

Dr. Fetzer gave a slight, sarcastic smile and walked back into the facility. Ben and Elira followed her. She had Wanda call for an ambulance while Ben and Elira signed in. When they walked to Dad's room, Dr. Fetzer accompanied them.

Ben couldn't believe how close to death Dad was. He was gaunt and shriveled. His eyes had lost all their luster. They were fixed and glassy and staring at the ceiling. He lay in the bed with only a thin hospital gown and already looked like a corpse. Tears he couldn't control ran down his cheeks as he drew close to his dad's side. All he could think of was that his dad did not deserve to die for something that should not have been fatal if given the proper care for recovery. He took his dad's hand in his and held it. Elira put one arm around Ben as she also gazed tearfully down at Simon.

The paramedics arrived with a gurney, and one of them asked the director for any information on his medications and health issues. Dr. Fetzer led one of them back to her office, where she gave him a list of medications. Finally, two paramedics using bed sheets gently transferred Dad from his bed onto a gurney and then to the ambulance. Ben was relieved to see that his dad was now out of this abominable facility and on his way to the hospital.

At the front counter, Wanda brusquely handed Ben the discharge papers, and he and Elira ran for the car. Ben drove trying to keep up with the ambulance. He was wondering just what the paramedics might be doing with Dad now, if anything at all.

At the hospital, the paramedics removed the gurney from the ambulance and transported Simon to the emergency room. As one of them was leaving, Ben overheard him say to the other, "According to the facility, this patient has been resistant and noncompliant, and probably got what he deserved."

"Oh," the other replied, "I figured that already!" They both laughed as they exited the hospital.

Ben was furious. *What? That wicked director must have spoken badly about Dad! Her feelings about Dad should not be communicated to anyone. That's so unprofessional! I must get him seen by an ER doctor now. He can't die.*

A young ER doctor walked in with green scrubs and a face

mask. "Hello, my name is Dr. David Flagler. I am the attending ER physician for your father. We'll run some tests immediately, and I will have our neurologist on call, Dr. Sandra Higginbotham, notify you of what we find."

"Okay, please keep me posted. I'm so grateful for your help," Ben replied.

While waiting, Ben and Elira couldn't distract themselves with their phones or the hospital TV screens for long. All they could do was sit and stare into space without saying a word. Both were gravely concerned about the outcome.

Ben whispered to Elira, "I'm reflecting on all the wonderful years I was privileged to have growing up with Dad and Mom. I was so blessed to have them. Our lives were filled with love and laughter, even when Mom found her new religion. Dad always accepted what she had decided to follow, and he always loved her no matter what her beliefs. It was so painful to find out that Mom was one of those who went missing in The Disappearance, and now how it stings to think I might also lose Dad because of Duncan's senseless, violent act."

"Ben don't go there. You don't know that yet. Wait for the doctor to tell you what's going on."

"I rebuke the havoc this time has created for all of us, and I know it comes from the Devil," Ben said. "These things were foretold in the Bible, and I'm sad that you, me, and my family were part of the generation to experience it." Elira rolled her eyes, but Ben prayed fervently in his heart to God that his dad would come out of his condition long enough to pray to receive Jesus as his Savior! Then he could be at peace with his dad's eternal destination even if he were to lose him. Waiting seemed like an eternity.

Finally, in walked the neurologist Dr. Higginbotham who addressed Ben. "We have run tests on your father, and his brain activity is severely reduced. We have your father on heavy antiseizure medications that are masking the multiple grand mal seizures he has had that have likely caused brain damage and led to his many symptoms. I assure you that we are monitoring his progress closely. Right now, he will need to be in the ICU. I want to be honest with you—I don't know whether he will pull out of this, but we're giving him the benefit of the doubt. We'll keep you posted as any new updates become available. If you would like to see your dad, you can see him one at a time in the ICU."

"Doctor," Ben asked, "did you say there is some brain activity?"

"I see a little brain activity, but not anything to write home about. Our hopes are for a limited recovery. We'll have to just wait and see how this plays out."

"What do you mean by a 'limited recovery'?" Ben asked.

"Should he survive his current condition, we don't know at this time how much cognition, speech, or motor ability he may have for the future," the doctor explained.

"Okay, I would like to go in and see Dad," Ben said.

"Just go down this corridor and walk into his ICU unit 12. Please wear a mask, as he is highly compromised."

"I will." Ben looked down at his watch. It had been four hours since his dad had entered the ER. He gave Elira a kiss and scampered down the hallway with the joy of a child ready to see friends who were near and dear. When he approached his dad's ICU unit, he saw various tubes, IVs, and a monitor for his dad's vitals. *What would happen next?* He prayed the fearful thought away.

"Dad, I love you. How are you doing? I brought you here to be taken care of by hospital professionals. Are you feeling any better?"

Simon just lay there with open, glassy eyes. There was no recognition of Ben or of any of the words Ben spoke.

Ben began to cry and pray. "Dear God, I need your precious Holy Spirit to touch Dad now and to give him the ability to understand what I am asking. Please, God, I want to tell him about Jesus."

Ben sat there for what seemed like an endless period of time holding his dad's hand. He continued to pray that his dad would awaken long enough to speak to him about Christ.

"Holy Spirit, I need you to be present as I speak to Dad tonight. I thank You in advance for a miraculous evening as I tell him about Jesus."

A few hours went by, and Ben was ready to ask Elira to come in, when suddenly, Simon briefly blinked his eyes.

"Dad, is that you? Are you awake?" Ben gripped his dad's hands tightly in his own.

Simon moved his eyes slightly from side to side and began to breathe as though he were himself again.

"Dad, are you there? I'm worried about you and want to make sure everything is okay."

Simon turned his head ever so slightly to Ben and weakly said, "Hello, Son."

Ben could hardly believe his dad had the understanding to address him as "Son." "Hello, Dad!" Ben cried out. This was the miracle he had prayed for.

"I'm so glad you recognize me! I've missed talking with you, Dad. I love you so much. How are you feeling?"

"I feel tired, Son. Where am I?"

"You're in the hospital. Apparently, you've had a brain bleed. It has caused you to have some seizures, but they are trying to get you better here."

"I'm concerned for you, Son. How has it been for you?"

"Just what I thought it would be. What's happening to us is what Mom used to talk about. We are living during the Great Tribulation when the Antichrist takes over the world."

"I miss your mother so much."

"I know you do, and I do, too! You know Mom warned us about this time and that we could escape it like she did by giving our lives over to Messiah Jesus."

"Son, do you believe in this Messiah Jesus that your mom believed in? I know the Jewish Messiah will free His people, Israel," Simon feebly whispered.

"Dad, Messiah Jesus will return to eradicate this horrible time and establish His kingdom of true peace on the earth. The first time, He came to die as the Passover Lamb of God for our sins. This is the reason we need to receive Him into our hearts as our Messiah and Savior."

"Really? Have you done that, Son?"

"Yes, I've received Him into my heart just as Mom did. Dad, I want you to receive Him also so that all three of us can be together again one day in Messiah's kingdom."

Simon didn't answer Ben, but Ben could see his dad's mind was slowly considering what Ben shared.

After a long pause Simon spoke. "Son, what did you do to receive Messiah Jesus?"

"Oh, Dad, I just prayed to ask Him to come into my heart and life, save me from my sins, and become the Lord and Master of my life. When I did that, I felt peace and purpose, and I desired to read Mom's Bible to learn more about Him."

"Really, Son?"

"Yes, Dad; and if you would like, I can pray with you to receive Jesus into your heart and life. It is a very simple request for you to make."

"Benjamin, 'son of my right hand,' as your name means in Hebrew, I put my trust in what you're saying. I know your mom felt blessed to know the Messiah. She became a better person than I, and she had such joy. Yes, I would like to pray with you."

Overwhelming joy flooded Ben's heart and mind. Tears

streamed down his face. His dad would join with Jesus just like he and Mom had.

"Dad, just repeat along with me: Dear Heavenly Father, I ask Your Son, Jesus, to come into my heart and life, forgive me of my sins, become my Lord, and direct my life. Thank You. In Jesus's name. Amen."

When they finished the prayer, Simon had a peaceful smile on his face. It was the first time in a very long time that Ben saw Dad smile.

"Son, I do feel peace all over me right now, and I'm not afraid of what will happen to either of us. I know that God is in control. If I don't survive, it doesn't matter to me because I am in Messiah's hands."

"These words bring peace to my heart, Dad. I'm so joyful and glad to know it, and I now feel confident about your eternal destination. Mom, you, and I can be together again someday."

"Yes, Son, me too! I love you!"

"I love you, too, Dad!" Ben bent over Simon's frail body and gave him the longest, tightest hug he could. Ben kissed his dad's forehead. "Dad, you've always been a great father and husband. Mom and I were so blessed to have you. I'm going to leave you now because Elira is in the waiting room and must be wondering what has taken me so long. She would also like to see you. I'm so glad we had this time together. I will send Elira in to see you now."

"I'm glad that you and Elira have each other. If she hasn't already, I hope she will share in the faith of Messiah Jesus, too." Dad said in the loudest whisper he could muster.

"Sadly, so far, she's sticking to what she terms 'scientific facts that don't corroborate with faith.' I am praying for her, Dad."

"Son don't worry. God has it in His hands like He has you and me. I love you!"

"Dad, I love you always and forever." Ben pulled his father's hand to his chest. "I will send in Elira." With that, Ben gave his dad another kiss on the forehead, longingly looked at him for a few seconds, and then left the room.

He felt so light that he skipped down the hallway to the ICU waiting room, where he found Elira slouched in her chair napping. He stroked her hair. "Hi, Honey! A wonderful miracle has happened! I waited and prayed and prayed for Dad to awake. Dad eventually opened his eyes and spoke to me!"

Elira's face brightened. "He did?!"

"Yes, isn't it wonderful?"

Elira could hardly articulate a "Yes" as astonishment appeared all over her face. "That doesn't even seem possible, I'm beside myself with amazement!"

"I told him I would send you in now to see him. He's happy that we have each other."

Elira momentarily frowned. She didn't know how long they would have each other. "Okay, I'll go in to see him now," she said.

Within two minutes she returned, running all the way back to him. Ben stood when he saw her returning so fast. A horrible thought suddenly jumped into Ben's mind. *Dad died!*

"Ben!" she shouted. "Something's happened to your dad. The neurologist and nurses are working on him right now! The doctor said to give them some space to work."

Ben's eyes broadened as he took in the brunt of what Elira was saying.

"Elira, not one minute before you came to announce this news, I felt Dad's presence in this waiting room. I'm not really surprised that you returned with this news. I felt it before you got here, but I was hoping it wasn't true."

Elira hugged Ben as tears rolled down their faces. The doctor appeared at the waiting room door and signaled for Ben and Elira to come closer.

"I have some bad news for you," Dr. Higginbotham said. "We tried all we could to bring your father back, but he flatlined. No amount of intervention could help. I'm sorry. If you have any questions, I'll be glad to answer them. Otherwise, if you choose to, you can go in and see your father."

Ben broke out in a huge, shuddering sob; but deep inside, he was so glad that God had given him those precious, miraculous moments with his dad.

"I do have one question," Ben said. "Dad had full cognition, opened his eyes, and spoke with me not more than a couple of minutes ago. How could he have been able to wake up for such a fleeting amount of time and then suddenly deteriorate?"

"There are some things that medical science can't explain. That was nothing short of a miracle. Perhaps your dad wanted to have that time with you," Dr. Higginbotham said. "I will have the nurse prepare the paperwork for you to make funeral home arrangements. Now let me take you to see your father. I have to hurry because I'll have to head out of here fairly soon to get my implanted chip today."

Ben shuddered again. Dr. Higginbotham would soon receive a chip from the New World Order and all that it stood for. He held hands with Elira as they walked somberly toward his dad's ICU room. When they got there, a nurse escorted them in and the doctor left.

Simon was lying there completely still, but with a peaceful expression on his face. Ben put his arms around his dad's neck and hugged him, now weeping more. Elira put her arms around Ben.

"I love you, Dad, always and forever!" Ben kissed him on the forehead again, just as he had only a few minutes before.

Chapter 15
An Unswerving Commitment to Christ

Not more than two days later, Ben and Elira were standing with Ruth Newman by Simon's grave. Ben had found no rabbi who would officiate a Messianic Jewish service where anything about Jesus Christ would be mentioned.

When Ben called Simon's friends and family, he let them know that the service would be Messianic, but they were not interested in attending such a service and some even ridiculed it, especially those who had recently received their chips. Many felt Ben and his family had gone rogue and suspected him of being a troublemaker. They were afraid of identifying with Ben by attending his dad's service and burial.

Ben pondered the rapidly changing world around him. It didn't make sense how quickly things were changing. Even the sun and moon now gave out only two-thirds of their normal light, and a third of the stars no longer appeared in the night sky. *"What's going on here?"* Ben thought, *"Things are changing so rapidly."*

Ben led the small graveside service for his dad with passages from both the Old and New Testaments and told how his dad had prayed on his deathbed for Yeshua, Jesus, to come into his heart. Ben spoke a closing prayer and signaled for the two funeral staffers standing by to lower his father's casket into the ground. As they did, Ben, Elira, and Ruth each threw a rose on the casket.

All three then turned to walk toward their cars. Ben was pleased with the service and burial he was able to give his dad. Mom would have loved it, he thought. Ben and Elira turned to bid farewell to Ruth.

"It was great to have you here!" Ben said.

"It was nice to meet you!" Elira added.

"Thank you! It was my pleasure," Ruth responded.

When Ben and Elira were alone in their car, Elira spoke up. "I feel like a minority! Now that your dad received Christ, and you and Ruth are believers, I feel excluded from all of you! I don't feel that you and I have common ground anymore because, as I've been telling you all along, this will divide us further."

"Why do you focus on what we don't have in common and lose out on what we do?" Ben asked.

"Ben, you know this can't go on, because our differences will grow. What's more, the government will eventually catch up with you. Your life is in danger and so is mine by being with you. I'll be caught in the crossfire!"

"Elira, let's stay together and support each other for as long as we can. You know I can never accept that chip into my body; but, as I've said before, you don't know what will happen to us until it does happen. Let's try to find a way. I'll protect you as much as I'm able to from all this evil."

"Ben, I'll never NOT get the chip. In fact, I'll be getting it implanted soon! There's no reason to delay it to the very last day, because it's inevitable that we'll need it for you and for me to survive. Don't you see?"

Ben quivered. He had tried to delay her implant so that maybe she would come to her senses and finally receive Jesus as her Savior and Lord.

"Elira, there's NO rush! You can wait until the last week. My accounts are probably unfrozen, and I've inherited everything from Dad. Let's see if there are any changes on the horizon," Ben pleaded. "We've seen good people's attitudes change for the worse after receiving the chip, even though Ibrahim said that it will help people unite into the one world he envisions establishing."

"You're believing a lie from religious fanatics that this chip can change people and keep them from being who they are. You also believe they will go to hell, which is another myth!"

Ben ended the conversation here, but deep inside he prayed to God that she would see through the rhetoric of Ibrahim and his New World Order.

When they pulled into the driveway, Duncan and some of the other neighbors were standing around talking with each other. *Uh-oh! Not again!*

"I'll come around and open your door, and we'll quickly head inside together," Ben said cautiously stepping out of the car and heading toward Elira.

Duncan didn't even wait for him to reach Elira's door. "You had to bury your dad today! As for us, we're glad he's gone! What happened with him? Couldn't he survive?" Duncan chuckled.

Ben saw the vicious gleam in Duncan's eyes, and he refused to engage with him. He opened Elira's door and gripped her hand as she stood up.

That seemed to be the cue for the other neighbors.

"You probably are so fanatical you won't get the implant!"

Lauren said, glaring at Ben. "You're a fool like your parents, and you'll die of poverty and starvation!"

Ben shivered to think of the fact that he would be cut off from being able to financially survive or to survive at all in this New World Order now that the chip implant was mandatory.

Sheryl offered her opinion. "You can rest assured that you will lose everything and die like your dad!"

"Or, are you going to disappear too, just like your mom?!" Wimberly quipped, and then all of them burst into loud laughter.

Ben wondered whether his neighbors had already received their chips, as they seemed more venomous and demonic than ever. *They seem to want me dead just like Dad.*

Finally, Wimberly addressed Elira. "Are you a crazy believer now, too, and will you die because you believe in such hysterical fairy tales?"

"I'm not crazy, and I don't believe in fantastical myths and fairy tales. I am scientifically minded, and you know that!" Elira shot back and pushed her way past the neighbors to the front door. Ben followed closely behind her and swiftly bolted the door behind them as they stepped into their home.

"I'm so sick and tired of these aggressive neighbors!" Elira declared. "They can't be polite or kind anymore. I'm over it!"

"I think the growing darkness and lawlessness has dampened proper decorum with others." Ben said and hung his keys on a hook in the pantry. "In fact, and I just read this, the Bible says that because 'sin will abound, the love of many will become cold.' It describes that in the New Testament, and that's certainly true of today."

"Okay, Ben, you don't have to religionize this. These people are just difficult personalities. That's all. I've told you that before. Maybe you should consider selling your dad's home and living in a kinder community."

"That won't help." Ben smirked as he sank into the armchair and rested his forearms on his knees. "I think that more and more people will become angrier, more hateful, and evil when they receive the chip. I've noticed that people's personalities seem more agitated and aggressive when they receive their full identification with Ibrahim and his one-world government."

"What does identification with the current world system have to do with personality?" Elira piped back. "Once again, you are dealing in an alternate reality made up of stories about the end of the world."

"Let's scrounge up some dinner." Ben couldn't deal with another confrontation especially with Elira at the moment.

In the kitchen, Elira turned on the countertop TV. More crazy news, Ben thought. Doesn't she tire of a steady diet of it?

"This is a Special Report," the news anchor said. "Master Ibrahim has been fatally injured in an assassination attempt! I repeat: Master Ibrahim has been fatally injured in an assassination attempt! It's believed that a sect of Christian or possibly Jewish believers have purportedly shot him in order to destroy the one-world government with its obvious exclusion of them. Master Ibrahim lies dying at an undisclosed location in the Middle East surrounded by his closest staff. His condition is grim."

Elira gasped. "Wow! No way! What'll happen now?!'

"This was predicted in the Bible, Elira!"

"Oh, shut up, Ben! You know I'm tired of hearing biblical predictions. Keep them to yourself!"

Ben prayed in his heart for what he knew would come next. Ruth had given him more articles about these very days. This is a big turning point, he thought. Master Ibrahim will come back from death! He is the exact opposite of Jesus Christ with a similar resurrection to fool the world. *It's so obvious that he is the Antichrist.* Sick to his stomach, Ben turned off the TV.

Elira grabbed the remote and turned it right back on. "What are you doing? This is breaking news! A Special Report! What will happen if Master Ibrahim dies? Who'll take over the mess he's trying to fix?"

Ben shot her a stunned look. *She's really bought into this--as though this Antichrist is the savior of the world! How could she think he's helping with all the chaos they're living in? She's blind and brainwashed.* "Elira, no matter what happens, the world will go on in God's perfect will for it. Don't you see that?"

"No, I don't believe in God's will. If God were real, the madness of what is happening now wouldn't exist. We need a strong leader to set the world straight and at peace again. Where is this God you speak of? Has He done anything for you, your mom, or your dad?"

Ben stood up and went into his bedroom to pray and meditate on God's Word. *How could he get through to her?*

A scream came from the living room. Ben rushed out, only to find Elira frantically pointing at the TV and the announcement that Master Ibrahim had died.

"Plans are now being hastily made to exit his body from a hospital where he has died to a morgue," the news correspondent reported. "His closest staff is convening right now to plan the next steps for the New World Order and its government in light of his death."

"This is a somber time for the world where so much tragedy has been experienced in the last few years," the news anchor added.

"Yes," stated the news correspondent, "His close staffers are now saying that extreme scrutiny of those who consider themselves Christians or Jews will escalate, especially since the deadline is nearing to get the implant. There'll also be a full retribution to those who might have been involved in Master Ibrahim's untimely death."

Reality hit Ben hard. *All these events are unfolding just as Scripture predicted.*

Beside herself with grief, Elira cried, "Ben, we and the whole world are now more doomed than ever!"

"Elira, that isn't quite accurate. Ruth and I have talked, and we are not doomed. Sure, there will be a coming persecution and martyrdom of Christian believers and Jews who've not received their implanted chips. In fact, it seems as though it's just around the corner! But I know where I stand. I can't accept the chip. I know if I die, God will receive me into His kingdom, or He just may allow me to survive through this Tribulation period, but I'm not doomed."

Elira turned away from Ben, marched to her bedroom, and slammed her door. Ben turned off the TV and returned to prayer and Bible reading in the living room.

Just as he opened Mom's Bible, the phone rang. It was Ruth.

"Hi, Ben, I just wanted to check in with you. There are a lot of new events happening before our very eyes that corroborate with Scripture."

"Yes, it's all happening so quickly, and I know that the persecution of Christian believers and Jews will be growing to lethal proportions now."

"How are things going for you and Elira with all this?" Ruth asked.

"Very poorly. Her heart is closed to the light of the gospel. She thinks that Master Ibrahim was the man of peace for the world. Little does she realize that the only person who could bring peace is the Prince of Peace, Jesus, our Messiah!"

"I figured things were going to get ugly between the two of you, coming from opposite spiritual viewpoints. I'm praying for your encouragement and strength during this evil time. Don't forget that God is our Refuge and Strength, and you will not be moved. Ben, you must realize that, at some point, you may have to sacrifice your love for Elira by letting her go. You'll never regret anything or anyone you give up for Jesus. You know that, right?"

"I know that, but I dread facing that time. I know it's approaching fast. I don't think our relationship will survive unless Elira sees the light real soon. It's almost time for her to receive her chip." Ben could feel his eyes moisten at such a sad thought. *Elira wouldn't be herself any longer.* How horrific for such a nice, intelligent, and beautiful young woman.

"God will help you to get through it, and you'll be blessed. Oh my! I have the news on my computer screen, and it has just been reported that, miraculously, Master Ibrahim has come back to life while being transported to the morgue. Apparently, the head of the One World Church, Alexander Baganov, has performed unknown rites and incantations over his body as it was being transported. This head bishop of the One World Church is definitely the False Prophet we read about in Revelation. I'm sure of it now."

Elira rushed into the living room. "Have you heard? Master Ibrahim lives! He's alive! Now that's a miracle! That's the closest thing to being supernatural that I have ever known!"

Ben quivered, as Ruth also heard Elira in the background.

Ben continued to speak with Ruth in Elira's hearing. "The Bible had already predicted this event, hadn't it, Ruth?" Elira fumed at this and stomped back to her room.

Ben ended his conversation with Ruth and came to Elira's bedroom. Her eyes were glued to the computer with a blow-by-blow recount of Master Ibrahim's miraculous resurrection. How counterfeit this is to the glorious resurrection of Jesus from the tomb on the very first Easter Sunday long ago. *I wish Elira would recognize the difference God makes in a person's life!*

As Ben turned and trudged out of Elira's bedroom, he heard Bishop Baganov in the background touting the power of Master

Ibrahim to come back from the dead. "I now state to the whole world that they need to give their unequivocal trust and allegiance to him," Baganov declared.

A chill crept over Ben. The persecution would begin full force now.

Ben returned to reading his mom's Bible, and this time turned to Revelation 13, where the fatal injury of Mizrah, and Head Bishop Baganov's praise of Mizrah's miraculous ability to come back from death, were described. While Ben read, Elira came in.

"Ben, we do have faith and religion in this New World Order and a god to worship. Head Bishop Baganov is now calling for universal worship of Master Ibrahim as truly God." Ben shook inside. *Elira is so deceived. I know what's coming next.*

"Elira, you've never, ever believed in the worship of anything! Your faith has always been in science and experiential truth. How could you consider this sound?" Ben pleaded.

"I saw him get up from death. Yes, it defies science, but it's reality!" Elira said. "If I never worshiped anyone or anything before, I now see that it's feasible to worship what is real and can be seen with one's own eyes!"

Ben nervously scratched the back of his head and looked out the window. He now understood how even an educated, bright mind could be duped. Maybe she was right--He now didn't see how things with Elira would be able to progress to marriage for him. Their relationship was coming unglued, and he felt sorrowful because he really loved and cared for Elira with all his heart, but it could never work. He broke out in a torrent of tears.

Elira rushed to his side. "What is it, Ben?" she asked. "Why can't you accept my belief? Is it any different than what you and your mother believed, which you never saw for yourselves?"

"Elira, you believe in something you supposedly saw on the

computer with your eyes, but what if I tell you that I experienced a total life change when I invited the Lord Jesus Christ into my heart? How could such a change occur, where I would devote my life to Him without the experience being so real? All I encourage you to do is to ask Him into your heart just to see if He is real. If you mean it when you ask Him, God will come to you and show you He's real. I guarantee it."

"Ben, that's hogwash! I must ask a dead carpenter who lived thousands of years ago to come into my life, mean what I am asking, and then I will experience Him. It sounds like some sort of psychic interaction with the dead. That's insane! You're a fool to believe this and say you experienced it."

Ben had to accept it. Elira's heart could not be won to God. She was closed to Him and was not one whose heart could ever be penetrated by God's Holy Spirit. He wept some more as Elira left the room.

The following week, Elira received her implanted chip just inside the skin of her wrist. Ben grieved for days. By then, Head Bishop Baganov ordered an image of Master Ibrahim erected for all people of the world to worship. If not, they would be put to death. Unfortunately, it wasn't long before miraculous, unexplainable occurrences took place, such as the image speaking exactly like Mizrah himself, and fire falling from the skies above, down to the earth below, at the command of Mizrah's image. The image now seemed like an exact clone of Mizrah and spoke with his same voice and authority.

The relationship between Elira and Ben now became intolerable. They argued constantly, and Elira had a deceitful, impudent look in her eyes and attitude. The chip had solidified her allegiance to the Antichrist, Mizrah himself, and there was now *no* hope for her to turn back. Where she'd once loved Ben and was devoted to him, she now despised him and thought very poorly of him. She frequently derided him, and sought to sabotage anything he was doing so that he didn't even feel safe or secure with her in his own home. This was exactly what he dreaded would happen—she'd become like the neighbors—and he found himself praying daily around the clock for his situation. He hardly wanted to stay in his own home and took his meals outside when he could.

Finally, one day he came home to find that she was moving out. He was relieved.

"Ben," Elira said, "I'm giving you one more opportunity to get the implanted chip and live with me so that we can live and work together in the New World Order. If you don't, all my bags and boxes are packed, and I will move in with Duncan next door! I have more in common with him now then I have with you."

Ben felt sucker punched. Move in with Duncan? There was hardly a greater demon she could intertwine her life with than him! *What was she thinking?* Clearly, she wasn't. *Had she gone mad?*

"Elira, as I've told you over and over, I would gladly die than take the chip into my body. You never understood that it is the mark of the Antichrist, Mizrah himself, and it will separate you from God and His Messiah, Jesus, forever! I begged you so many times not to receive that chip into your body. Now you're doomed to be like Duncan, and your mind and personality have already changed. You are not the woman I fell in love with. I know that I may die for what I am doing, but I know I'm doing what is best for me in my precious eternal relationship with God. I am committed to God, and I will not waver."

"Then you are a fool as I have said, and I have wasted all these months with you and your family, living as an outcast because of my intellect and scientific knowledge. You will die, Ben, because Head Bishop Baganov has ordered death to all who do not give homage to Master Ibrahim, who is the real messiah! It's only a matter of time until they track you down, and you'll die for your foolhardy, fictitious beliefs. For my part, I'm glad I will not be there to witness it."

Ben reeled at the words coming out of Elira. He knew it was no longer she that was speaking to him, but some sort of evil spirit that was now inhabiting her. In his heart, he rebuked it in the name of Yeshua Ha Mashiah.

"Soon, you will no longer have this home or food or clothing. You will be forced to walk the streets and run into the wilderness to hide until they hunt you down like a rat and kill you! Why would you want to be forced into this when you can be part of a one-world government system of peace, security, and prosperity?"

"Elira, you're brainwashed. There's *no* peace or prosperity. Look around you. Don't you see it? There's only destruction for those who do *not* accept Mizrah and his grip over the world. The horrors of what you'll see next are just beginning. Yes, death will come to all who do *not* follow Mizrah, but those who do, will not see God forever."

"Ben, goodbye and good luck. I'll probably see you around the neighborhood, but we're through. And remember it was your choice."

"I loved you and will always love you. I'm deeply grieved to see you go, and to see the end of our relationship. But as much as I had hoped against hope and prayed for you and me, I knew you were right. It was inevitable we would part because we're going in different directions spiritually."

Without so much as a tear or a hug, Elira walked out the front door and out of Ben's life forever.

Chapter 16
The Determination to Overcome

Ben rose from his chair after what seemed like hours where he had wept, prayed, and thought. It was dark outside, and he faintly heard the voices of Elira and Duncan laughing while drinking together in Duncan's backyard. The sense of Elira's betrayal with the likes of such a hoodlum as Duncan overwhelmed him. Dad had never recovered from the man's attack. How could Elira live with him?!

The phone rang. It was Ruth.

"Ben, how are you? I know you've heard what's going on with this wicked government and One World Church. How are you making out with the new developments?"

"Oh, I'm so glad you called, Ruth. I could use a Christian friend right now. As we already had figured, Elira did receive her chip last week, and things went south in a hurry. There was nothing in common left for us, and there was no longer hope for her. She left me today for Duncan of all people!"

"Yikes! No kidding! Duncan?! How crazy is that?! I'm so sorry, Ben, but it doesn't surprise me at all. She was never opened to receiving the gospel of Jesus Christ. It was only a matter of time before you two would part. We spoke about that possibility, but I never foresaw her going to Duncan!"

"Yes, you were right that we would split. I was just hoping that somehow, through God's Holy Spirit, she might be changed, but it never happened. She surely wasn't one of those destined for salvation."

"What are you going to do now, Ben? Without the chip, the mark of the Antichrist, we'll eventually lose our homes and ability to buy food. The door is closing in on us in a few days, and severe persecution will begin for us, since we have not given allegiance or homage to Mizrah or his image."

"I'm already feeling very unsafe in my neighborhood, and the neighbors will come down on me more especially now Elira has joined their ranks. I really do think it's Duncan's desire to take possession of my home for his own. I fear even going out of my front door!"

"That isn't good," Ruth replied. "Perhaps you can just leave your hostile neighborhood and come live in my home for now. So far, I've not experienced the hostility you have. You are welcome here. I have a spare bedroom, and maybe we can walk through this dark time together until the Lord takes us to be with Him."

"I'd normally take time to think about it; but right now, it sounds like a plan. I think there'll be more benefit in joining together as we face what comes next. I'll just take some personal items and a few photographs of Dad and Mom and abandon Dad's home. It'll be of no use to me any longer anyway. The New World Order will take possession of all our properties and goods soon."

"Okay, awesome. I think our mothers would've been glad for us to face these dark times together since they two were such great friends. They must be smiling down from heaven at us right now."

"Give me about an hour, and I'll be there. Please pray all will go well. It's late, and hopefully neighbors are retiring for the night, and I will not be harassed as I leave."

"I'll be praying for you right now! Get started, and I'll see you soon."

Ben pulled a backpack from his closet and placed some underwear, toiletries, and other clothes into it. He also pulled out a pair of soft loafers and his athletic shoes. He then went into his parents' bedroom and lovingly gazed at his parents' wedding picture and a picture of them with him as a small child. He dropped the photos into his backpack. He then added a picture of his parents right before Mom disappeared and a picture of himself as a grown adult.

Ben carried his backpack into the kitchen and grabbed some canvas grocery bags and placed into them all the remaining food that he could. Food would become a scarce commodity for himself and Ruth in the coming days. No more grocery shopping or any shopping at all. He wasn't going to leave the food he had behind.

He paused his packing to hesitantly look out the front window of his home. So far everything looked clear outside and quiet for the night. He decided to make a run for the car. He wouldn't even lock his front door. It wouldn't matter anymore.

He opened the front door and bolted to his car. He locked all his car doors with one push of his lock button on the driver's side. He started his car but didn't turn his headlights on. He was backing out of the driveway when he caught the outline of a figure in the dark in his rearview mirror. He slammed on his brakes and stared at the reflection of the figure behind his car. *Is this a person or a demon?*

The person slowly walked around to his closed window on the driver's side. Elira! Her eyes burned with malicious fire. She beat on his window until he lowered the window down slightly.

"Where do you think you're going in the middle of the night?" she hissed. "Trying to escape the inevitable?" She snickered and then laughed.

Ben cringed, and a cold sweat ran down his back. He was face-to-face with sheer evil, and he didn't know what to do but pray. He couldn't believe she was up and had seen him.

"Elira, you left, and there's nothing more for me here. Do you understand that? What difference does it make if I leave?"

"You're a coward and headed to Ruth's!" Then she added, "I wonder if you had something going on with her to begin with, and now, I'm conveniently out of your way!"

Ben felt the Holy Spirit telling him not to be baited by Elira. He calmly responded, "I have always loved you, but now all I can do is to survive another day by being with other believers, not just with Ruth."

Elira laughed and cursed at him. "You'll die soon!"

"I know that." Ben accelerated his car backward out of the driveway. He could still hear Elira shouting and cursing as he sped off and turned his headlights on. Out of his rearview mirror now, he saw Duncan running out to meet Elira in the driveway as other neighbors also poured out of their homes. They seemed like hellish beings oddly dancing in the street.

When Ben turned into Ruth's driveway, she had her outdoor lights on and was waiting for him.

"I was praying for you! I'm glad you made it safely. Was everything okay?" Ruth asked.

"I couldn't believe it. But just when I thought the coast was clear, I saw Elira, and I could see sheer evil in her eyes. She accused me of having an affair with you all along, and she cursed me and threatened me. Said I would die soon!"

"Oh my! I'm so sorry you were confronted by her, but I'm so pleased that the Holy Spirit got you here safely. Come on in and let me help you with your things."

"Thanks. I also brought all the food I could. We'll need to put it away in the fridge and your pantry."

"Thanks for bringing what you had! I'll grab the bags of food."

Ben entered his new home and thought how ironic it was that he and Ruth ended up together during this horrific time and how their mothers had also been so close.

THE NEXT MORNING, Ruth didn't wake up until noon! She was shocked she had slept so late. Was Ben still asleep? *How odd for her to sleep this late,* she pondered. She tiptoed into the hallway and noticed that he must still be in his bedroom because he was nowhere to be found in the house. She decided to make some coffee and toast, and maybe he would wake up soon. She doubted he typically slept late either.

As the coffee was brewing, she clicked on the TV. Wrong thing to do. CNN was reporting that Ibrahim Mizrah had broken his covenant with the nation of Israel. Now he was sacrificing a pig on the most holy site of the third temple, which he himself had allowed the Israelis to previously build in Jerusalem. Amazing how Scripture was being fulfilled daily!

Ruth heard Ben coming into the living room where she was watching TV.

He looked at Ruth, bid her "good afternoon," and then said, "I slept in and it's afternoon already, but I heard your TV as I was coming in here. Things are moving at warped speed toward the return of Messiah Jesus!"

"Yes, they are!" Ruth took a sip of her coffee. "I can't believe that Mizrah has already fulfilled yet another fundamental part of the end time—what is called 'the Abomination of Desolation,' where the new altar of God is desecrated."

"Yes." Ben perched on the arm of her fire-red sofa. "Now his true character has attained its diabolical peak in what he's done within the sacred temple of God. Such ultimate sacrilege!"

"It won't be long before we'll need to flee into the wilderness in order to survive," Ruth declared. "The deadline for Antichrist's mark will arrive in a couple of weeks, and then we can no longer interact with the rest of this new world." Ruth cupped her coffee mug tightly in both hands. *Who knew how much longer she'd be able to drink this lovely brew?* She frowned. "It's really down to the wire now."

"Yes, but remember we're also in God's hands. He'll see us through!"

"That's true." Ruth nodded. "Many will die though. Maybe even us, but He'll be with us. We'll be targets because we have not received our chips, and we'll be condemned enemies of Mizrah and the New World Order. The Bible already foretells what will happen to those who are believers and live during this time of Great Tribulation on earth. If we should die, we'll make up those saints who come out of this horrendous time in earth's history."

So much evil has already occurred, Ruth thought, *and yet it was going to get worse for them and for the entire world.* But she couldn't allow herself to think ahead to the future. She just had to survive for today and enjoy what she had.

"Why don't we enjoy that coffee and toast you made?" Ben said, echoing her thoughts.

Ruth broke out in a smile. "Coming right up!"

Chapter 17
The Courage to Move Forward

Before the implanted chips became mandatory for transactions, Ben used his New World Order currency to purchase hiking gear, sleeping bags, a small tent, and food preparation utensils and kits. Oddly, everywhere Ben made his purchases, he did not attract suspicion, which he attributed to the covering of the Holy Spirit over him and Ruth, who often accompanied him. Yet, there was an eerie feeling that eyes were watching him and that he could soon be caught.

Ben arrived at Ruth's local gas station to fill his car's tank with gas and thought to himself about how things were about to drastically change. This is the last time I will ever pump gas into my car. With sanctions growing against those not yet implanted with their chips, we soon won't be able to have our cars anyway. What's the use? License plates would be an instant source of identification for sure.

Ben got out of his car to pump gas, but suddenly noticed a gas station attendant staring at him from a distance. Shivers went down his spine. What is this man looking at? Could he be monitoring what I'm doing? This hasn't happened here before.

Ben quickly finished, paid at the pump with his New World currency, and pulled away. As he sped down the road, he looked up into his rearview mirror to find that the attendant had exited the station and was taking a picture of his car. Ben started to perspire and shake. *He's got my tag number! This can't already be the end for us!*

He got to Ruth's home and entered the front door. Ruth was working on gathering items they would need after the deadline for their chips.

"H-h-i-i, Ruth!" Ben stammered.

Ruth quickly turned to look at Ben--his face very pale. "What's happened? You look like you've seen a ghost!"

"I went to your local gas station to get gas for what is probably our last time, but the gas station attendant kept looking at me; and when I left, he came out to take a picture of the back of my car as I went down the road."

"That never happened to you before, did it?"

"No, never, but things are getting tougher now for us. We are part of the very few who haven't converted to the implanted chip. I think suspicion about us is growing. I was hoping to avoid it a little longer, but I think I won't be able to use my car now. Thankfully, you have a garage, and I'll keep it hidden there. I will siphon some gas out of my car if we need to use yours."

"Sounds good to me but sit down, relax, and take some deep breaths. Looks like you're having some anxiety."

TWO WEEKS WENT by as Ben and Ruth enjoyed what was left of their freedom and prepared for life on the run. The day for the deadline for implanted chips finally arrived more quickly than Ben had ever imagined. There was no turning back.

"Ruth, I want you to know how much I have enjoyed the

moments we've shared in cooking a meal together, talking about our mutual faith, and praying individually and together over the last two weeks; but, as we've been discussing all along, we can no longer stay here at your home or at any other residence for that matter. We need to leave now and implement our survival plan."

"Yes, I know, Ben, but now I'm feeling anxiety. I've never had to do this: leave my home, carry just a few survival tools and provisions, and live in the wilderness as a fugitive of the law. I'm so scared!"

"Look, we're not alone. We have our almighty God with us. He will help us. Staying here is not an option." Ben nervously scratched his forehead again as he always did when he, too, felt anxious. "You know the plan. We'll leave under cover of darkness at about 2 A.M. when the least amount of people might be up and about in our neighborhood and city. We will follow our predetermined route right into the outskirts of the city where a huge forest and open wilderness begin. We'll walk until the sun rises, at which time we'll cease walking and find shelter somewhere to rest during daylight hours when we cannot be seen or heard. Are you with me on this?"

"Why, yes, of course."

"Ruth, please remember we have the Lord helping us! We've prayed for this day for a long time, and we've already committed everything into His capable hands. It'll go well for us. You believe that--don't you?"

"Yes, I do!"

"Good! You know we'll need to go as far as we can into the forest to avoid capture, but you never know, Ruth, there's got to be other fugitive believers just like us whom we may find on our journey. If that happens, we may be able to band together."

"Why that would be wonderful for all of us, don't you think? There's more strength and help in being together."

"Before we rest up one last time in your home before our journey, let's pray." Ben took Ruth's hand into his and bowed his head. "Dear Lord, Ruth and I have come this far by your strength and your love. We have refused the chip of the Antichrist and his New World Order. As you know, Lord, we are now fugitives of the law. In the wee hours of tomorrow morning, we will leave what we have known for all our lives and journey into what we do not know awaits us. But Lord and Savior Jesus, you already know the end from the beginning for us. We trust in Your almighty wisdom, guidance, and direction to save us from this evil regime until you come to put an end to it or until you come to call us to You. We trust You with our lives and know You will be with us in whatever happens to us. As Jesus, our Messiah prayed, 'Your kingdom come; Your will be done on earth as it is in Heaven'. We commit ourselves to You as unto a faithful Creator Who knows and loves us and Who has a perfect will and plan for us. Amen."

"Amen," Ruth said as she let go of Ben's hand and looked into his eyes. Tears filled hers. "I never thought I would live to see this day nor that it would ever happen to me. Now begins a dreadful time of fleeing capture and living on bare necessities we would be blessed to come by. Jesus warned of such a time in the Gospel of Matthew, Chapter 24."

Ruth reached over to pick up her electronic Bible lying on the coffee table and turned it on. "Let me read a bit of what it says. It will be a good reminder for us both: 'There will be famines and earthquakes in various places. All these are the beginning of birth pains. Then you will be handed over to be persecuted and put to death, and you will be hated by all nations because of me. At that time, many will turn away from the faith and will betray and hate each other, and many false prophets will appear and deceive many people. Because of the increase of wickedness, the love of most will grow cold, but the one who stands firm to the end will be saved." Ruth paused and quietly placed her Bible back down on the coffee table. She looked over at Ben.

"Thanks for that reminder, Ruth! Now let's rest up for the journey and pack any last-minute items we need to bring in our backpacks."

"Yes, I will rest now, and I'll gather up the rest of what needs to go into my backpack. Later, I'll place my backpack close to the front door for our departure."

Ben got up and left Ruth to rest on the couch. He studied a map of the surrounding area one more time and put a compass in his backpack. *Unfortunately, our phones had to be turned off a couple of days ago and destroyed,* he thought. *How I wish I could use them for our journey, but that would be impossible! We'd be discovered immediately.*

Ben took the picture of his mom and dad he had brought to Ruth's home, lovingly gazed at it, and gently placed it in his backpack. He also put in a small paperback Bible. No way to use or charge electronics anymore. How ironic! With all the techno-logical advances of humankind, evil and destruction brought about basic survival all over again, he mused.

Ben laid on his bed to rest. *Last time I will ever have a comfort-able bed like this!* Being hunted down like an animal will cause Ruth and me to hide in caves and under trees. *Not much sleep or rest for us from now on.* How I wish I had listened to Mom about Jesus. Tears flowed down his face. "Dear God, I pray Ruth and I will be up to the strength and wisdom to make this journey for as long as we can. I, too, am concerned about fleeing at such a dreadful time. Have mercy on us during this Great Tribulation!"

Ben soon drifted off to sleep but was awakened a few hours later by Ruth coming into his room. "I've set all my necessary things in my backpack by the front door, and I'm ready," Ruth said. "We already had our provisions packed, but I found another flashlight to add to your bag. Of course, I packed my anxiety medication. Unfortunately, I know I'll need it. With God's grace and help, I hope to conquer any lingering anxiety as we go longer into our journey and the medication runs out."

"I'm so glad you're ready, Ruth, and everything you did sounds great. How long have you been awake?"

"I woke up about an hour ago and I feel rested for tonight."

"Good! You'll need it! What time is it now?"

"My watch says it's about 8:00 P.M."

"Wow! We still have about six hours to wait. How about if we get a last good bite to eat now?" Ben asked with a smile.

"Sure thing! Let me see what I can cook up for our last 'civilized' dinner. I'm surprised that the authorities have not cut off the electric and water to this home yet."

"I'm sure they will at any time. The deadline for the chip was today."

"You don't think they may suddenly come knocking at our door? I couldn't bear the confrontation. I'm so afraid. I cried a little today when I woke up. I pity myself, but I'm to blame for my own suffering."

"Ruth, calm yourself down! We're in this together, and I assure you that we're not the only ones. Being a fugitive is better than being separated from God for all eternity because we've taken the Antichrist's mark, isn't it?"

"Yes, you're right. But I'm a flesh and blood person just as you are, and I'm afraid of the torture and death that may come upon us even though we try to flee."

"Ruth, don't you think that Messiah Jesus was also afraid of the suffering awaiting Him, the torture of His passion and the cross? We know He was when we read His prayer to His Heavenly Father in the Garden of Gethsemane, where He asks God if this 'cup' of suffering and crucifixion could pass from Him, but He confirms, despite His fear, God's will be done. Jesus has already walked in our shoes and knows what we're facing, and He's with us."

"Thank you for repeatedly reminding me of that! Hey, I've got a couple of steaks that we would have to leave behind. I'll make them for us to eat. Would you like that?" Ruth asked.

"What a terrific last real dinner to have! If you have potatoes, I'll be glad to make them," Ben added.

"Okay, but I will not make the steaks on the grill outside tonight. I think it's safer for us to be quiet and stay in until we both must leave."

"Agreed, Ruth!" Ben replied.

Soon, Ben sat down at the dining room table with Ruth to enjoy their last meal of steak and potatoes before they had to leave.

"Let's pray, Ruth! Thank you, dear Lord, for the sustenance You've provided in this last real meal for us tonight. You are good to us all the time! Let it nourish our bodies for what comes next. In Messiah Jesus's name, Amen." Ben cut into his steak and took in a mouthful.

"Yum! This is so delicious! Thanks for making it, Ruth."

"You're welcome. I'm glad you like it. The potatoes are good, too. They're fried just right."

When they had finished, Ben got up to rinse off the dishes and put them aside. *Last time I'll wash dishes in a kitchen sink,* he sadly thought.

"Hey, Ruth! Do you have any leftover coffee from this morning?"

"Yes, I do. Do you want me to warm it up?"

"Yes, please warm it up for us and let's just sit on the couch a little while longer to pray, and relax."

"Okay," Ruth responded as she got up from the table.

Ben and Ruth spent the last couple of hours of their freedom sipping coffee, talking, and praying together. Before they knew it, the clock struck two. The designated time had now come for them to leave. They put on their gear, picked up their flashlights, and unbolted the door. Ben peeked out of the crack of the slightly opened door and peered around the corner. Seeing no one, he motioned with his hand for Ruth to follow him out. They crept down the sidewalk. The forest was not far away because Ruth's home was close to the outskirts of their town. With each step, Ben scanned the space around them for anyone or anything that might pick up on their presence.

They remained dead silent, not even speaking a whisper to one another, but as Ben and Ruth passed a small alley, Ben noticed a shadowy figure standing across from them. His mind reeled. Who could that be? Were they being followed? Did someone already know they had left? The figure seemed to be waiting on them. Ben was terrified.

"Ruth," he whispered, "we need to cut out of this path and run down the nearest street that's coming up. Do you see someone up there that seems to be waiting on us?" Fear and anxiety suddenly gripped Ruth. She started to hyperventilate. "We'll be okay, Ruth. We just have to stop and change the direction we're going in."

"Okay," Ruth spoke in a low, breathy voice, "Let's do it!'

They turned the corner of the nearest street and ran out of sight. As Ben looked back, he couldn't see the stranger, but still wondered who he might be at this time of night in their small city.

"Wait a minute!" Ben exclaimed. "We're close to your local gas station here. Right?"

"Yes," Ruth responded, "why?"

"What time does the station usually close?"

"I think about 12 midnight, but by the time they shut down everything and leave, I believe it's usually 1 A.M."

"I'm wondering if that isn't the gas station attendant who's usually on duty."

"What would he be doing just happening to walk in the direction we took?" Ruth asked.

"I'm wondering if he doesn't live close to the station. He may have recognized me because the last time I was at the gas station, he was the guy that took a picture of my car. Remember I told you? I was still using the New World currency and I hadn't used a chip to pay."

"Oh, how eerie! Let's continue running until we can get to the forest, Ben. It's quiet down this street. The businesses seem all closed and dark inside."

Ben appealed to Ruth. "Okay, we can run a bit more, but we have to be careful not to draw attention to ourselves by running."

"Yes, got it!" Ruth acknowledged.

Soon they arrived on the edges of the forest at the outskirts of the town. Ben and Ruth both gave out a huge sigh of relief, but Ruth was suddenly apprehensive about entering the forest at night. She abruptly stopped in her tracks.

"Ben, I'm scared to enter the forest. What if our flashlights will be seen in the darkness? What if every little crackle of a twig or movement through the brush can make sounds that anyone close by may hear, especially if they're out here to capture us. I'm afraid I'll step on a snake or that we'll be in range of wild animals—raccoons or rats. I didn't want to say anything about my fears to you before now. I was praying that I could get better about this, but now that we're here, I'm not. I could cry!" She began to sob.

"Ruth, as I've said lots of time before, God's got this. You know that!" Ben repeated and patted her on the shoulder. "We have to get in as far as possible into the forest tonight. They'll be looking for us in the morning, and we need to put enough distance between us and them."

"Just like I've said many times before, how I always wish I didn't have to go through this, and how horrific to be ousted from my comfortable home, to live under open sky, and to be hunted down and always looking over my shoulder, dreading the inevitable. Maybe we should just surrender! I can't take it, Ben!"

Ben shifted his backpack up on his shoulders. "Let's see how far we go before we can't go any farther and must give up our lives. I really believe we're doing what God would have us do!"

"Okay. Let's just pray, and I'll hold your hand as you lead us. I'll be right behind you," Ruth replied.

Ben prayed that God would lead them through the dark and bring them to another day in His perfect will for them. Then he took Ruth's hand and stepped into the forest.

Chapter 18
The Beginning of an Unknown Journey

Ben turned on the flashlight and moved them deeper into the darkness. He found what he thought was a deer path. Sometimes the underbrush and thick trees scraped them, but they trekked on.

After a couple of hours, Ben turned and gazed at Ruth. She seemed tired. He prayed in his heart for the Holy Spirit to indicate if they had gone far enough and if they could set up camp for the rest of the night.

"There's a pretty good clearing here where we can set up camp. It's almost morning anyway, but we can get a couple of hours of sleep. What do ya think?"

"That'd be great. I'm exhausted," Ruth said, immediately dropping her backpack to the ground.

Ben took out the small tent from his backpack and set it up in the dark, with Ruth holding the flashlight. When he was done, they each took a sleeping bag, entered the tent, and dropped off to sleep.

Daylight streamed too early into their tent. Ben awoke to birds chirping and the sound of a breeze flowing through the trees. He was grateful to God for the beautiful new morning and that Ruth, and he, were alive for another day.

While Ruth slept on, Ben rose and started a small fire with dried brush he placed in a small mound. He would toast bread over the fire and boil coffee grounds in water. He gazed wistfully at the food and wondered how long what they had would hold out or if they would starve before they were apprehended by any authorities. *What a depressing prospect!*

Soon Ruth stirred from the tent and peeked out.

"Good morning!" Ben said, holding up a tin cup of coffee. "I've got fresh coffee. How are you feeling?"

"Great," Ruth said, "except for feeling a little stiff from sleeping on the ground and for feeling like I'm still a lawbreaker and a fugitive!"

Ben laughed. "Get used to it! You and I are now officially lawbreakers...criminals! It may feel odd, but when the authorities are 'the Devil,' we need to do what we can to keep our lives intact."

"Yes!" Ruth said as she joined him by the fire. "What else do you have cooking besides coffee?"

"Just toast," Ben replied. "Want some?"

"Oh, boy, do I ever! I'm hungry."

"I bet you are! We did some hiking last night for sure!"

Ben handed Ruth two pieces of toast. He looked out over the forest and took in all the beauty of the sun shining through the trees and the fresh breeze blowing over them. What a pity that, despite the beauty of this day, they were both living in the darkest period of human history.

"Want any more toast or coffee?" Ben asked.

"No more toast; only some coffee." She hesitated. "Ben... where do we go from here?"

"I think we have to always keep moving forward. We can't stay in one place, or we'll be found. Today we need to walk until we find another place to camp for tonight. What do you think we should do?"

"It's still only the first day of our journey, and I'm already so unhappy with it!" Ruth declared.

"You and I both!" Ben responded. "But this is life for us now, and God, 'Hashem,' walks with us in it." He placed a hand on her arm. "Get enough to eat, because we won't break for lunch, but we'll go on until about five p.m. when we stop for the night."

"Oh, I'll be fine. I've had enough to eat for now. After all, my anxiety keeps my stomach pretty upset anyway. The good Lord willing, I'll be able to eat again tonight," Ruth said and smiled.

"Okay. I'll break down the tent, pack everything, and put out the fire. I'll try to bury any evidence of our being here, and then let's head out again. At least we'll be moving by daylight."

Ruth stood up to gather her things together. "How peaceful a place this is! What a pity to have to move on," she announced to Ben while taking a look at their surroundings one more time before leaving.

As they started their journey again, Ben gazed at the paper map long and hard in his hand. "By my calculations, we should go another day in this small forest. That'll be today; and then tomorrow, we'll need to wait until dark to skirt the periphery of another small city to get to an even bigger plot of wilderness where some mountains exist. When we get there, I hope we'll be able to hide in those mountains for a while." Ben indicated to Ruth as he showed her the map.

"Oh my!" Ruth exclaimed, "It's hard for me to endure the rough terrain in this wilderness for another day! And then, having to skirt around another city where we might be exposed to others!"

Ben wrapped his arm around her tiny waist and gave Ruth a

few seconds to catch her breath as the realization of the next steps in their journey sunk in.

After a few moments, Ben put his arm down. "Are you feeling okay now?"

"As best as I can for right now. I just have to take it a moment at a time."

"That's right. Okay, then! I'll try not to tell you more than the very next step we'll need to take each time."

Together, they proceeded to walk hand in hand through the forest so that they could hold and balance one another through rocks and crevices. After fifteen miles, in thick forest and rough terrain, and in the late afternoon when the sun was far down in the west, Ben found another alcove to settle in for the night. They were exhausted. *Not bad progress*, Ben thought. They sat down to eat some bread and beef jerky and soon after fell right to sleep.

In the morning, Ben and Ruth woke up again to streaming sunlight through their tent and birds chirping at them, all clearly oblivious to the dangerous world around them. Ben turned on the battery-operated radio for the first time since they had left on their journey, and then leaned in closer to Ruth to hear.

"Already happening! Christians and Jews are being apprehended, incarcerated, and put to death by beheading," the newscaster reported.

Fearing especially for what Ruth had just heard, Ben jumped up to instantly shut the radio off; but to Ben's surprise, Ruth reached over and turned the radio back on. "I may be afraid, but I have to know what's going on," she exclaimed as she nervously ran her fingers through her tussled hair and added, "You know the Bible speaks about this type of execution as Antichrist's choice during this time."

"Yes, I read that in the book of Revelation, too, but it didn't take a day or two for it to begin! The swiftness with which it has begun is mind-boggling! During the French Revolution, a guillotine was used for beheading, but this demonic Antichrist is beheading by the sword. How barbaric!! I'm sure he's especially ordered this type of execution to get a ghastlier reaction from those who are his followers and to also instill terror in believers like us," Ben replied.

Ruth suddenly broke in on Ben's comments "Wait...listen..."

The newscaster continued, "Apparently, an unprecedented plague of sores has surfaced, whose etiology is not yet known, and which is spreading on citizens across the New World Order in the aftermath of Master Ibrahim's retaking of the Jewish temple at Jerusalem. Thousands of citizens have already been afflicted and the World Health Organization and Centers for Disease Control cannot determine a treatment or cure for it at this time, but they are working on it.

"Yikes!" Ben exclaimed to Ruth.

"Yep, no doubt the world hasn't a clue of what's happening!" Ruth responded. "Let's conserve the batteries and turn off the radio for now."

Ben sighed with relief that any anxiety had not occurred beyond their abilities to handle it. "Sure thing!" Ben turned the radio off. "We do need to conserve those batteries since we'll unlikely be able to get more! If it's all right with you, let's eat a heftier meal tonight with the canned hash we brought."

"Agreed, and I will help to prepare it. I do suggest we rest now and start a fire later, well before nightfall, so that it won't be seen by the time it gets dark," Ruth replied.

Ben took off his shirt and stretched out on the ground. "Rest right now sounds good. I'll certainly light a fire later and with enough time before sunset so that we can heat the food and eat."

Ruth got down into her sleeping bag. "I'm so glad to get more rest."

What seemed many hours later, they both awoke to some nearby rustling that startled them. Ben caught sight of the fright in Ruth's eyes and quietly got up to tip-toe to where the rustling could be heard. Ruth clasped both of her arms together and rocked back and forth to comfort herself. She silently prayed. "Dear God, I trust you now. Let this be nothing serious and that we'll be okay."

As Ben walked spryly towards the rustling noise, he saw what looked like a small animal that was sniffing, nibbling, and moving through brush. He breathed a sigh of relief and shouted back to Ruth. "From what I can see, Ruth, it's just an animal, perhaps a raccoon moving through the brush. Don't worry!"

Ruth exhaled. "Oh, thank God! Thank you, Lord, for answering my prayer!"

Ben returned to begin a fire. "That frightened me, too. Let's get out the hash and heat it up. It'll soon be time for us to head out."

"Again, I'll say it. How scary to live looking over our shoulders! Even the rustle of an animal in the brush can trigger so much fear and panic."

"No doubt about it, Ruth, but so far, God's kept us, and remember we've only just begun our escape."

Together, they fixed their meal and ate. Darkness began to fall, and Ben put out the fire in time for them to have loaded their possessions for another night of travel. "Are you ready, Ruth?"

"As ready as I'll ever be! I'm glad we rested."

"Then let's head out!"

They gingerly and quietly proceeded on toward the forest's edge. Ben turned his flashlight on only to point it as low to the ground as he could so that they wouldn't be detected and could see where they were stepping. Their goal was to eventually exit the forest and then make their way around the periphery of the next small city, always observant of who or what might be around.

Suddenly, they heard a loud helicopter overhead with a huge spotlight scanning the forest. Ben quickly shut his flashlight off. *Did they find us? Could they know where we are already?! That gas station attendant might have reported our direction,* he thought. Perspiration formed over his entire body. His hands began to shake and become clammy. He pulled Ruth over to hide under a cluster of trees.

The helicopter hung over their area for what seemed like an eternity scanning the ground. Ruth began to cry, and Ben clung to her as he also shook uncontrollably.

Chapter 19
A Hope for the Future

T o not be detected, Ben and Ruth slowly slipped onto the ground to lie completely flat on its surface. Both were praying fervently that the helicopter would move on without spotting them. Finally, the helicopter soared higher and away, but Ben and Ruth continued to wait, wondering whether it was safe to exit their hiding place. Soon, Ben whispered to Ruth, "Let's get up and move on. I think we're okay now. Danger has passed."

Ruth whispered, "Are you sure? They could be waiting for us to come out and then they'll strike."

"We can't continue to lie here, or they'll come back. We need to move on. Let's pray now." Ben reached over to grasp Ruth's hand and bowed his head. "Dear Lord, thanks for covering us from being detected and giving us this narrow escape. We give you praise and glory, Most High and Mighty God! Help us the rest of the way tonight until we can reach a safe place to rest. In Jesus's name, Amen."

"Amen!" Ruth repeated as Ben helped her up.

Soon, they were forging ahead in complete darkness, this time with no flashlight after what had just happened.

"Will you be all right walking in darkness, Ruth?"

"I think I'll have no problem as long as you and I can hold on to one another."

"Okay, let's do it. I'll take your hand. I think my eyes are adapting to the darkness. I can make out some things. Of course, I have no idea where we're stepping, but the Bible promises us that with God we'll not stumble or fall." Together they continued deeper into the forest.

WHILE BEN and Ruth were finding a way to survive in the forest, Elira and Duncan were actively at work in the New World Order. Elira, who took on technological research again, scanned the neighborhood on her screen. Aha! There it is! Everyone showed as chipped except for one home. "Pete," she yelled back to her immediate supervisor, "come over here and take a look. Here's a home that has not shown any chip status for three days now. We should send out a team."

Pete bent over to glance at Elira's computer. "Yeah, no kidding! You're right! Looks like we have a stand-out! I'll send a team out right away. Good job!"

Could it be Ben? Elira thought. *His dad's house turned up empty, but it's only a matter of time for Ben! Such a waste! Could he be happy? How foolish indeed!*

She heard a knock at her office door. She opened it to find Duncan stepping in with an impish, lustful grin. *How gross and repulsive!* He lusted after her with such gusto that she felt he would throw himself on her right there! How different he was from Ben, who was always a gentleman and respected her as a lady. Yes, Ben was peculiar...yes, peculiar when compared to other men—his faith must have made him that way, she thought. She certainly missed that about him, but also blamed his faith for their break-up.

"Hey, Elira," Duncan sneered. "Maybe you can get home earlier this afternoon—like right after our meeting."

"I thought you came in here to get the number of outstanding individuals who have not been chipped so that you can report that information back to our local authorities whom you now represent."

"First things first, my dear!" Duncan smacked his lips.

Elira could feel her body repulse at Duncan's words and demeanor. *He looks like a toad, frumpy, vile, and lecherous!* Elira pushed Duncan away with a shove of her hand.

"Let's just work on solving Ben and Ruth's escape from justice...Local law enforcement officers have already been dispatched to check out a home in the neighborhood that has not had any occupants chipped, but we have reason to believe Ben and Ruth are not there, but most likely have made their way into the forest surrounding our town. An eyewitness reported seeing them head that way. He's the gas station attendant, Bruce Adams, at the gas station closest to Ruth's home. We believe they fled together because Bruce reports a man and a woman matching their individual descriptions walking quietly, but hurriedly together to the edge of town after midnight of the deadline day for their implanted chips. Since a few more days have gone by, they must have covered some substantial amount of territory by now and are much farther away than we think."

"Okay," Duncan retorted, "they won't get away. We'll find them, and Ben will meet his end just like his foolhardy father and mother!" Duncan let out a long, ghoulish laugh.

How relentlessly Duncan hated Ben and his family! Somehow, it had to give Duncan delight that she was now with him when she was previously Ben's girlfriend, Elira thought.

"What's the next step?" Duncan prompted Elira's mind back to their discussion. "Have helicopters been dispatched to survey the forest overhead? That will make it easier to spot them."

"Yes, they've already been dispatched and have made a search, but to no avail. The helicopters reported finding no one. At this point, other authorities of the New World Order will become involved. Eventually they will expose every hiding place for all these Christian and Jewish believers. I'll notify the larger authority of the New World Order that we were unable to locate any escaped believers in the forest that was surveyed by the helicopters."

"Good." Duncan said, his face exhibiting a wide grin from ear to ear. "May they smoke them out like rats and may their end come as soon as possible!" He laughed again, this time with such a bloodcurdling laugh that sent shudders through Elira, but she had to agree. She did not want any Christian or Jewish believers to escape.

"They need to bow their knees to Master Ibrahim or die!" Elira added. "After all, Master Ibrahim is the closest to a real miracle. He's ushering in world peace by unifying the planet into one. That has never been done before in human history! Being chipped will bring us all into the promise of a new, unified society. Why do these fringe elements persist in thwarting Master Ibrahim's great power and plan? They deserve to be caught and punished!"

In that moment, Duncan reached out to grope Elira. She cringed, which ignited his anger. He got in her face. "What do you mean by drawing back from me? You're mine now, and we're all part of this same world order. You'll satisfy me just as we must Master Ibrahim. To hell with anything outside of us!"

With that, he brushed up against Elira, swooped her up in his arms, and passionately kissed and fondled her. "Come home soon!" he commanded. "I'll be waiting! Master Ibrahim is supposed to speak tonight, and I want to make sure we don't miss him." With saying that, Duncan turned from her and walked out, grinning again from ear to ear.

Elira hated Duncan for the fiendish animal he was. She would now have to make her way home quickly to avoid his ire. It was unfortunate for her but living with Duncan was her only option. She no longer had a home of her own and she was accustomed to the support and companionship of a man like Ben; but, with Duncan, she felt trapped and used. Even though she wanted it to be different, this was her new way of life now, and she resented Ben more because of it. Hopefully, the time with neighbors and friends later in the evening would be a source of pleasure for her while listening to the Master she loved and respected so much.

Elira quickly sent a message to the New World Order about the inability to locate Ben and Ruth. She asked for them to assist in a continued search, and then shut her computer off and headed for home.

BEN MOVED to help Ruth put out the fire in the cave they'd hid in for the evening, when Ruth suddenly froze. They'd been getting ready to read their Bibles and to pray together, but now Ruth was immobilized by sounds outside. Ben jumped up to look out the cave. He could hear human voices in the distance.

He immediately threw sand on the fire to extinguish it. They remained silent in the dark hoping that the voices would not get close to them or their cave. However, the voices came closer. Ben prayed quietly. "Dear Lord, I pray for a miracle that these voices are friendly and not here to capture us. Please protect Ruth and me until you ordain differently. In Jesus's name."

"Ben," Ruth whispered into his ear, "I'm so afraid. My heart is beating so hard. It feels like it's going to pop out of my chest, and I can't breathe."

"Remember Hashem is with us. He goes with us and is around us by the power of His Holy Spirit. 'Do not fret because of evildoers,' as the Word says," Ben reassured her.

Ruth took several long, deep breaths, for her anxiety to settle down.

As the voices grew closer and closer, Ben spotted beams of light, like flashlights, near the cave entrance. A group of people--perhaps the authorities, or possibly a family or friends looking for a place to hide.

Ruth prayed in her heart that God would surprise them with other believers, either Christian or Jewish.

Soon, the voices got close enough for Ben and Ruth to hear what was being said.

"We are almost to the base of the mountain, and it looks like there's a cave. Praise the Lord!" a male voice yelled out.

"Good. Let's set up for the night. God has been faithful to find us a place to lay our weary bodies down and for us to worship Him," a female voice called back.

"Perhaps we can stay here for several days without being noticed!" another male voice chimed in.

Ben looked at Ruth as best as he could in the complete darkness. "Do you hear what I am hearing?" he whispered to her.

"I sure do!" Ruth replied. "It looks like God has been good to us, and we've found fellow believers!"

"Yes! But we must not startle them. I'll let them know we are believers too."

"How do we do that?" Ruth asked.

"I'm praying about it. I get the feeling that if I call out to them and let them know we're believers too, that they'll be happy to hear this and not be startled."

"That sounds like a good plan, but I pray it works," Ruth said. "They may think it's a set-up for capture. We would!"

When the voices reached much closer to their cave, Ben stepped out and yelled, "Please don't be alarmed! We heard your voices, and we're believers of the Lord Jesus Christ. We've escaped the New World Order. Would you like to join us in the cave?"

The voices and footsteps stopped short. There was a long pause. Not an extra word or step was taken. *They're probably skeptical of me; afraid that the authorities have cornered them.*

Ben spoke again, "Please don't be apprehensive. We were afraid until we heard your conversation as you got near the cave. If you are doubtful of us and our intentions, you know the Holy Spirit will reveal truth to you about us; and when you feel comfortable, please come forward."

There were some whispers and rustling within the group and then Ben could just make out a man cautiously stepping forward. "You would have to be Christian believers. No one undercover would refer to the Holy Spirit as the Revealer of truth. I'm Adam."

"Adam, I'm Ben. You and your group are welcome to come up here to stay in the cave with us. We were praying that God would unite us with other believers fleeing death. We feel there's strength in being together."

After more vigorous whispering within the group, where Ben overheard some skeptical dissent, Adam responded, "All right. We'll be glad to enter your cave tonight, but we'd like to get to know you and any others with you first."

"Great! Come right on up. I'll shine my flashlight at where I'm standing," Ben replied.

Soon the shadowy figures of about seven people filed into Ben and Ruth's space as Ben shone his flashlight into the cave.

When the group were all inside, they turned on a couple of their own flashlights.

"There is only one other person besides me. This is Ruth. My mother and her mother were close friends whom we both lost in The Disappearance. Now we're glad that both of us are friends, too, to flee capture together."

"Yes!" Ruth exclaimed. "How wonderful to be together during this time."

The group along with Ben and Ruth sat down together in a circle to continue their conversation.

"Well, it's good to meet you both." Adam said. He was a tall, strapping man of six feet or more. He had dark brown, almost black hair, and dark eyes and a heavy muscular build.

Ben gazed at Adam in the dim light. "I'm glad someone like him is on our side!" Ben mused. "He looks the perfect model of brute physical strength."

Adam pointed first to a slim, shy teenager who couldn't have been more than 16 or 17 years old. She had sandy-blonde hair and blue eyes. "This is Elaine," Adam said, and then pointed to the next person, a man in his late fifties, chubby with graying hair and a receding hairline. He seemed poised and confident. "This is John."

Adam pointed again to the next person, a woman in her early fifties with white-blonde hair and blue eyes. She had a huge grin on her face. "This is Evelyn, John's wife."

Next Adam pointed to a man in his thirties who also had a hefty body build and with brown hair and brown eyes. "This is Noah," Adam said. "He's my brother."

Adam gestured to another young woman in her mid-twenties or thirties with auburn hair and hazel green eyes. "This is Katie, my own wife," Adam announced with warmth and tenderness. "Before we had to flee, Katie had been studying to become a nurse. She enjoys medical science."

Finally, Adam pointed to the last of his group, another young woman in her early twenties who had ink-colored eyes and long brunette hair that reached to her hips. "This is Noah's girlfriend, Elizabeth. We call her Liz."

After these introductions by Adam, Ben spoke first. "Ruth and I are Messianic Jews. We were left behind because we didn't heed what our moms told us about God and His Son, Jesus. My father, Simon, received Christ on his deathbed and is with my mother now. Ruth's father never did receive Jesus Christ as his Savior as far as she knows, but he was also not part of her life or her mother's life for many years and they lost contact with him. Ruth and I both have no siblings. I had a girlfriend that I wanted to marry, but she never did believe in Christ, or even God, for that matter. She would chide me about my mom's beliefs and later the beliefs of my father and me. Ruth and I...., he hesitated, "well, we now look forward to going to meet the Lord if we should be captured and executed."

Adam, along with the rest of the group, looked empathetically at Ben and Ruth. "My brother, Noah, and I are both sons of a Godly pastor," Adam replied. "He and our mother both taught us God's Word. However, when we were a little older, we went our own separate ways apart from those of our parents. When The Disappearance occurred, Noah and I found we were left behind along with my wife and Noah's girlfriend. We have since spoken to each of them about what really took place, and all four of us have dedicated our lives to Jesus Christ as our Savior and Lord. We, too, await what God has for us, and we understand death could very well be next for us. Although we can be apprehensive about it, we trust God for what will happen to us and that He will give us the courage and strength for it. As far as Elaine, Evelyn, and John are concerned, all three are members of our dad's church. Elaine is one of the young people from the church. Her parents were taken up in The Disappearance, along with her older sister and brother. Evelyn and John have grown children who never became believers. Their adult children weren't expected to be part of The Disappearance and have received their implanted chips. Evelyn and John don't want to receive the Antichrist's mark and have prayed to rededicate their lives to Jesus Christ. Elaine has also prayed to receive Christ as her Savior. We're now all fugitives together. The name of my father's church was Maranatha Christian Fellowship. Today, it is abandoned, of course, and most likely demolished by the New World Order by now."

When Adam finished, Ruth said, "Now that we're together, let's share whatever we have in common just as the early New Testament church of Jesus did!"

"That's a great idea!" Adam agreed. *It's obvious that Adam must be both the leader and spokesperson for the group, Ben thought, since he responds each time for his group.*

"Have any of you heard anything more from the outside world?" Ruth asked. "We only have an old-fashioned battery-operated radio which we use sparingly."

"I don't know if you've heard," Noah answered, "but God is raining down His judgment upon the Antichrist's earth and government. It was reported just yesterday that all the oceans of the world have turned to blood. As if they weren't already angry, people hold anger now in lethal proportions toward God after this newest plague! For us, we know that the next great punishment by God will be that fresh water will also be turned to blood. Since we have some fresh water to drink now, we thought it prudent to add extra fresh water to our flasks and canteens before the freshwater ponds, lakes, and streams turn to blood."

"What's more is that we have heard rumors that a huge meteor fell somewhere in the Middle East or Far East closer to China. We don't know if it's true; but if so, it's left a gaping hole from which legions of locusts with stingers like that of scorpions have spread throughout the countries of the New World Order. These locusts have become yet another tormenting plague for those who've received the Antichrist's mark," Adam added. "All this trouble is happening almost simultaneously."

"Wow! The scorpion-like locusts have got to be a torment from hell!" Ben exclaimed. "It's a good idea for us to take all our water containers and fill them with fresh water as soon as the sun rises in the morning. In the meantime, perhaps we could try to get some rest."

The larger group of nine now each staked out places within the cave to place their mats or sleeping bags and turned in for a night of peaceful rest.

~

DAYBREAK CAME EARLY. The rays of the sun began to shine far into the cave, where all were stirring. Ben looked over at Adam, who lay on the ground fully awake, but blinking upward toward the ceiling.

"Hey, do you want to take the water containers we have and go find a stream to fill them?" Ben asked.

"Yes, of course. Let's gather the containers and head out before the others get up," Adam replied.

With that said, Ben rose and gathered the containers he and Ruth had and aided Adam as he, too, went around to each person's equipment in his group and gathered any water canteens or flasks.

Soon both men were outside the cave making their way to a watering hole. As they surveyed the gorgeous morning, it was hard again to believe that this morning was part of the Great Tribulation. It was beautiful and the air was crisp and cool. Everything still seemed so peaceful and bright.

"I spot a stream! Adam exclaimed as he put down his binoculars.

"Excellent!" Ben added. They made their way down to it, and observed the clean, rushing water. The sound of it calmed Ben's spirits, and he voiced a prayer out loud, "Thank you, Lord, for this Your gracious blessing to us!"

Adam responded, "Amen!"

Each man took some water containers and dipped them, one at a time, into the stream to fill each with clean, life-sustaining water. When they had received their fill of water for all the flasks and containers, they proceeded to turn in the direction of the cave, being mindful of their footsteps and any possible enemy that could be surveying the area. They consistently looked in every direction when taking a step, to avoid being discovered. In short time they made it to the cave entrance and took one more glance around. When they did, they couldn't believe their eyes at the sight of the stream. It was now blood red! They had just made it to receive the water they needed before the water turned to blood! Already the fish appeared to draw up to the surface, gasping for breath. God's continuous judgment of the earth was apparent.

When they stepped into the cave, some of the others were awake and chatting while setting out snacks. Adam and Ben appeared with the water.

"Hi, everyone!" Adam announced. "Ben and I returned just in time with fresh crystal-clear water. As we turned to glance around us before entering the cave, the pristine, pure water had already turned to blood! The fish in the stream are already rising to the surface and dying. There'll be a mighty stench soon."

"Oh my!" Elaine gushed out as she gripped Liz's arm next to her. "This is it for any more water, right? How will we make it without water?"

Liz patted Elaine's hand which was tightly gripping hers.

"Isn't it just like God to have withheld His judgment of the water turning to blood until we could fill up our containers? Think about it! Don't worry!" She stroked Elaine's hand. "God hasn't allowed us to get this far to leave us. Do you believe that?"

Elaine shook--her panic evident to all the group. "Yeah, I do believe it, but it's so frightening for me just the same."

"Now, except for reservoirs that have already been filled, it will be difficult for the people of the earth to have water to enjoy," Noah noted to everyone.

"Oh, yes, indeed," Katie sighed. "And yet earth's people will not be able to repent because they have all become one with the enemies, Antichrist and Satan."

"How about if we sing a chorus of praise to God?" Liz asked. "And, while we're at it, we could read some passages from Scripture and have a morning prayer together."

Each person nodded in agreement. Liz, whose voice boomed above the group, began to sing a chorus in which they all joined in. The group, who were once again seated in a circle, took turns to pray out loud and to praise the Lord for all their blessings.

Ben spoke out the final prayer for the group, "Dear Heavenly Father, we pray for all other believers who have not received the mark of the Antichrist to come out of this Great Tribulation period, that You would keep them in their escape from the authorities, and see to their safety, protection, and provision as You have so graciously done for us till now. We pray you would comfort them in persecution, torment, or capture, as we all look forward to eternal life with You. In Jesus's name, Amen."

When Ben finished, the group gathered to share a little of their food together and to enjoy some of the fresh water brought in by Adam and Ben. "What a wonderful time of fellowship and joy in a dark time," Ben thought.

A FEW MONTHS LATER, Elira paced back and forth biting her fingernails with angst. Not only couldn't the forces of the New World Order find Ben and Ruth in their initial search for them in the nearby woods, but they seemed ill-equipped to endure a search into the forest and woodlands further away. *How lame can they be?! This isn't happening fast enough. We're losing our window of opportunity! What does it have to take for them to succeed?* She slammed her fist on her desktop and glared at her computer. *What's made it difficult are the disasters that have consistently taken place. Unbelievable! You would think that the earth is coming to some catastrophic end! If there was a God to curse, I'd curse Him because this is sheer torment and an impediment! Everything that's going on is only weakening the authorities. How can they survive with sores on their bodies, a lack of fresh water supply, and the constant, horrible stench of blood and decomposing fish? It's preposterous!*

There was a light knock at her door, and in walked her co-worker and supervisor, Pete. "What's happening with the search?"

Elira was suddenly jogged away from her thoughts. "What's happening you ask?! Why nothing at all is happening! That's what! The search party has not been able to find any fugitives; and what's more, they seem badly overcome by the elements."

"Let's refresh the computer for new updates that may have just come in." Pete suggested.

Elira pressed the refresh button on the computer and looked at the screen. "Okay. I see a military regiment has made their way through to a larger search area. Good. It's about time! But wait, wait...wait...What's going on? Uh oh, Oh no! They're kidding! They're saying the sun is getting closer to the earth's surface?! What utter nonsense! Military forces are dropping from heat exhaustion?!" Elira stared incredulously at her computer.

Pete humped over the computer next to Elira. "Incredible! Great time for that! I'll be damned if this isn't some sort of fictitious delay! What's really happening there?" He scratched his head.

Elira shot up out of her chair to look Pete in the eyes. "Look, I'm calling in to see that the troops will not abandon this search. Not only is this one for the good of the New World Order, but this is justice for me! I've a vested interest here, and I'm not quitting and neither should they!"

Elira turned to walk away. *Those troops can drop alongside the road for all I care, but I'll see to it that they persevere in their pursuit or there will be stiff penalties by the Order.*

Frustrated and angry, she pulled her office door open with all her might and slammed it shut behind her leaving Pete wide-eyed in the wake of her fury.

BEN TRIED VENTURING OUT of the cave the group of fugitives had been staying in and fell back putting his hands over his eyes. "Wow! What has happened this morning? The rays of the sun are infernal and so fiercely penetrating! My protective sunglasses aren't helping at all! My face and skin are burning like wildfire," he bellowed out to the group within. "Hey everyone! This has got to be a newest judgment from God. The sun seems closer to the earth, and it's burning hell-hot!"

"Well, in a way, I praise God this latest judgment is actually going to escalate our protection from the movement of the enemy to capture us," John said.

"Yes, and the coolness and darkness of the cave still shelter us from the heat," Evelyn chimed in.

"At some point in time, though," Ben said, "we'll need to move on to not be discovered. We've been blessed to be able to stay here for as long as we have; but, despite the burning heat, it's only a matter of time before the New World Order will be standing at the entrance of our cave. I'm sure they've continued making attempts to find us, but we've alluded them. We still need to be diligent to travel by cover of darkness farther away to stay ahead of them. I don't know when to pursue a new path, but we must discuss that soon."

Adam hesitated, glancing quickly at each of the others in the cave. "It seems we can stay here another night or two. Then, yes, we must leave by cover of darkness, as you've said, Ben. Where's your map of this region so that we can see it and move in a direction that can take us to another cave farther ahead?"

"Wait a minute! Have either of you thought about the possibility that the New World Order might have sent other military personnel from the opposite side of this forest to corner us?" Evelyn excitedly asked, eyeing her husband inquisitively. "We must be wary, don't you think?"

"Well said." Ben replied. "Perhaps we should branch off to an entirely different location, which might take us through some cities before we reach more untapped wilderness."

Katie coughed, catching a strand of her hair falling over her forehead and in front of her eyes. "That sounds like a good plan."

"Yeah," Ruth replied. "Maybe we'll need to start off the day after tomorrow, depending on the intensity of the heat. But if we move by night, the heat won't burn us."

"We just need to pray about this," Adam suggested.

"You're right!" Ben said as he took up his Bible to read a Scripture verse to the group. "I want to encourage all of you with this Scripture verse God reminded me of. It's from Deuteronomy 31:8. It says, 'The Lord Himself goes before you and will be with you; He will never leave you nor forsake you. Do not be afraid; do not be discouraged.'"

"Hallelujah!" shouted Liz from behind the rest of the group. "How appropriate to keep in our minds and hearts right now."

Adam stood up to pray. "Once again, dear Lord, we thank You for Your promises and Your great faithfulness to us. We ask for Your guidance in our travels. Reveal to us the place You have for us next. In Jesus's name. Amen."

Ben eased onto the cave's floor and sat with both legs crossed. "Join me in a chorus of praise." As the group joined in, Ben saw some of them lifting their arms and hands in worship, their faces raised upward.

When they were all done, Adam said, "Let's pray that God will provide for our needs in the foreseeable future as we will need food and water to sustain our lives during our escape from capture."

"Yes," Ben nodded in total agreement. "We will need provisions from God's intervention at this point. I know many of us are getting hungry and losing a lot of weight. We expected our lives to be this way as we flee apprehension by the authorities."

Adam raised his shirt sleeve up to wipe his face. "Yes, our supply of food and snacks has dwindled to almost nothing, and none of us, of course, could have carried large amounts of food with us to last the entire time we'd be running from the authorities. We have done well to stick to our daily rations, which has prolonged our food supply, but now we must look to our surrounding environment for the food we need. I would love to catch some fresh fish, but the streams and waterways are now polluted from God's punishment." He hung his head. "I don't know what more we can do except to hunt down an animal to kill and eat it."

"Don't be concerned, honey," Katie put her arm around his

shoulders. "God will provide the food we need. I saw berries and dandelions in the forest we can pick and eat."

"Yes!" Elaine declared. "I'd like fruit or vegetables to eat rather than having to kill an animal."

"I would like to pray," replied Ruth with a wide, confident smile and shifted her weight on the cave floor. "Dear Lord, you know all we need. We lack food and drinkable water right now, Lord. Provide for us as you did for the Israelites in their wilderness wandering. We praise you for it! Amen!"

At dusk, the group came briefly out the mouth of the cave. Ben held his nose as he focused his eyes in the darkness. "The water smelling and looking like blood is flipping me out! Dead, rotting fish all over the surface of the water and the shoreline!"

Katie cupped her hands over her mouth and nose. "I'm gagging. I have to go back in."

"Me, too!" Elaine added. "I've got to get out of here! Hopefully, this smell won't continue on our journey, especially as we head away from water."

"Let's go back in now and light a fire." Ben softly said as he stepped back into the cave. "My gut feeling is to be out of here sooner rather than later. I'm concerned. I have a former girlfriend who is very resentful of my turning to God, and she's a technology buff with the Federal government. I get the unmistakable sense from God's Holy Spirit that she's not letting up from her work with the New World Order in hunting down Christian and Jewish fugitives, especially me and Ruth."

"In spite of what you're personally feeling about your former girlfriend," Adam added, "I, too, feel we must keep moving. Even though the natural elements are corrupted by God's punishment, I know the New World Order's forces will stop at nothing to eventually capture and execute us. I also say we move out no later than tomorrow night. Unfortunately, we must move through a smaller village to get to wilderness that is farther away from here and where our steps cannot be easily traced."

"We have no other choice," Ben announced. "I see concern on all your faces to leave this cave because we all know the alternative for us is capture if we stay. We need to keep moving for as long as we can."

"Okay," John said, "I think the whole group is with you both on that decision, but we'll need to prepare for our move and get rest for the night! Not all of us are young, you know!"

"I'm so afraid!" Elaine interjected. "I am the youngest but feel like at any time I will face punishment and death. I don't know if I can do this any longer." A shiver ran through her, and she placed a hand on her chest. "My heart is beating hard again. I wish I could just wake up from this nightmare!"

Two of the other women gathered around her to hug her trembling body. "Don't worry. Have faith," Liz said.

"I'll try," Elaine responded.

"Look. God has our beginning and our end. He'll see us through. He knows how much we can all handle!" Evelyn added.

"Hey, everyone," Adam said, "let's get some sleep tonight. Tomorrow we'll prepare for our move and look at the shortest distance to a new place far enough from here. At nightfall, we'll wait until it's early morning and depart for our next destination. Do we all agree?"

Ben nodded along with the others. "I feel I should sleep closer to the mouth of the cave tonight. I want to be a lookout for anyone that I might hear or see nearing the cave, and I'll be able to alert the rest of you."

Elaine started shaking again as Evelyn reached to hold her. "Oh no! You're scaring me! Are you feeling someone or something just outside our cave?" Elaine asked.

"Shhh," Evelyn tried to hush Elaine as she hugged her tight and rocked her for comfort.

Adam studied Ben's face in the fire's dim glow while the rest of the group gazed at them both. "Brother, are you feeling capture is imminent? Do you feel we need to move out tonight?" Adam asked Ben.

"I do feel it is imminent, and I want to be prepared, not surprised! I don't think we need to leave tonight. We can rest; but as I already said, I'll be on the lookout for any sound or light."

"Okay, do what you feel is best. May the Lord give us all peace and rest tonight!"

Ben lifted his sleeping bag out of its place and dragged it to the front of the cave. He gazed outside the cave one more time before lightly lying down on top of his sleeping bag. He clasped his hands together in silent prayer as his eyes glanced up into the darkness. His thoughts wandered into the possibility that the eerie feeling he was having could come through.. *This may be a long night,* he speculated as he tried to fall asleep.

Chapter 20
The Threat of Death

Ben hardly got a wink of sleep, tossing and turning the whole night. He heard a twig snap, and he was up with a jolt. He listened more carefully. *Could that be someone coming up to the cave? I can't just step out. I must get close enough to make out who or what it is.*

Ben picked up a knife by his side and readied his flashlight. As his eyes focused into the darkness and became accustomed to it, he made out the form of an animal, possibly a small fox. He saw it cross in front of the cave and make its way to the lakeshore, sadly with no water for it to drink. Ben sighed in relief. His beating heart calmed down for the moment and he lay back down. *I'm glad no one awoke. They're sleeping peacefully.*

After that, the night passed uneventfully, and in the morning, Ben gathered the small band of believers to prepare them for exit from the cave. "Everyone, just remember that our primary weapons are prayer and praise! God fights our battles for us. Amen?" Ben said.

"Amen!" Everyone answered in unison.

"At 1:30 A.M. I will lead you out of the cave to our next

destination with the map I have already studied. I'm turning on the battery-operated radio now for us to hear reports of the outside world."

"We are proud to say that as of today, fifty thousand rebels to our sovereign Master Ibrahim and his New World Order have been captured and executed," the news broadcaster reported. "This is just in the last nine months. Despite never being implanted with their chips, they were discovered miles from their homes or cities and apprehended. Each was beheaded publicly."

"What a ghastly spectacle it must be to view daily on TV or Internet!" Katie exclaimed.

"Yes, can you imagine the horror of this? Mizrah chooses executioners who can use swords or hatchets to increase the macabre scene of these executions. Ben and I had already talked about it when they first began," Ruth added.

"Unbelievable! Yes, it's chosen to instill fear on those not captured!" Evelyn noted.

Adam drew near to comment. "Mizrah is the Destroyer, the Devil Incarnate, the Antichrist! What else would one expect? He would have a penchant for killing, and certainly beheading just increases the shock and horror of it all to his benefit."

Ben nodded. "Exactly right! And no doubt about it; he's a vicious psychopath."

"Now our lack of a fresh water supply will slow down the authorities in their pursuit of us, but it will also slow us down, too." Adam noted. "We will have to be mindful of how much we each drink on our journey. If the Lord provides us some rain, we can hopefully fill our water bottles with rainwater."

"On another note," Ben added, "we need to be prepared by 1:30 A.M. to head out. Once again, we'll go under cover of darkness when hopefully others in pursuit might be resting from their day. We'll depend upon streetlights as we skirt around the village, and we'll carry a few flashlights pointed down as close to the ground as possible to guide our way." The group nodded consent.

At about 1:00 A.M. they prepared to head out from the mouth of the cave. Each person had items they carried for the group such as bedding and supplies. Each also had their own backpacks.

"All these items we need to carry can eventually bog us down," Liz spoke out. "At some point they can become a deterrent for us to walk further."

"I don't think we need to worry about that yet," Noah said grabbing her extra items to help her out.

Lifting just her backpack onto her shoulders, Liz snickered. "Yes, I guess there's time for ditching this backpack later, too."

At 1:30 A.M., they advanced out of the cave and into the wilderness with flashlights, looking for a path to the next large city and around it to the next forest. They proceeded to walk in the darkness, with bushes and trees that stood in their path. They pushed aside tree branches and bushes and kept moving in a line without speaking a word to one another as they followed Ben.

Once Ben saw the lights of the next large city, he led the group onto the outskirts of it using only the city lights to lead them to the beginning of the large forest that followed. The others walked as silently as they could, tiptoeing around the outskirts of the city— praying for success.

At about 7:30 A.M., Ben came upon the edge of the forest. He took a deep breath. "We made it to the edge of the forest!" he declared. The others knelt for a prayer of thanks with him.

"The curfews imposed on cities across the globe made it impossible for anyone to be out at night," Adam whispered. "But now, people should be getting up for the day, and we should walk deeper into this forest to look for a place to camp."

"Yes, siree!" John replied. "The rays of the early morning sun have started coming up. Thankfully, because of the forest's dense canopy of trees, we should be more shielded from the burning hot sun so close to the earth. Great time to start into the forest!"

Ben wiped perspiration already forming on his face. "Okay, turn off your flashlights to conserve their batteries," he said as he led the group forward into the wilderness. After they trekked for what seemed like miles, they came upon a natural clearing in the woods, where he halted them.

Adam spoke first. "Ben, do you think this is a good place to put up camp for the night and perhaps to remain here for a little longer?"

"Yes, I do," Ben responded. "I feel the Holy Spirit telling me that this is our next resting point. We can shelter under a canopy of trees and have a fire in the small clearing."

"Unfortunately, it's not a cave like we've had before," Noah noted, "but it will give us a place to lay our heads and to enjoy our time with one another in fellowship, prayer, and praise."

"Yes!" Ruth exclaimed. "This is a good resting spot. Let's camp here."

Adam and Ben signaled to the others to drop their gear and set up camp. Quickly, the group transformed the clearing into a campsite. The women lit a small fire and divided what final snacks they still had left among them along with some berries and edible leaves they picked up along the way. Ben called the group to worship and praise by breaking out in a chorus for them to follow.

From the small clearing where the fire was lit, Ben turned on the battery-operated radio, and the group gathered around to listen. A booming voice spoke. "We have breaking news that Master Ibrahim's kingdom has come under complete darkness so thick that persons cannot see one another. This has presented a new challenge for the government to work on its far-reaching agenda. This new phenomenon will be researched to combat it quickly. In the meantime, lights will be used around the clock."

From the small clearing where the fire was lit, Noah looked up into the sky. "Hey, as a matter of fact, I can't see a star shining," he announced to the others as they also looked up.

Curious to see for himself, Ben walked out from under the trees of the nearby forest to look up into the sky. "You're right! I just thought, where I was standing, was covered by a dense canopy of trees, but I don't see anything in the sky here either."

"Wow!" Adam exclaimed. "We are in total darkness except for our flashlights and fire. The bad news is that total darkness now covers the earth. It's another one of God's judgments we read about in chapter sixteen of Revelation. The good news is that with total darkness and the other judgments that have come upon the Antichrist and his New World Order in the last several weeks, there's less chance we can be discovered. With that in mind, we can possibly stay here for several days without having to move. Let's extinguish our campfire so as not to draw attention to ourselves. We'll be in utter darkness. The morning and day to follow may still hold scorching heat even though there is no daylight."

Ben aimed his flashlight at himself. "Although we are not in a cave, we are covered by a thick canopy of trees providing cover for us. However, the sun has been so close to the surface of the earth that the uppermost branches and leaves of the trees have turned brown, but now we will be hidden from view anyway because of total darkness. Two good things about this is that the underside of the tree canopy helps to provide shade for edible plants and fruit below and any crackle of burnt leaves or branches from above can alert us of anyone's presence in our area so that we can make a quick move. We must always have our gear packed and ready for a moment's departure, got it everyone?"

"Yes!" the group responded in unison.

The next morning came with continued, unrelenting heat, though the world was covered in thick darkness. Ben surveyed their food and water supplies.

Ben shrugged. "The water supply is very low, no doubt because of the group's thirst in such unprecedented high temperatures. The food supply is all but completely gone. The only food we still have are the few leaves and berries we were able to find on our way here." Ben had an empty feeling in the pit of his stomach. He felt panic rising, "Holy Spirit, give us direction; give us insight," he prayed clasping his quivering hands together and upward. "I give this problem to you."

While the others stirred awake, Adam lifted his voice in prayer, "Lord, help provide us food as you did the ancient Israelites in their wilderness wandering. You can make it appear for us and to also increase our existing small water supply. Thank you in Jesus's name."

"We've all lost weight and are weaker than ever before and very dehydrated, but I think it's come to where we must allow ourselves food only once a day, no snacks." Ben said while staring at his small bite of food. "We will need to continue rations of each person's water intake until we are able to get some rain."

"Wait!" Evelyn fidgeted in place. "There are some who suffer from medical conditions and we need food to sustain us, or our bodies will become more vulnerable."

Ben stared at her blankly. *What a dreadful time to be living in,* he thought. "I don't know what to tell you, Evelyn. We know suffering is part of our common experience right now. We only have our faith in our Heavenly Father to rely on. We'll take it a day at a time, okay?"

"Okay, no worries!" John pulled his wife closer to him. "Don't worry, honey. It will be all right. We knew this would eventually happen to us."

Liz turned on the battery-operated radio again.

"Master Ibrahim's government is now conducting an all-out search for fugitives from Chillicothe Falls and its surrounding communities. What is your role in aiding the search?" asked a news reporter doing an interview on the ground.

Ben jerked when he heard the voice of Elira respond. "I am the technological whiz behind finding where these fugitives are hiding and bringing them to justice."

"Really? And what is your role in all of this?" the reporter asked another.

"If those who are listening don't know, I'm on the Board of County Commissioners representing the town of Chillicothe Falls for our county. Since two of the fugitives are from Chillicothe Falls, I am overseeing their capture," Duncan responded, "and I'm proud of it!"

Ben squirmed and beads of perspiration formed on his forehead. The group stared wide-eyed at the radio, speechless.

"I see," the reporter said, "what are their names?"

"Ben Goldberg and Ruth Newman, who have escaped together in what we believe was the middle of the night. They are on foot, and they could not have made so much progress to be across the country. We've just not been able to reach them yet, but we will. It's only a matter of time!" Duncan paused and then laughed.

"And there's another group of seven persons that came from a nearby community, the city of Salisburg, is that correct?" the reporter asked Elira.

"Yes, that's right. We are closing in on them also and working with the local city authorities there to find them. They cannot be much farther away either. They are on foot and have a larger group to keep together. We believe that with this abhorrent heat and the lack of access to water and food, they should be very weak and easy to capture now, if not already dead." Elira retorted.

Ruth shot an ominous glance at Ben, while the rest of the group also sent panicked looks toward one another.

"Hey, we know that this is happening even when we are not hearing it on the radio," John reasoned. "We can't live in fear."

"I think they'll soon lock onto us," Liz said. "We agree to keep moving, right?"

"Unfortunately for us, it's hard to continuously move, but it's a solution to keep on living and making it less likely for them to find us," Evelyn pouted, repeatedly rubbing her arm.

"I agree," added her husband, John. "We're the oldest in this group, and we know we have to do what's necessary to avoid certain death until it may be what God has for us."

"I'm still scared," Elaine voiced in a loud whisper. Everyone turned to look at her.

"It's that great fear factor that convinces more people to bend to the manipulation of the Antichrist. Messiah Jesus said in Matthew, chapter 16, and in Mark, chapter 8 that 'whoever wants to save their life will lose it, but whoever loses their life for me will find it. What good will it be for someone to gain the whole world, yet forfeit their own soul? Or what can anyone give in exchange for their soul?' In other words, if you only focus on your physical life and your fear of death, you may gain your physical life for a time by taking Antichrist's mark and avoiding death, but you will certainly lose your eternal life with God in the end," Katie responded.

Elaine stared intently at Katie for a long moment. "I only pray that the Lord will help me be courageous if I face death and that it'll be quick and as painless as possible," she whimpered.

"I'm the closest to you in age," Liz said, "and I just leave it in God's hands and try not to think about it. I trust Him for that."

"We read about Stephen in the Acts of the Apostles who was martyred for his faith," Ruth spoke up glancing at Elaine and leaning her head back against a tree trunk. "He was stoned to death, and the Lord Jesus Himself was with him in the suffering he endured. We read that Stephen, full of the Holy Spirit, saw Jesus standing at the right hand of God. I believe Jesus was standing because He was ready to receive Stephen into heaven with Him."

"True!" Ben said. "When we walk through death, our Lord is with us. Now we must focus on leaving here by night. Since our food is all gone and our water supply low, we'll have a lighter load to carry but, at some point, we will have to rely only on what the wilderness has to offer us, whether animal, fruit, or leaf. For a substitute for water, we'll need to find fruit that has a higher water content to keep us hydrated as much as possible. Death may not occur only through being captured, but from the adverse conditions we face with food, water, and travel. We need to keep that in mind."

Chapter 21
Gathering Evil and Doom

Thanks to wind-up watches, Ben was able to know that night had fallen, though thick darkness continued around the clock. It seemed a matter of moments since they had packed their equipment and supplies and took time to pray. Now it was time to head out again for what lay before them.

"I'm so glad we took the time to go over the map. Important!" Ben handed it over to Adam for safekeeping.

"I do think heading northwest where there are smaller towns, and a bigger wilderness is key," Adam said, as he took the map and tucked it away in his backpack.

"Entering the larger, steeper mountain range is ingenious! That should throw the authorities off our trail. But what about John and Evelyn? Can they do it?" Ben asked with a sigh.

"That's where I think that we should talk to them, Ben. Don't you agree?"

"I do! Let's talk to them now."

"Let's do!" Adam exclaimed.

The group was scurrying about getting ready to leave on the

next leg of their journey when Ben and Adam approached John and Evelyn. *I hope this goes well!* Ben hoped and prayed.

"Hey, John, Evelyn! Adam and I want to chat with you. Got a moment while you're preparing your stuff?"

John looked up from packing his bag. "No problem! Get over here, Evelyn!" Evelyn left what she was doing and headed towards her husband.

"Listen," Ben said, "we've looked at the map and the plan is to go up a steep mountain range to make it harder for us to be followed and found. Adam and I are concerned for you two. How do you feel about this?" Ben held his breath for the reply.

"As you already know, my wife suffers from high blood pressure and anxiety, and she's not at all athletic."

"Oh, John, you don't call what we've been doing all this time on our journey exercise?" Evelyn asked.

"Evelyn, we will be scaling a steep mountain range!"

"What? You're kidding me! We're not mountain climbers!"

"Neither are we!" Adam reassured her. "We're all going to try our best."

"This sounds a bit crazy to me. Why not just take an easier path?" Evelyn wrung her hands in dismay.

"We'd be easier targets with an easier path!" Ben reached out to take her hands in his. "You've got to trust us on this one!"

John looked earnestly into his wife's eyes. "Well, Evelyn, what do you think? We can try. We can't dismiss the plan without trying."

"I suppose you're right. Will we take it slow?" Evelyn asked Ben and Adam.

"As slow as possible!" Ben said gently letting go of Evelyn's hands.

"We'll do everything to ensure you're both safe and can keep up," Adam reassured.

"Okay, then! Let's go with it!" Evelyn agreed.

Under earth's total darkness, the group stealthily wound their way through the wilderness, quiet to not attract any undue attention. The pace was slow, but steady.

"Keep your flashlights off as we head around the towns we pass. Only turn them on when we are in the wilderness but keep them low to the ground as possible," Ben ordered. "After all, we have some lights from the towns we will pass."

"I'm not feeling well. How much longer?" cried Elaine.

"What's wrong?" Katie asked as she came up beside her.

"I don't know. My breathing is becoming difficult."

"Our altitude is getting higher. That could be it, unless you're getting anxious."

"My heart is racing; I know that. Must be fear. I don't know." Elaine clutched at her throat. "I have to sit down."

"Hey, everyone! Need to stop here! It's Elaine!" Katie shouted to the group.

Ben and Adam rushed to Elaine's side. Ben put his hand on her shoulder. "What? ...What's going on, Elaine?"

"I...I...I don't know. I'm winded." She gasped. "I can't keep up."

"Maybe we need to help talk you down. Whatta you thinking?" Katie asked.

"M...m...my family has l...l...lung disease—asthma," Elaine replied.

Adam pulled at his growing beard. "We need to carry her. We're not far."

"You bet! Elaine, we're going to lift you and carry you. We're each taking a side. Don't do a thing. Someone, please pick up her stuff," Ben shouted to the group. "We've got to get around this small town."

Adam stumbled forward as he lifted Elaine onto his arms and chest. "Where are we?"

"We're at Spring Valley. It won't be long for us to stay on its periphery until we get to the mountain range. The elevation is even higher there. How are you doing on your end?" Ben asked.

"No problem right now! I'm concerned about carrying Elaine in the dark. We can't have any light while going around the town," Adam emphatically affirmed.

"No worries, Adam. The town has lights enough for us to see. At least, we're not in total darkness until we get to the mountain range. How are you doing, Elaine?"

"Better...I can breathe better without the exertion."

"Great!" Ben and Adam said together.

"Although there's darkness day and night now, don't kid yourself that others won't be getting up soon in this town. It's almost morning," Ben said and re-shifted his portion of Elaine's weight to help him assist Adam in carrying her.

"Ben, I hardly think that makes a difference. Do you think it does? Day and night are the same now. Body clocks are out of sync."

"I never even gave it a thought! You're right. We need to look out for any persons up and about at any time. We're nearing the end of the town. It's completely dark up ahead. Must be the beginning of the mountain range," Ben spoke up to the others.

"I certainly hope so. I'm exhausted. You and I can't carry Elaine much longer after a full day. I think we've made excellent progress, don't you?" Adam asked.

"Yes, but we're not there yet."

As they rounded the final edge of Spring Valley, Evelyn showed signs of slowing down.

"I need to rest! I can't continue like this," Evelyn told her husband, winded and gasping for breath.

Ben heard what she said and looked back at her. As much as

he could see in the darkness, she did look exhausted as she collapsed against John, who lowered her to the ground.

Katie ran back to where Evelyn was and took her pulse. "Her pulse is racing, and she looks flushed," Katie said as she shone a small flashlight on Evelyn's face. "I've no way to determine Evelyn's blood pressure, but I can only imagine that it's high."

"Okay," Adam whispered loudly as Katie quickly turned off the flashlight. "We'll have to find cover nearby and rest. We'll not be able to put up a campsite or spread out any sleeping bags because we must be ready to go at a moment's opportunity. Thankfully, there's still darkness during the daytime, which can hide us while we're so close to this small town."

"Okay, everyone, sit or lie on the ground quietly and continue keeping your flashlights off," Ben said as he and Adam gently placed Elaine down. "I think we're only about a mile away from the foot of the mountain range. We're close now; so hopefully, we shouldn't see any human activity around here."

"I'm beginning to catch my breath and I feel better already," Evelyn said just loud enough for Ben to hear.

Adam, who sat near Ben, leaned in toward Elaine. "How are you feeling?"

"I feel better, but the thought of going further for more hours is intimidating," Elaine responded. "I don't know if I have the physical stamina to walk several miles in a day. I'm glad you and Ben carried me for a bit."

Ben nodded, though he knew Elaine couldn't see it. *Wow! How scary that Elaine and Evelyn are showing signs of fatigue and illness. Please help, Lord!*

Ben got up and moved toward Evelyn and John. "Evelyn, my concern is for your high blood pressure, age, and weight. Would this steep mountain range be tough for you? What do you think?"

"I think that a steep uphill climb is daunting for me, but I'll try it. If we're on level ground and I have an opportunity to rest often, I would last longer, especially since my meds have finished up a long time ago, and we're not receiving proper nutrition or hydration."

Adam got up and went over to Ben, Evelyn, and John. "We understand. We just don't know what to do. We would never leave you and John behind, because capture is certain unless we can get away fast enough. Do you think you could try to walk enough of the way into the mountain range and onto the edge of the next forest?"

"I'll assist her, and we'll walk as far as we can," John replied. "If Evelyn and I ever become a hindrance to the group, I speak for her and me that we'd want you to leave us behind. We know that God is with us and we're not afraid to die. We understand death may come for all of us at some point during this horrible time."

"Okay," Ben said. "Understood. But for now, we'll rest. Soon, we'll need to press on. We're still too close to the town."

After a few moments of rest, Evelyn stood up with John's assistance while the rest of the group also stood, including Elaine, who could now walk and breathe comfortably on her own. They slowly moved around the remainder of the town and into the foothills of the mountains. Unfortunately, due to Evelyn's inability to walk swiftly, everyone else was moving at a much more relaxed pace.

Suddenly, Evelyn cried out in pain. "Ouch! Ugh! I've twisted my ankle for sure!"

Ben quickly pivoted around to look at what happened. She had just stepped off a large rock and her ankle twisted to one side. She was breathless and hyperventilating. The group gathered around John and her.

Ben flashed a red-bulb flashlight downward. "Her ankle is swelling quickly," he said.

"I can't go on like this anymore!" Evelyn cried. "I just give up. This is no feat for me to accomplish."

"Please don't say that," John replied. "We can do all things through Christ Who strengthens us."

"You're being unreasonable!" Evelyn grimaced. "I can't go further with a twisted ankle, and the pain is excruciating."

Adam, Katie, and Ruth knelt to examine the ankle with a flashlight. The ankle was swollen to the size of a baseball.

"She could use a cold pack," Liz said. "I have something like that somewhere in my equipment." She stuck her hand into her backpack and drew it out. "Here, Ruth, take this and place it on Evelyn's ankle."

After Ruth applied the cold pack, the group waited.

"It's giving me some relief from the pain," Evelyn commented, "but it's still very swollen and my guess is that the swelling won't go down soon enough for me to walk again real soon."

Ben, Adam, and Ruth gazed at each other by the glow of the faint flashlight. Adam spoke to the group. "It looks like we'll have to stay here. We cannot move forward in the condition that Evelyn is in. Besides, she has other issues, like her high blood pressure. We'll have to stay. We're not into the full mountain range yet."

"No," John announced loudly. "You all cannot stay here with us. It would be a tragedy to do so. Evelyn and I can fend for ourselves walking at our own pace. If we're captured, we're captured. Although we would've still escaped on our own, we were so blessed to have a group like all of you to join with us for all this time. Please go on, and we'll follow along as we can until we can find you and meet up with you in the mountain range. I'm sure you'll be staying somewhere in the mountains hiding for a few days. Evelyn will need to heal more before we can tackle the steeper terrain, if we can."

"True. She will need to heal before moving forward," Katie agreed. "That could take several days."

"I think hanging together is best!" Ruth said. "We can't...we shouldn't...leave both of you."

John insisted. "Evelyn and I are weary of running like rats ready to drown in rising water. The Bible declares saints will come out of this Great Tribulation. Some will survive, but we know that many will not. God knows the best for each of us."

Ben conferred with Adam, Katie, and Ruth in a hushed voice. Adam became perturbed and shook his head. Finally, he made what sounded like a sigh of resignation.

Noah walked up and joined in with them. "What's going on? What are you all thinking?"

"I am weighing the risk of two people against the whole group," Ben responded. "If we go the pace that Evelyn and John now require, capture is certain for all of us. In fact, right now, Evelyn won't be able to travel on foot at all for several days. I know that she and John recognize their vulnerability and limitations, and I believe from the very beginning they knew that their age and health issues might eventually present a handicap not only for them, but for the whole group. John is being very reasonable about it."

"Does that mean we'll leave them?" Noah asked.

"I don't want to make that decision; but unfortunately, I believe seven people may live a little longer if we do," Ben sighed.

"I am thoroughly against it," Ruth said, "but Ben has reminded us that John has urged us to leave. I think he knows his wife just might die trying to make it up and through a mountain range with her lack of stamina, plus her anxiety and high blood pressure."

"I know God can cover us, and we can pull through without leaving them," Noah said.

"No, Noah, we're still somewhat close to where they know we last were," Ben insisted. "We don't have enough distance between us and them. We should be further away."

Noah's frown was evident in his voice. "I really am conflicted about this. On their own, they surely won't survive."

"We'll leave them with more of the remaining water," Ben responded. "That should keep them somewhat hydrated while Evelyn is recuperating. They'll just need to depend on the forest for food and further hydration as we are going to have to do. Evelyn needs to stay in one place for now. Two persons will be a smaller target."

With this comment from Ben, the discussion between the four ended with their resolve for the courage to part from Evelyn and John. They stood up and came to where Evelyn and John were seated on the ground.

Ben addressed John. "This is not an easy decision for any of us to make, much less follow, but I know you already understand that Evelyn will not be able to travel by foot for several days. I know you also realize that we've not traveled far enough away from our last known location enough to not be discovered or picked up. You've suggested that we go on ahead. Considering our plight, that's a sound solution for the other seven of our group members who are also at high risk of being captured. By dividing up, we do think that we both have a better chance to make it. Do you still feel okay with that, John?"

"I told you before that you should move on before the authorities catch up to us. I feel that having just myself and Evelyn to think about is easier than for me to have to think about all nine of us trying to dodge capture," John replied.

"Okay," Adam said. "We'll leave you with some extra water and a few items of food from our natural environment we'd already saved up. We'll keep you in prayer and look for you to join us later just inside the mountain range. We'll try to wait there a few days to see if you appear. God protect you both as we part one from the other. Here is one of our compasses. We are headed directly northwest. There are no deviations from keeping straight in that direction. You should come upon us that way."

Adam then turned to the entire group. "Come around John and Evelyn. Let's lay our hands on them both as we pray for them now as they stay behind."

The group gathered around John and Evelyn. Ben led the group in prayer, his concern heard in the hesitation of his voice. "Dear Lord...we commit John and Evelyn into Your hands. You alone know the end from the beginning for all of us. Please watch over them as they are absent from us. Keep them safe and bring them to us as soon as possible. We trust You with our lives. We know that we'll ultimately reign with You in Your kingdom with all the saints of all the ages and with the holy angels. Holy Spirit, bring swift healing to Evelyn's body and give her and John Your supernatural strength. We ask, Lord, You seal them by Jesus's shed blood and Your precious Holy Spirit until we meet again. In Messiah Jesus's name, Amen!"

When the prayer was over, each member of the group hugged and kissed Evelyn and John. Most of them wept as they said their goodbyes and geared up for travel.

The group of seven now made their move away into the darkness, with Evelyn's voice heard trailing off behind them.

"This is my fault," she sobbed. "If I hadn't had health problems..."

Ben's heart wrenched as her sobs faded away into the distance.

Chapter 22
A Victorious Celebration

Helicopters from the one-world government of the Antichrist circled where Elira directed them. By her and Duncan's calculations in the hunt of remaining Christians and Jews who had not received their chips from the New World Order, they believed that they would be closing in on Ben, Ruth, and the others who had escaped. The helicopters were equipped with night-vision ability. In a short time, they were over the place where two people had hunkered down.

Two helicopters circled. From her control room, Elira directed the pilot of one of the helicopters to shine the huge floodlight onto the ground, followed by a special camera and mic she'd made sure for each pilot to have aboard. The pilots made out the forms of the two persons below, and she relished in their discovery. She wanted to hear the voices of the two persons the pilots had found.

A woman's voice choked and stammered. "L...l...loo...look! They have...fou...found...us, John!" She began to sob and shake violently. "I know this means...," and with another huge shaking of her body in waves, she hysterically uttered, "CER-TAIN...DEATH!"

John wrapped himself over her in a huge body hug as if trying to shield her. "Don't say that. We are...in...in God's hand...especially NOW!"

Elira scoffed. "They're in MY hands now. Lower your helos down."

The helicopter with the huge floodlight lowered to the ground. The pilot radioed Elira. "We got them! It's a couple!"

A wicked smile of satisfaction broke on Elira's face. "YESSSSSS!" she cried. "I heard. Brilliant, Captain Caldwell!"

The helicopter landed, and Elira could just make out, from the camera on the helo, several government agents tumbling out and surrounding the frightened couple.

"Put your hands up and behind your heads! No movement whatsoever or you'll be killed!" Caldwell stated.

The couple complied, though the woman looked very pale and continued shaking uncontrollably.

"Please, Officer," pleaded the man. "My wife is beginning to wane under this intense pressure. She is under too much anxiety and has been known to have very high blood pressure."

Caldwell gave out a derisive laugh. "That's incredibly ridiculous and stupid of you to say. You are headed for death anyway. What does your wife's anxiety and blood pressure have to do with your impudence to the New World Order and Master Ibrahim? Your blatant insolence has gotten you where you are now."

Elira's voice broke in on the radio to the capturers, "Do you have them in custody?"

"Yes, ma'am, we do!" Caldwell declared.

"What are their names?" Elira asked.

"What are your names?!" shouted the pilot over the roar of the helicopter blades.

"John and Evelyn!" hollered John.

"Did you hear that?" Caldwell asked Elira.

"No, I cannot hear voices in the background. I need for you to repeat their names for me into the mic!" Elira retorted with annoyance.

"John and Evelyn!" projected the pilot.

Elira became irate. "John and Evelyn? Who are they and where are they from?"

Another law enforcement officer, Sergeant Sean McCoy, yelled above the sound of the chopper. "Where are you both from?"

"Salisburg, near Chillicothe Falls," John answered back.

"They are from Salisburg, near Chillicothe Falls!" shouted McCoy to Elira, who listened intently.

"Chillicothe Falls?" Elira gasped. "What church congregation?"

"Redemption Community Church," John replied.

The sergeant repeated the name of the church for Elira, and then she asked, "Do you know anyone from the Messianic congregation in Chillicothe Falls?"

"Our church is not Messianic, and therefore we never interacted with the Messianic temple," John responded.

McCoy repeated John's reply to Elira.

After a long pause, Elira retorted with stiff sarcasm. "It seems odd that the churches of the area would not interact with one another at some point after The Disappearance, but I will have to accept that from you, John...for now. Place him and his wife under arrest!" she commanded.

Captain Caldwell brought handcuffs toward them. Evelyn screamed and broke down further into deeper guttural sobs. John just stared blankly at the officer and then mechanically put his arm around his wife. His hand was pried off Evelyn by one of the other officers, and both his arms were stiffly pulled behind his back. Caldwell placed the handcuffs on John and then turned toward Evelyn. She became uncontrollable.

"NOOOOO!" she screamed.

Caldwell looked at her incredulously and continued to do his job. He grabbed her arms that were now flailing in the air and forced them behind her back. She began to hyperventilate. She shook like a leaf and became flushed and sweaty. John thrust himself forward to protect her but was stopped by McCoy.

"Not so fast there, sport!" McCoy forcibly pulled John away from Evelyn.

Caldwell then grasped both of Evelyn's arms, roughly bent them behind her back, and handcuffed her. She fell to the ground unconscious. Several officers merely picked her up and placed her in the helicopter, and John followed. Soon the helicopters rose upward.

Evelyn continued to be unresponsive. One of the officers aboard, Ed Lewis, who was medically trained, had a look at her condition.

"She's had a hypertensive crisis. I believe she has suffered a stroke. She'll need emergency medical attention. I have no way aboard this chopper to measure her blood pressure," Lewis stated flatly.

Elira could have stopped watching the chopper's internal cameras at any point. But she couldn't! What was it about this couple that fascinated her? She had never seen them before.

The helicopters landed in Chillicothe Falls, and both John and Evelyn were taken out. An ambulance was waiting for Evelyn. She was lifted onto a stretcher for paramedics to check her vital signs. Her breathing and pulse were shallow, Caldwell reported to Elira. Meanwhile, John was booked into jail awaiting arraignment by a judge.

∼

AT RUTH'S REQUEST, Ben ran to his backpack to get out the radio and turned it on. As they gathered some nuts and berries they had found in the forest, the group listened to the news. The newscaster announced that a couple of fugitives had been captured in the vicinity of Spring Valley. One of them was in critical condition in the local hospital with life-threatening conditions, and the other was in jail awaiting arraignment. The newscaster then announced their names. Ben froze, and the others also stopped suddenly to gaze back at him in shock.

"Oh noooo!" Ruth lamented. "John and Evelyn are captured! That means certain death for them now. How I feel so badly about leaving them."

"Evelyn has extremely mitigating health issues," Liz responded. "She's in the hospital in critical care. She knew, and we all knew, that she might not be able to make this journey. It has proven true. She and John tried their best, but we can see that she wasn't up to making it, and we were all targets of capture because of her health."

"Yes," Ben answered, "unfortunately, we did the right thing for the group, but we knew they might be captured because they could not move from their hiding place quickly enough."

"We'll need to pray for them both!" Elaine emphasized.

"Let's pray now!" Adam added.

"They're in God's hands for sure now," Noah said. "If we never see them again, we'll be reunited with them someday."

Katie broke into a prayer for the couple and especially for Evelyn. The others took turns praying for them too, and, when they felt the peace of God's Spirit over them, they ended their prayer and began to sing in praise to God.

JOHN FELT SO ALONE without Evelyn and so afraid for her safety.

Questions were swirling in his mind. How is my wife doing? Is she still alive? I will be facing a judge soon, and what will happen to my wife? Oh, dear God, I pray I get some word of her condition soon! The silence is maddening! If she dies while under medical supervision, I see it as a blessing from You, Lord. This might be Your perfect will for her to bypass jail to be brought before a judge to eventually be executed. You know it would be more than what Evelyn could handle. John dropped his head into the palms of his hands and wept.

It was several days later when a prison guard came to John's jail cell and unlocked the door. Another guard came into the cell with him.

"Get up!" the first prison guard ordered. "Your day of arraignment has come, you scum!" John started to get up when he was grabbed violently from the pallet on which he sat by the other guard.

John's eyes widened and his face flushed with angry frustration. "What are you doing? I was getting up."

The prison guard who grabbed him, now slapped him in the face. "Mind your manners! You're an enemy of the state and the criminal here! You'll take orders from us, not the other way around!" He then forced John's hands behind his back and handcuffed him.

The two guards shoved John outside his cell down a long corridor. John thought of Evelyn and prayed for her. What's happened to her? Could he know today...maybe even see her? Would that be possible?

At the end of the corridor was an exit door that led to another longer corridor that appeared to have floors that had been newly polished reflecting the lights that came through the large windows along each side. The guards walked quickly and brusquely. John saw tall, polished wooden double doors ahead. Undoubtedly, this must be the judge's chamber or courtroom.

Once they arrived at the doors, one guard pushed them open for all three of them to enter. A very ornate, small courtroom came into view. The guards released their prisoner to the bailiff, who was waiting next to the judge's bench. The bailiff escorted John to a chair before the judge's bench. No one else was present, but John felt that soon the courtroom might hold local authorities and witnesses to testify against him.

John faintly heard voices coming from another direction outside the small courtroom. All at once, he saw doors fling open on the opposite end from where he'd entered, and in walked several people. Their faces seem grotesquely distorted with fury, loathing, and evil as they cast their eyes on him. He shuddered to look at them and instantly turned to prayer within his heart to God. Shortly after each person had settled into place, the judge came walking into the courtroom as the bailiff proclaimed, "All rise for the Honorable Judith Schlesinger!"

John stood up and looked directly at the judge. She was glaring at him with disdain. He knew that she was part of the New World Order, and that justice would more than likely not be upheld. After the judge sat down, each person except the bailiff sat down in their chairs.

"Mr. John Bennett, please stand!" Judge Schlesinger ordered. "The list of charges against you are as follows: One, treason to the New World Order by noncompliance to its laws; two, evading justice; and three, aiding and abetting other fugitives in treason and the evasion of justice. Are these correct, or do you need verifiable witnesses and testimony against you? What do you say to these charges?"

"These charges are correct, Your Honor," John announced. "You don't need to bring further witnesses or testimony."

The judge scowled at him and then let out a pernicious

laugh. "At least you have the presence of mind to understand that you're a criminal and breaking the law! How then do you plead: guilty, not guilty, or no contest?"

"Guilty, Your Honor, as charged regarding treason and evading justice. I plead no contest to aiding and abetting other fugitives of the law."

"How interesting!" Judge Schlesinger exclaimed. "You refuse to plead guilty for aiding and abetting. Yet law enforcement has discovered that you had been with a group of seven other fugitives from your church who are still at large and have not been apprehended."

"Yes, but I did not aid or abet them. Instead, they took me and my wife into their group."

"Oh, is that it?" declared the judge snickering. "And where is your wife now?"

"Frankly, your Honor, I have no idea. She suffered a stroke when we were captured and she was taken to the hospital. I don't know if she's still in there and has survived it."

"Bailiff, get the hospital on the phone," commanded the judge. "I want to speak with the doctors that are attending John Bennett's wife...What is her name?" She directed the question to John.

"Her name is Evelyn Bennett."

John and the judge waited for the call to be put through, and it wasn't long before the courtroom phone buzzed. The judge requested the hospital for information on Evelyn Bennett and asked that her attending doctor be put on the phone immediately. There was a pause while Judge Schlesinger placed the phone on speaker so John could hear the conversation clearly.

"She's deceased," her doctor reported to the judge when he came to the phone. "She died this morning at 9:09 a.m. We have disposed the body in accordance with the laws of the New World Order for all those who refused the mark."

"What happened?" John asked.

Judge Schlesinger let out a laugh, and snapped back, "And why would you care to know?"

The doctor replied, "When she came into the Chillicothe Falls hospital, her blood pressure could not sustain a healthy level and we ordered tests on her brain. It appeared to us she had suffered a blood clot to her brain due to a stroke. Her brain activity was seriously affected. They put her on a ventilator to keep her alive; but, her body eventually shut down anyway."

Judge Schlesinger thanked the doctor and ended the call.

"Your wife is dead!" the judge shouted gleefully. "She met her just reward for her treason and attempted escape from justice."

John hung his head. Tears flowed down his cheeks. *Evelyn is with Jesus now. I don't need to be concerned about her any longer, although I ache for her passing. I love You, Lord Jesus, for taking Evelyn this way, and I love you, Evelyn! I know I'll see you soon!*

"You're not crying, are you?" Judge Schlesinger asked sarcastically. Several people in the courtroom laughed. "What do you think would've happened to her and you in your rebellious actions against the government of the world?" Judge Schlesinger asked. "Wouldn't you think that you would eventually be apprehended and that both of your deaths were certain? Fool!"

John continued to weep.

Judge Schlesinger ordered John, "Please stand. With the power and authority vested in me from the New World Order, I sentence you to death by beheading for your crimes of treason against the Order and your treason to our eminent Master Ibrahim Mizrah!" She banged the gavel on her desk.

The bailiff shouted, "All rise," and Judge Schlesinger left the courtroom without so much as a glance back at John. The rest of the would-be witnesses also quickly exited. John was left with the bailiff, who escorted him back to his cell to await his execution.

It all happened so swiftly! It'll be a short time now before I will be with the Lord and reunited with Evelyn. John knelt next to the cot in his cell. Time to pray and sing hymns of praise. Soon, he fell fast asleep.

While he slept, he dreamed of Evelyn and her passing. He saw Evelyn at the hospital feebly lifting her head from her pillow. "It's so blinding bright in here. What's happening?" she quietly asked in his dream. "I feel my spirit lifting out of my body toward the outstretched arms of Jesus! He's reaching His hand out to me. I'm going to take His hand into mine." When she took His hand, the two of them vanished out of the room into the light; and, as she glanced back at her lifeless body on the bed, the heart monitor showed a flat line.

John stirred awake from his dream. *Thank you, Lord, for revealing Evelyn's beautiful and peaceful passing to me,* John mused, and soon fell back to sleep again.

About a week later, John's execution day came early in the morning. The prison warden woke John up and led him for the first time outside of the prison into the open-air courtyard where a group of people were gathered for executions. As his eyes scanned the crowd of witnesses, he noticed some of the same ones who had been in his courtroom. Most notable were two he had especially noted on the day he stood before the judge. One was a young woman in her thirties who sat with another brash and defiant man in his fifties. Both seemed to hold particular importance in the capture and execution of Christians and Jews. They had stood out to John then in the courtroom and again today. They began speaking with others in the crowd. Suddenly, John recalled their voices. They were the same two he'd heard on the radio whom Ben claimed were specifically hunting for him and Ruth. He also remembered hearing the voice of the woman over the mic when the helicopter landed to apprehend him and Evelyn. *These must be the diabolical duo Ben had spoken of! Wow! They succeeded in capturing Evelyn and me!*

The executioner was dressed in black with a black hood. Only his eyes could be seen, which revealed pure devilish delight for those he stood ready to behead. John prayed quietly in his heart.

Two others were in line before him to be executed. One was a beautiful young woman. Tears streamed down her face as she raised her hands in worship to the Lord. The executioner forced her hands and body to her knees, bent her head forward, and quickly whacked it off with his ax.

John turned his face away in horror and disgust at the gory sight. It was so sick and depraved, and how like the Devil.

The next person, an elderly, frail woman, was pushed forward. She stumbled and fell but managed to utter, "I love you, Lord Jesus!" The executioner erupted in fury, grabbed her feeble body, and slammed her to her knees as she had her head bowed. Then with one swift stroke of his ax, her head fell from her body and her body fell forward. Although being aghast at the inhuman sight, John knew that she was now with the Lord Jesus.

Finally, John's turn came. He walked the few feet to the executioner and whispered one last prayer to the Lord. He knelt with the joy and peace of Jesus as he smiled toward the witnesses of his execution. The executioner taunted him and spoke with an eerily guttural voice.

"You realize what a fool you are to die for a dead carpenter who lived centuries ago when you could've been part of our New World Order. Fools like you deserve to die rather than to live and enjoy the great future ahead for all of us!"

"You obviously don't know Who you call a dead carpenter. If

you did, you would truly have a great future!" John replied. "But now, that you've received the mark of Antichrist Mizrah, you'll never know Jesus!"

The executioner's eyes lit up with the pure fire of destructive hatred. He pushed John's head forward and down, swung his ax fiercely and swiftly, and off came John's head.

What the executioner and the others could not see or know is that in those few seconds, John saw the Lord Jesus standing at the right hand of God to receive him. He also saw Evelyn with Jesus, and when his spirit left his body, he was joined with them both in victorious celebration.

Chapter 23
Wilderness Wandering

After climbing to the highest part of the steep mountain range, Ben, Ruth, and the group huddled together inside another cave farthest away from any city or town. Here they felt safe enough to hide for several weeks. They had settled in for the night, and Liz turned on the radio.

"Good evening!" spoke a newscaster. "Today we are hearing reports that the ancient Euphrates River has completely dried up. For several years now, rising temperatures and drought have affected this region where the Euphrates had supplied much-needed water. New World scientists believe that since the water had already turned to the color and consistency of blood as other streams, lakes, and rivers have, it's not deemed a great loss at this time."

Ben got up on his feet to turn the radio down. "Hey, guys, this is what the Bible also predicted in Revelation! It was fore-told by the apostle John that this great river would dry up in preparation for those nations who would bring warriors to the Battle of Armageddon, the final war against God and His Christ before the Millennium, when Christ would rule and reign on earth for one thousand years." Ben turned the radio volume back up and sat down again on the cave's floor.

The newscaster went on. "Today's count of executions of rebel Christians and Jews who fled our Order within the last three years has now totaled 250,000 from over fifty different countries. Many of those captured are still awaiting trial and execution in prisons and jails. Now, to local and regional news this hour…"

This time Adam got up to turn the radio off, frustration covering his face. "Listening to a report of executions is depressing for us. Of course, it makes the New World Order seem like a hero to everyone else. How ironic!"

Ben shot up and turned the radio back on. "Brother, they were about to play the local and regional news from our area. Let's listen to what the authorities might be up to there."

"…yes, and there are only four rebel deaths to report in Chillicothe Falls today: Marian Davis, age 80, Alexa Zimbalist, age 26, and John Bennett, age 56, all executed, and John's wife, Evelyn, age 53, who apparently expired at the hospital before she could be sentenced and executed." Shock and horror were painted on each face in the group. This time Ben jumped to his feet to shut the radio off.

"I knew it would end this way!" Katie said. "John knew that Evelyn couldn't keep up with us, and he was wise to insist on us going without them."

"Exactly right," Ben replied. "They fought valiantly with us evading the authorities for as long as they could. Sadly, they were limited by Evelyn's health issues and her untimely fall rendering her unable to walk any farther."

"They're now with Jesus!" Adam proclaimed, "They certainly were a great spiritual influence to me, and I bet to all of us in the way they handled themselves and their circumstances."

"Yes," Ruth piped in. "I often looked at Evelyn as a role model. She was older than any of us and with physical limitations, too, but she always made the best of it and pushed forward for as long as she could."

"I remember how inspiring John was to me," Katie added, "when he knew that Evelyn had twisted her ankle and could not go any farther. He accepted what had happened to them but insisted on our safety. What a hero! What selfless love, just like Jesus's!"

"I just think it's awful they were captured!" Elaine said bursting into tears.

"Now, there," Ruth said comforting Elaine. "We know that they're okay because the Lord Himself gives us the peace and strength to 'walk through the valley of the shadow of death' as it says in Psalms 23."

"We all fear capture!" Liz responded. "That's a normal human reaction, but our Lord operates in the superhuman by His Holy Spirit in us."

"I do know that with all my heart. It's just still hard for me to accept it," Elaine replied.

Ben suggested they all pray together. The group bowed their heads in prayer. "Dear Lord, we thank you for the lives of John and Evelyn and for the fact that they are now with You. How magnificent it must be! Continue to be with us in our journey down here until You come again, or You take us to be with You and John and Evelyn. Amen." Ben looked around at the others. "Would any of you want to add to this prayer with prayers of your own? If so, please go ahead."

Each group member voiced a prayer including Elaine, who prayed, "Father, help me and us to keep the faith until You come for us, or You come to establish Your world order at the end of this time. Please keep our bodies alive and supply us with the daily provisions of food and water like you did for the Old Testament Israelites in their forty years of wilderness wandering. You were faithful to them. You've not changed. You will be faithful to us now. In Jesus's name, Amen."

Adam closed all the prayers with his: "Heavenly Father, You have heard all these prayers before we ask them. Please allow us the opportunity to rest in this place peacefully for several days or even weeks before we must move on with our journey. Have mercy on us during this time and encourage our hearts in You. Amen."

After the prayer, Ben, who was sitting next to Ruth, spoke directly to her. "I was so taken with the beauty of the companionship and love that John and Evelyn shared with each other. They not only had the love of the Lord in each of their lives, but His love for each other. Ruth, you and I have been together for a while now, fugitives from the Antichrist. I've come to realize that I spent so much of my time and life in a relationship with a woman who was not a believer because, at the time, I was also not a believer. But now I realize what a difference it makes to know genuine love because we're both believers, and I don't want to die without making you my wife. I would love to be joined with you in marriage. Our mothers would have loved to see that. We have so much in common, not only our faith in Messiah Jesus, but we are both of Jewish heritage. You've already been such a close friend and helpmeet. Would you marry me?"

Ruth's eyes opened wide with shock and surprise, and then only melted with love as tears filled her eyes.

"Yes, yes, yes!" she said.

The group erupted in heavy applause, whistled, and shouted, "YESSS!!! Yay!!!"

"Is there anyone in this group who could marry us?" Ben asked.

"I can!" Adam raised his hand.

"I can also!" Adam's brother, Noah, said. "We're both ordained by our father's church."

"Well..." Ben looked at Ruth. "What would keep us from being married here and now?"

"Nothing!" Ruth said. "And we shouldn't waste any time. Each day is precious."

Adam and Noah stood up to officiate the union while Ben held out his hand to Ruth so they could stand together.

Adam picked up his Bible and began the nuptials with the recounting of how God brought Eve to Adam and ordained the union of one man for one woman for life. He read from First Corinthians 13 on love. "Love is patient, love is kind. It does not envy, it does not boast, it is not proud. It does not dishonor others, it is not self-seeking, it is not easily angered, it keeps no record of wrongs. Love does not delight in evil but rejoices with the truth. Love always protects, always trusts, always hopes, always perseveres. Love never fails." Adam flipped some extra pages over in his Bible to First John and read, "God is love, and all who live in love, live in God, and God lives in them."

When Adam finished, Noah asked Ben and Ruth to turn and look at each other and to hold each other's hands as they spoke their marriage vows.

"Ben," Noah said, "repeat after me these words: "I take you Ruth as my wife. I promise to love you, protect you, support you, and care for you with God's help for as long as we live."

Then Noah led Ruth in the repetition of the same vow to Ben.

After Ben and Ruth had spoken their vows to one another, Adam led in a prayer over the couple. Then Noah pronounced them husband and wife according to the laws of God and the power vested in him by ordination to gospel ministry.

"You may now kiss your bride!" Adam announced.

Ben tenderly took Ruth in his arms and kissed her. It was the first time he had ever kissed her like a man kisses the woman he loves. They embraced for a moment while the group stood up and exuberantly applauded—this time for what seemed like several minutes.

"How great to have something to celebrate! We need to celebrate!" Elaine shouted hugging them both.

Adam smirked. "Yes, we will, but . . . not so much with our low provisions. We've almost nothing to eat as usual these days."

Ben smiled and let out a howl. "We may all be too thin, but...still...Ruth and I are married! We can celebrate without food!" Ben said. He swept Ruth up in his arms. "We'll dance to lively praise and worship music, as all of you clap and keep the rhythm going."

"That's a wonderful idea!" Ruth replied. "I would love to have this first dance with you as my husband."

Noah led them in fast-paced praise and worship songs, clapping his hands, as Ben and Ruth danced within a circle of the all the group members also clapping at once. *There is such laughter and joy,* Ben thought as he looked over the scene. *It seems as if life has become as it should be all over again, but for how long?* He winced thinking about it. When the song was over, Ben embraced Ruth and kissed her again. The celebration continued into the night.

Finally, when the celebration died down for the evening, Adam and Noah got up to speak. "Listen up, everyone!" Adam shouted out to all of them. "In the morning, we should scout around for any more fruit, berries, or other edible plants that could hydrate us. If we want to, we can also look for wildlife we could eat, but fish would be out of the question since they continue rotting on the surface of the blood-filled lakes and streams."

"Okay!" Liz responded. "I'm speaking for all but the newlyweds. We'll be glad to get up and do a search tomorrow for food."

"It's time we probably should 'hit the sack,'" Noah suggested, "and leave the newlyweds some space for themselves tonight."

Ben was grateful the others arranged their sleeping bags closer to the mouth of the cave so that Ben and Ruth could enjoy some privacy at the back of the cave.

Ben kissed Ruth tenderly. It was by no means a usual wedding or a wedding night they might have experienced in better times, but they nonetheless enjoyed them both. How Ben enjoyed the physical union and consummation of their marriage! They lay for a long time in each other's arms.

THE MORNING CAME QUICKLY as Noah roused up Adam. He did not want to disturb Ben. Both went outside the cave with flashlights to see what provisions they could find to bring back to the group. At this point, what they could find would mean the difference between life and death.

Adam and Noah walked the forest, and prayed for guidance to quickly find the native, wild foods that would help nourish them. Adam pointed at the ground, and they grabbed up hazelnuts and placed them in a pouch that Noah had slung around his torso. Next, they stumbled upon a huge patch of dried dandelion. They picked up as much as they could. They stumbled on pawpaw, a fruit which contained water for hydration and which was still not completely dried up or ruined due to the darkness and heat.

"Adam, we have a bow and arrows, a slingshot, and large pocketknives, why don't we try hunting any wildlife we can find for food?" Noah asked his brother.

"I don't think it would be a good idea. It's a project to hunt in thick darkness, to wrestle and kill the animal, skin it, and adequately dispose of its skin and bones so that we are not discovered if the authorities might be right behind us. The whole process would take a lot of time plus we don't have water to wash the pocketknives and the meat," Adam pointed out.

"Yeah. You're right! We don't need the work or trouble!"

When the two brothers had gathered what food they could from the surrounding forest, they headed back to the cave. By then, Ben and Ruth were up with the rest of the group, talking about how wonderful the companionship of marriage can be in a time like the Great Tribulation.

Noah glanced in Liz's direction. "I often thought of marrying Liz before this terrible time. I feel cheated of a union with her that we could've had before now, but I've just suspended any thoughts of marriage while being fugitives."

"You don't need to do that," Ben urged. "Just do what Ruth and I have done. Two people are better together in confronting this time." Everyone watched for a reaction from Noah or Liz.

"You're right, Ben, but I think Liz and I feel it's just too much to go through a new marriage with the pressure of evading capture. Isn't that right, Liz?"

"Yes, we talked about it after The Disappearance when we were both left behind. We're mindful of what Jesus said about this time in Matthew, chapter 24. We personally feel that major life activities should take a back seat to the pressures we face during this time."

"Yeah," Noah added, "we feel the opposite of you and Ruth, but each person has to be guided by their own conscience before God in the face of what we're enduring."

"I can understand that!" Ben answered.

The rest of the group continued listening as Noah

announced, "Hey everyone! Adam and I found some food in the forest to eat. Come and get what you'd like!"

Right away, hungry group members bounded up towards the stash to grab what they could eat. Soon they sat back down together for a breakfast of hazelnuts, pawpaw, and dried dandelion.

"Who would've known humankind would come back to the same days when primitive humans foraged the forest for their food?" Adam asked. "Uncanny how we've come full circle."

Once again, Liz turned on the radio for everyone to hear news of the outside world.

Thankfully, we always turn on the radio sparingly, and we have enough batteries between us as a group to last for a while, Noah mused.

"Today Master Ibrahim has made plans with all the armed forces of the New World Order to move into the Valley of Megiddo to fight the forces against him for one last time," the news anchor announced.

"They must be referring to the Battle of Armageddon, against God and His forces in the Valley of Megiddo," Noah interrupted.

"Just at this moment, we also have breaking news—an earthquake of the highest magnitude ever known to humankind has struck the New World's capital city," the news anchor continued.

"The capital city is what the Bible refers to as 'Babylon, the Great' in Revelation!" Noah interjected. "It carries the splendor and marvel of ancient Babylon for our era, but it also holds responsibility for the blood of all Christian and Jewish martyrs it has slaughtered from its beginning."

"The resplendent capital city has split into three parts due to this very destructive earthquake. Wait...wait a moment....oh my! Word is just in that an unknown number, but possibly several thousand people, have been killed and swallowed up into the earth! The authorities in the capital city are attempting to assess the accurate number of those killed or lost, but they are saying that the search, rescue, and recovery will take some time."

Noah's jaw dropped. "Incredible! I know the world will be in such an uproar now more than ever and hell bent to fight the Battle of Armageddon." He turned to glance at Adam and Ben's reactions. They were trying to listen.

"It has been reported that Master Ibrahim has now declared this earthquake an attempt to destroy him and his government. He has also stated that he will continue to mete out justice to anyone opposed to the New World Order, including God Himself, Who Master Ibrahim declares to be the most foolish religious myth and figurehead still believed by those opposed to our Order."

"I told you!" Noah exclaimed.

"Yeah, bro, you're right, and all of us have read about these events in Scripture, haven't we?" Adam asked the group. They all nodded in response.

"Let's continue listening!" Ben urged.

"Right now, we are connecting to a correspondent on the ground in our capital city. What are you seeing, Cedric?"

"Well, Dave, there is so much destruction and chaos here. People have been running to the huge cracks in the earth trying to rescue survivors from the rubble. It's an enormous mess! It may take weeks and months to uncover all of what lies beneath, but the human toll is believed to be unprecedented."

"Can you get us any comments from anyone around you?" the news anchor urged.

"Yes, absolutely! Let me approach this man near me that looks completely shell-shocked. Sir, can you give a comment as to what just happened and how you feel....Oh....oh....oh, noooo!"

"Cedric, what's happening? Cedric, can you hear me? Cedric....Cedric.....please...tell us what's happened!" A long pause of two to three minutes ensued, when finally, the news anchor spoke again. "Well, for our viewers and listeners, we've lost our connection to Cedric. We certainly hope that everything is okay with him. We'll be back after a short break."

The group stared at each other in wonder.

"Unbelievable hearing all that was predicted occurring in the moment!" Ruth exclaimed.

"Yeah! No kidding!" Elaine responded. "This is freaking me out all over again!"

"The Bible tells us in Matthew, chapter 24, the same chapter Liz referred to earlier, that if these days weren't shortened, no one would survive." Noah noted.

"Okay," the voice of the news anchor returned. "We have it on good authority that now hailstones the size of small boulders have additionally hit the capital city. These hailstones have also been reported in other parts of the world. We're still trying to find out what has happened to our news correspondent, Cedric. Sheer anger and frustration are apparent here in the survivors of these two disasters, and we hear that Master Ibrahim will make a comment to the world on all these happenings this evening. We understand he's now meeting in emergency session with his advisors and plans are already being discussed to step up an all-out search for any remaining Christian and Jewish believers to bring every last one of them to justice as he has promised. Extra forces would be deployed to take charge in the search."

Liz shut off the radio. *Enough is enough,* Noah thought, as Elaine began to cry again.

"Whenever we hear the radio, there's always bad news, and it always involves us as targets," Elaine said. "Why do we try so hard to survive?"

"Hey, Elaine, take a deep breath. All this is going to pass

soon, and we'll be living with the Lord for eternity. Yeah, it's hard to hear, but we're so honored to be the last saints inhabiting earth," Ben responded. "We share so much with the New Testament saints and martyrs."

"That's absurd. We're suffering emotionally, mentally, and physically. All we have now are memories of how life was. How stressful to live, eat, sleep, or interact with anyone outside of us!" Elaine said between sniffles. "How much I wish over and over again that I had known Jesus earlier!"

"We get it, Elaine! We're in the same boat. It's a done deal. We didn't do what we were supposed to, and we're here now! We're with you in it. We may not want to be where we are now, but if you can change your thinking about it, you may just see it as a blessing!" Adam said.

"We've said it before--because God knows how you feel, He'll see to what's best for you." Liz reminded Elaine.

Can't come soon enough for Elaine, Noah pondered.

Chapter 24
Evil's Culmination

Back at intelligence headquarters in Chillicothe Falls, Elira was focused more than ever on her work. *Can't lag here. Master Ibrahim is doubling down on these despicable rebels. Ugh! Where's Ben? Or…Ruth, for that matter? If I get her, I know he'll probably be close by—the coward! Ugh!* She slammed her fist on the computer stand, eyes flashing and nostrils flaring.

As always, Duncan showed up. Elira rolled her eyes. "Whatta you doing here?"

"What are you up to, my dearest?"

"Dumb question. You know."

"Hasn't worked, has it!"

"Stop taunting me, Duncan, I swear—you want to pick a fight? I don't have time."

"No, nothing of the kind, dear!" Duncan let out a pernicious laugh. According to news reports, the combined forces of Master Ibrahim have come together from around the world to converge in the Valley of Megiddo for the last great battle these rebels and any of their forces will ever see. You and I know Master Ibrahim will win this battle easily. His conquest over these rebels and their hair-brained religion will succeed, and he'll certainly solidify his grip over the entire world and end forever the foolishness of faith. He can rule unopposed because 'God' would soon become a sadly defeated opponent."

"Yep! You can't deny the Euphrates River drying up over the past several months makes easier passage for armies from the east. The hunt for Christians and Jews has heightened to a frenzy. Master Ibrahim wants every one of them captured. Ben and Ruth still allude me. Damn them! I need to find them before the military forces not being used for the great battle will search and capture any remaining Jewish or Christian believers. What an embarrassment for me if that happens! So, get out of my face! I need concentration!"

Duncan let out another devious laugh and slithered his way out of Elira's office.

BY NOW BEN, Ruth, and the others had taken refuge higher into another adjacent mountain range to escape capture.

"I think we can perhaps stay here for months now." Ben told the group, "If we make camp at the steepest mountaintop, I'm thinking the enemy forces will not venture up here anytime soon. They would have to make an extended effort to reach us. We just must push on. How do you feel about it, Adam?"

"I agree we will be out of their reach for a while. Let's try it, but my concern is that the steep mountaintops in this range might be bare of vegetation for food. It already looks as though the terrain is dry and rocky. Plus, there should be thinner air up there and it will be harder to breathe."

"Okay, gotcha! How do the rest of you feel about it?" Ben asked.

"Thinner air concerns me!" Elaine replied.

"Lack of vegetation and food? A biggie!" Katie also replied.

"What I like about it," Ruth said, "is that we can possibly stay long term. That will help us physically and emotionally to not have to be running every few days!"

The group then erupted all at once debating different opinions when Adam finally stood up and said, "The easiest thing to do here is to take a vote! How many are in favor of the idea?"

Adam counted the hands. "It looks like four persons are in favor of it. That's the majority; so, we'll go with that. We need to prepare by finding some food to carry with us as we head up."

The group trekked slowly on foraging for all the food they could find to carry along with them up to the mountaintop. It was tiring work and sometimes Ben thought it might just be easier to give up going further. Each of us looks tired, older, and weaker. *Please give us strength and courage, Lord, to carry on!*

As the group finally ascended the steepest mountain peak, Elaine was displaying the same anxiety and difficulty breathing she had previously. She felt sick and dizzy as the climb to the top became difficult for her.

"Hey…hey…hey, everyone. I can't breathe. I need to stop," Elaine yelled as she dropped to the ground and turned over on her back."

Katie ran to her side and placed her hand on Elaine's heart. She then placed her hand on Elaine's wrist.

"Her heart is racing. I see she's hyperventilating. I will try to have her breathe long, deep breaths into a paper bag I carry."

"Okay, everyone! Let's take a minute and rest while we give Elaine time to rest!" Ben shouted out.

"I…I….I…am….afraid…the….authorities…are…very…close!" Elaine breathily whispered to Katie. "I don't have time to rest!"

"You are fine, Katie replied. "You just need to breathe normally again. You're panicking!"

"Hey, you know I also experienced windedness and dizziness by climbing higher and higher and once lost my footing, Ruth commented. "By God's grace, I did not break any bones. The large tear from my thigh up to my hip has continued to bleed a bit even though it is bandaged, and I'm badly bruised, but I'm fine. You'll be fine, too. Just take it easy for now."

Ben thought about how much these incidents with Elaine have delayed the journey. *How much longer can we keep ahead of the authorities longing to capture us?*

Soon, Ben heard voices in the distance. So did the others. They looked at one another in awe. Ben jerked. Had our worst nightmare really come to pass? Were the antichristian forces at our doorstep?

Elaine convulsed. Her pupils dilated. She was having a hard time breathing. "I'm a believer, but I dread being captured," she softly whispered to Katie who was still attending her.

Ben led the way as they climbed even higher. *The antichristian forces would have to climb higher. Not an easy job for them or us.* He smiled as he thought. *There's one difference. We've got God on our side!*

Adam and Katie helped Elaine to her feet, but she began to flounder, although they each took one of her arms in theirs to hold her up. They hoped to walk along with her and to drag her feet along the ground to guide her to safety where the rest of the group was heading.

"I can't keep up!" she confirmed to Katie and Adam. They held onto her tightly; but soon, she could no longer continue, and it caused Katie and Adam to terribly fall behind, too. Ben looked back at Elaine, Adam, and Katie slowly stumbling up the mountain together.

"I'm coming to help you!" Ben said.

"That would be terrific." Adam said. "Katie, why don't we sit her down on this rock embankment just a moment while Ben runs back to us?"

"Sure thing." Katie said as they helped Elaine sit. "Are you okay here?"

"Yes!" Elaine responded as she slightly leaned back when, suddenly and without notice, she lost her balance and fell backwards over the embankment. Everyone in the group gasped and some screamed in horror as they saw her tumble backward over a cliff.

Ben froze. Katie covered her face with her hands, and Adam cried out, "NOOOOO!" Ben ran back to look over the cliff, shining his flashlight down to see. Others came up, if they dared to, and gazed over the embankment to find her body dashed against the rocks. She was lifeless. Katie lifted her hands from her face and began to sob in horror. Ruth and Liz turned their heads away. Ben and the other two men simply looked wide-eyed with complete shock and deep sorrow.

"We've lost Elaine!" Ben teared up and wiped the perspiration from his brow.

Adam brushed tears away and said, "I didn't want her to die —No! Not this way. But I'm relieved God kept her from her worst fear: Being captured! If there's a blessing here, that's it."

WHAT THE BAND of fugitives did not know at the time was that a celebration was occurring in Heaven--the union or wedding of Christ with His Church. How dazzling in splendor and perfect was the Lord's Bride, the Church! John and Evelyn, Ben's dad Simon, and Elaine were there plus Ben's and Ruth's mothers, Adam's and Noah's mother and father, and many more too numerous to count--all the believers of all the ages from earth. What a time of celebration and feasting at the marriage supper of the Lamb, Jesus Christ! The Church and its Lord were now united forever!

The Bride of Christ was dressed in the brightest, purest white linen and adorned in such beauty with a diamond and jewel-encrusted tiara on her head. Her Husband, Christ, also in a dazzling pure single white garment to his feet, gazed on her with pure love. His hands that took hers in His still had the marks of the nail piercings He received at the cross to pay for her freedom and redemption from sin. His sandaled feet also bore the nail prints from His great sacrifice at the cross. Their union was a time where all the host of Heaven celebrated with boisterous applause and enthusiastic shouts of praise to God. The celestial music playing throughout the wedding and supper was utterly unimaginable to the human ear, and the feast at the table of God, the Father, like nothing ever experienced on earth. Indeed, the spectacle captured the verse of Scripture in I Corinthians 2:9 that says, "no eye has seen, no ear heard, and no mind has imagined what God has prepared for those who love Him. "

On Earth, however, all the antichristian forces were gathered at the Valley of Megiddo for the great battle. They looked with disgust and contempt over the battlefield. They were ready.

Suddenly, Messiah Jesus appeared in the skies shining in dazzling, blinding, bright-white light riding a brilliant white horse. The look of absolute rage was on His face. Heavenly warriors dressed in shining white and also riding bright white horses followed closely behind Him.

It was obvious the antichristian forces were in for a heavy, desperate battle. A name appeared across the thigh of the Lord Jesus reading "Faithful and True," and His head held many crowns. His bright white robe, dipped in blood, revealed His title: "King of Kings and Lord of Lords." The battle was set, and suddenly an angel appeared in the skies, crying out to all the scavenger birds of the air, saying, "Come! Gather for the great supper of God to eat the flesh of kings, generals, and the mighty, of horses and their riders, and the flesh of all people, free and slave, great and small."

This Great War lasted for several days, during which executions of believers had come to a halt. Mizrah was fretting over the outcome of the battle. His forces were being sorely defeated; and to his utter shame and embarrassment before the world, he and his False Prophet were finally captured by the forces of God. The Lord Jesus Christ Himself threw Mizrah and his False Prophet, Baganov, into the lake of fire, or hell, where hell's fire is not a literal one, but a spiritual one, which never dies out. This is spiritual separation from God and His love forever.

DURING THIS GREAT WAR, Ben and his group of fugitives reached the highest pinnacle of the steep mountain range they had been climbing and succeeded in evading the antichristian forces attempting to capture them. They set up camp and hunkered down for the long haul. Although they had done their best to conserve their radio batteries throughout their escape, their radios no longer worked. Only in their spirits could they hear the roar of dense celestial attack upon the earth and realized that major events must be occurring.

As the authorities continued to advance toward the fugitives, they were beginning to close in on the small group. However, there was concern on the captain's part about the reports that had surfaced about Mizrah and the defeat of the New World Order forces. If the rebel forces under Messiah Jesus had truly won the Battle of Armageddon, then the end had come for them and the New World Order.

"I don't know about continuing to pursue these fugitives," Captain Ragusa said to his New World troops. "I hear rumors that our New World Order has possibly been defeated in the Great War. Unfortunately, I hear that the bloodshed from that war has reached the height of a horse's bridle and that Master Ibrahim has been captured. I'm standing by for further instructions. However, I think we can still apprehend any fugitive whom we encounter along the way and bring them into custody while we wait for news."

Traveling up the mountain range to the highest peak, Captain Ragusa and his troops, using far-reaching infrared light devices, picked up on evidence of people together in an encampment. Under thick cover of darkness, they suddenly came upon Ben and Adam scavenging nearby for food. A small scuffle erupted in which both men were captured. Soon, Ruth, Katie, Noah, and Liz were also captured and placed in the custody of the New World Order authorities. They led them back down the mountain range.

"Hang in there, everyone!" Ben urged. "We'll see what comes next."

"Yeah, that's right! Everyone, hang tight. They are taking us to the closest law enforcement agency. That's all," Adam added as he rubbed a small bleed on his hand, no doubt from the scuffle, against his jeans.

Captain Ragusa squinted his eyes at Ben and Adam in the pitch darkness. "Why so impudent! You are in serious trouble with the New World Order authorities. I wouldn't take it lightly."

The captain and his troops slowly led the handcuffed group down the mountain toward final judgment in an antichristian court.

Suddenly, the group and their captors felt the surrounding elements becoming more hostile toward them. Torrential rain and excessively harsh winds rose.

"Take cover!" The captain ordered as heavy hailstones started to fall from the sky.

They and their captive fugitives ran to hunker down under some large rocks to await the outcome.

Chapter 25
Evil's Judgment

As the hailstones seemed to subside, Ben strained to peek out of their hiding place under the large rocks. He squinted and shielded his eyes with his hand. "It looks like daylight again!"

Adam spun around. "You're kidding!"

"You can see for yourself!"

The captain stood and crossed his arms. "We'll be leaving here right now!" he ordered, setting his jaw in defiance. "Let me remind you that you are still in the custody of the New World Order, and I am to escort you back for the justice that awaits you. Now let's go!"

When they all had exited from under the rocks, the captain and his troops cursed loudly. "What gives?" demanded one soldier.

"Yeah!" said another. "Is this light here to blind us? We're not used to this anymore."

Captain Ragusa hissed. "Shut up and walk!" He turned back around and was suddenly confronted by three people in dazzling white before him.

"We have come to escort you and our friends to King Jesus," one of them said.

Captain Ragusa flushed red hot. "What the heck are you talking about?"

"Don't play games. You were just told where you're headed," said another of the three, "You are headed to King Jesus for justice!"

A cheer rose up from the band of fugitives. They all jumped for joy.

"Well, guys, can you believe it? I don't think we have anything to be concerned about anymore." Ben declared. "We've made it through the Great Tribulation without being captured! Messiah Jesus has won, and we're free!"

"You bet!" Adam smiled broadly from ear to ear while he hugged and kissed Katie.

"Do you suppose that we can venture back down this mountain now?" Noah asked, his arms around Liz. "Maybe, Liz, we can now think about getting married!"

Liz elbowed him and giggled, "Oh, you think it'll happen that fast?"

"Uh no! Not so fast!" Ben joked. As emaciated and weak as Ben and his band of five were, they were overjoyed to live under Messiah's reign now. "How awesome to be among the few believers to come out of the Great Tribulation and to meet with Messiah Jesus!" Ben exclaimed and wept tears of joy.

Ruth looked at Ben with relief in her eyes.

"Ben, do you realize we could now begin a family together in the new millennial kingdom?"

Ben howled. "Do I ever!"

Adam and Katie held on to each other arm in arm. "Just think, Adam, we can walk peacefully in broad daylight now without having to look over our shoulders to see if our captors are close behind. The natural world is in divine order," Katie exclaimed.

"You got that right, baby!" Adam responded.

Noah gave Liz a strong hug and passionate kiss. "We're the most blessed, Liz! As the youngest members of our group, we can live longer into the peaceful kingdom the Bible describes as the Millennium."

Ben took a good look around at the three who made up the supernatural representatives from God before them. All at once, he recognized them—John, Evelyn, and Elaine in their new resurrected, celestial bodies! They looked handsome and beautiful, young, healthy, and full of life. They broke into a wide smile at Ben, as they must've also done at Ruth, when suddenly she let out a scream of glee.

"Loo ... Loo ... Look! Look!" she cried out as she frantically pointed in the direction of the three. Adam, Katie, Noah, and Liz turned to take a better look. Wide grins broke out on their faces.

All six quickly ran up to them and embraced them.

"All of you look so amazing!" Ben exclaimed.

"So, you're back here with us! Did you come just to see us?" Katie asked teasing them. "Of course, where else would you obviously go first in the world except to see us?!" Katie inquired and broke out in laughter.

"You don't know how much we missed all of you!" Noah said. "But we knew you were with Jesus and enjoying such joy in your new eternal existence."

"We're definitely jealous!" Adam chimed in. "We see how fabulous you look now without any age, ill health, or handicap. In turn, we must look very sickly to you!"

Liz reached out and hugged Elaine. "I was so sorry for the slip and fall that caused your death."

Elaine smiled wide. "I never knew what hit me. What a blessing that it happened so fast for me, and then I saw Jesus beside me lifting me up with His hand! I loved the immediate peace, love, and joy. My parents came to hug me and hold me again. There are no words to describe that great reunion."

"Death by beheading was especially scary for me to face!" John proclaimed. "My faith was being tested to believe Messiah Jesus would be with me as I faced it—and He was--I was not alone! I just praised Him and felt such peace as I walked up to the executioner. Immediately at the point of execution, I found myself in Jesus's presence and united with Evelyn and other believers I had known. What a reunion of sheer joy for all of us!"

"I know God was with me at the hospital," Evelyn added. "I saw Jesus and felt so much joy, peace, and comfort in letting go of my natural life to join Him. I knew He would be with John, if John were not already with Him. Being immediately in heaven was quite an experience of awe and wonder!"

"We believers who were in heaven before Jesus's current, second coming to earth took part in our wedding to Him as His Church! It was soooo glorious!" Elaine danced about with excitement as she spoke about it. "I never got to experience an earthly wedding, but this heavenly one was beyond my greatest dreams of what a wedding would be like, and it surely was the wedding for me! Right after, we had such a festive wedding cele-bration supper."

"Now we've returned with Jesus to do His work for His new millennial kingdom, and we didn't want to miss seeing all of you first!" John said.

As John finished his statement, Ben caught a glimpse of Elira out of the corner of his eye. He barely recognized her. She looked dark and desolate. Her eyes were empty and expressionless. She looked like a miserable, wretched, and disheveled creature, numb to what was about to happen to her. Duncan was at her side. He resembled some sort of demonic reptile who had handily taken possession of her soul to lead it to hell along with himself. As he held Elira's hand, his eyes emitted an unholy fire, filled with evil, and he hissed at Ben.

"Elira!" Ben called out, but Elira glanced back at him with empty, soulless eyes. Ben was shocked to see her like that and pitied her.

At once, a pronouncement went forth from Christ's new kingdom at Jerusalem, and Duncan and Elira disappeared before Ben's eyes. Ben knew what had just happened. He felt a sharp pain rise in his heart for Elira.

"Is everything all right?" Ruth asked him.

"Yes, everything's all right. I just pity Elira's fate and wish for her own sake she had come to receive Messiah Jesus. You know, although she was not of Jewish origin, her name means in Hebrew, 'the Lord is my light.' I hurt for the fact that the Lord was never accepted by her as her Light, and now she is in eternal darkness and separation from Him forever."

"Yes, wouldn't it have been so wonderful for all unbelievers to accept?" Ruth said.

The rest of the group nodded in agreement.

When John, Evelyn, and Elaine were about to part from the rest of the group to assume their duties for Christ's new kingdom, suddenly Ben's father and mother, Simon and Esther, came up, and along with them, Ruth's mother, Rhoda. Ben dropped to his knees with overwhelming emotion. He wept as he lifted himself up to hug his father and mother once again.

"O...O...Oh how blessed! How blessed it is to hold both of you in my arms again and to kiss you!" Ben exclaimed. "How I missed you so dearly! It hurt so much!"

"I'm so thrilled God answered my prayers for both you and your dad, and we're all together now in the new kingdom of Messiah Jesus! How I missed you, my dear son, but I know you received Jesus and married my best friend Rhoda's daughter, Ruth! How beautiful you both look together!" Esther cried.

Then Esther turned to her daughter-in-law, Ruth, but Ruth already had her arms around her own mother, Rhoda, and Esther joined them.

"Look at us, Rhoda, we're blessed with two children who followed what we taught them!" Esther declared.

"Yes, dear friend, and because of that I am holding my only child, Ruth, again!" Rhoda wept with joy.

"How I missed you, Mom!" Ruth cried.

While this was all happening with the women, Ben continued to hug his father tightly and whispered, "I want you to know how I tried to keep you from the evil being perpetrated on you by that rehabilitation center."

"Son, don't give it another thought," Simon replied. "The best thing you did for me is to pray with me to receive Messiah Jesus in my heart. It all worked out because today I am here with you and your mother! By the way, I'm so glad you never married Elira. Ruth was the girl for you! God gave you a fellow believer who would stick with you for the rest of your life!"

"I know, Dad! I'm so blessed to have her and to have all of you again!"

Soon, the group grew even larger. Adam and Noah's parents joined them and the joyous reunion continued. Adam and Noah's parents were thrilled their two sons, along with their sons' companions, Katie and Liz, made it into the new millennial kingdom—without encountering death—and they could live on in their physical bodies, possibly adding grandchildren to the family.

Esther winked at Rhoda "I'm waiting for grandchildren, aren't you?"

Rhoda put her hand on Esther's shoulder. "No truer words could be spoken right now, Esther!" They both laughed.

Ben put his arm around Ruth. "Hey! Give us a chance! We haven't even gathered at Jerusalem yet!" Wide grins broke out across the entire group.

Chapter 26
The New Kingdom

B en and the group entered Jerusalem. Such a throng of hundreds of thousands of people from not only all over the world, but also from Heaven were there so that Jerusalem couldn't contain all who wanted to enter it. Billions of resurrected believers just watched on from above. *What a wonderful time to be on earth,* he thought. Everywhere joy, peace, and love were evident in everyone. Taking Ruth by the hand, he moved to the center of what was about to take place.

"From here, I can just see King Jesus sitting on His throne."

"Really, Ben? There are so many people here." Ruth tried to lean on Ben to lift herself up to see.

"I think King Jesus is about to speak," Ben noted.

Jesus looked lovingly at the crowd. "Today, I proclaim one thousand years of peace on earth. No more war, crime, or strife on earth. The lion will lie down with the lamb and all instruments of war will be made into instruments for farming the earth. Those who have followed the Antichrist and his False Prophet have already met their fate in the lake that burns with fire forever. Now it's time for the Destroyer, Satan himself, to be bound for these one thousand years!"

Jesus then gazed up into the sky as an angel came down from God to earth to seize the Devil, known as the Dragon or Serpent, and bind him. By the command of Jesus, he was thrown into the Abyss for a thousand years where he could no longer deceive the earth's people.

Ben and the group heard ceremonial trumpets sounding. Jesus spoke again. "Now the time has come for Me to set up My new earthly kingdom at Jerusalem. Here, all natural and super-natural believers will gather to worship Me. The Jewish believers who had been hidden away by My Father from the Antichrist during the Great Tribulation have now come to know Me as their true Messiah. I have freed them from their hiding place My Father appointed for them during that time. I now take My rightful place as head of the entire government of earth to reign without opposition." Countless cheers followed as Christ sat on His throne and the crowd worshiped Him.

THE PEOPLE of earth left to go about their new lives in peace with one another. Even the animal kingdom was at peace. There was no more war. Literally, the prophetic words of Scripture came to pass—lions were seen lying down with lambs and the two playing together in a field. No wild animal would prey upon a natural human being or another animal.

Ben came out of the home which he and Ruth now shared together back in Chillicothe Falls to take in the morning air. *How amazing*, he thought, *to be with Ruth*.

He stepped back into the home while Ruth fixed breakfast for them. "Ruth, would you like to start our family soon?"

Ruth handed him his breakfast, a plate of scrambled eggs,

toast, and hash browns. "Ben, honey, I was just about to bring that subject up myself. I will have to go check with a doctor to be sure, but I think that family we want is already on the way!"

Ben almost choked on his eggs. "What...What did you say?"

"I said I think our family is already on the way!"

Ben rose from the breakfast table and swept Ruth up in his arms. "This is the third greatest day of my life: the first was when I prayed to ask Jesus into my life; the second was when I married you; and the third is to hear we're going to have a baby!"

"Well, let's make sure with the doctor first, and then we'll let everyone know."

"Yeah! Oh, baby, baby!" Ben wouldn't let up on his embrace of Ruth.

Meanwhile, Adam and Katie and Noah and Liz also settled back in Salisburg. Adam and Noah reestablished the church their father and mother had pastored before The Disappearance. Adam became the lead pastor and Noah his assistant. It soon grew as not only the two of them and their families became a part of it, but also Ben, Ruth, and others. The church became vastly involved in the community and represented in city government. In fact, Ben and Ruth now held positions in place of Duncan and Elira. "How ironic!" Ben mused. "How every-thing had circled back to its proper place—a place of justice, uprightness, wisdom, understanding, peace, and protection."

John, Evelyn, and Elaine went to work in the new millennial government in Chillicothe Falls, holding the administration of its policies at the city level.

In time, Ruth gave birth to a daughter, which she named in Hebrew, "Hadassah," meaning "Esther" in honor of Ben's mother. Ben was so proud to be a father.

"You know, Ruth, our child will live long into the millennial kingdom. Scripture tells us that the length of natural life will be like the patriarchs of the Old Testament. A person only one hundred years old will still be considered a child, and those that are one thousand years old will have lived a full, natural life."

"For sure, Ben, we have a new kingdom, and our child will have a wonderful opportunity to experience many good things in her long lifetime of nearly a thousand years! What a blessing for her and for us!"

Ben and Ruth's immediate family entered the hospital room to meet Hadassah for the first time.

"She has your eyes and nose, Ruth!" Esther declared.

"She has Ben's hair color and face," Rhoda exclaimed.

"Frankly, I think she looks more like me!" Simon teased.

"Oh, stop it!" Ruth countered. "She's just perfect, and Ben and I are so blessed to have her!"

Ben couldn't stop grinning from ear to ear. "I would say so!"

Soon Adam, Katie, Noah, and Liz walked in. They were delighted to come see the newest addition to the Goldberg family. Katie herself was six months pregnant, and she and Adam were excited to welcome their first child too.

"What a precious and beautiful baby!" Katie proclaimed. "Congratulations to you both. Praise the Lord Who brought about this blessing for you."

"We're so ecstatic to see Hadassah!" Adam added.

"Would you like to hold her?" Ruth asked.

"Oh! I don't know if I should. She is so small and fragile," Adam responded.

"Don't be silly," Katie replied. "You'll be holding your own baby soon, and you could use the practice!" She laughed and then said to Ruth, "I would love to hold Hadassah."

"Here you go!" Ruth gently placed Hadassah in Katie's arms.

Katie blushed with delight. She held Hadassah and kept looking at the amazing wonder of human life that could take place after so much death and destruction during the Tribulation.

Simon, Esther, and Rhoda smiled wide.

"God has brought about life, love, and peace again!" Esther declared. "What a blessing for this planet and its people."

"Yes," Rhoda added. "We are now grateful participants in Jesus's new kingdom!"

"Well," Simon said. "I also heard that we will be participating in another new joy—the wedding of Noah and Liz next month!"

"Yes, definitely!" Noah replied. "Finally, Liz and I will be married at the church my father began. My brother, Adam, will officiate. We're so looking forward to it."

"All of us are too!" Ben assured him. "We've been waiting a long time to see you both married."

"We've been so busy preparing for it. We feel so endowed with God's favor," Liz said. "Think of it—married at the beginning of the Lord's millennial kingdom!"

"Yes indeed!" Adam answered. "Our mother and father will be there, and our dad will give the closing benediction over Noah and Liz."

"Just wonderful!" Ruth exclaimed.

Chapter 27
The Promised Future

The following month, the rather large congregation of Adam and Noah's church, named again Maranatha Christian Fellowship, came together for Noah's and Liz's wedding. The church's name was certainly appropriate now more than before because of its meaning in the ancient Aramaic language: "The Lord has come." The church was decorated completely in white. The altar was filled with white flowers and a long, white runner was placed down the center aisle.

Liz had dressed in a beautiful stark-white bridal dress with a cathedral train. It was made of satin, pearl-colored beads, and white and clear sequins. Her hair was swept up and dressed in sequin and pearl applique. She looked stunning. "This is what I wanted!" she uttered to herself. "Thank you, dear Jesus, for this blessing! Couldn't have had this during that very dark time You took us through!"

Noah was dressed in a tailored black suit with a white sprig of flowers in his lapel. He had received an attractive haircut for the occasion from one of the town barbers. Adam was standing at the altar with Noah who stood before Adam and to his left side.

In the congregation were Ben, Ruth, Rhoda, Simon, Esther, John, Evelyn, Elaine, Liz's mom, and Adam's parents. The church was literally packed with people both in the natural and supernatural state.

Finally, Liz and her dad showed at the back of the church. He escorted her down the aisle as everyone stood and turned to look at the bride. Liz was beaming from ear to ear and focused her eyes forward only at Noah. As she came closer to him, he broke into a warm, broad smile. When Liz and her dad got to the altar, her dad turned and gave her a kiss, and placed her hand in Noah's. *Just think! My dad's here to do this. Wow! So wonderful!* Liz rejoiced in her heart.

Everyone in the congregation sat down, and Adam began the ceremony. The presence of God's Holy Spirit was so abundantly felt that overwhelming love and joy permeated the entire church. Noah and Liz pledged their lives to one another in marriage, and it was as if the Lord Jesus Himself shone His approval and blessing on them. *I so love You, Jesus, and I so love my husband, Noah! Thanks, Lord!* she thought to herself.

At the end of the ceremony, Noah kissed his bride, and Noah's dad gave the final benediction over the newlyweds. After the ceremony, there was celebration, dancing, and music far into the night. Liz pondered--*I wonder if this is anything like Jesus's wedding was to His church in Heaven.*

~

FOR THEIR HONEYMOON, Noah and Liz traveled to Jerusalem. There they paid homage to Jesus. Families would travel there yearly to honor Him at the seat of His millennial kingdom. The light of His presence spread throughout the city, and everyone visiting could see Him.

When Noah and Liz came before Jesus, they bowed low and thanked Him for their eternal life, salvation, and their marriage to each other. They also brought a tribute from their families. The Lord Jesus gazed lovingly into their faces and pronounced a blessing over them and their posterity.

When Noah and Liz were about to return home, Jesus spoke to them personally and said, "I commend you to continue the work of gospel ministry to all the new generations of children who will be born naturally. Although all those who entered the Millennium were believers, the decision for Me will still need to be made in the hearts of each new natural generation."

As a parting pronouncement to the couple, Jesus looked intently at all the people in Jerusalem, and at Noah and Liz, too, and spoke the same words He had at the end of His first coming, "Behold I am with you always, even to the close of the age."

In that very moment, Noah and Liz's hearts swelled with eternal joy.

About the Author

Dr. Lily Corsello is a doctoral-level licensed mental health Counselor with over forty years of experience working with clients in educational, denominational, church, and private practice settings. She has been a pastor and church staff minister. She has also been a church denominational consultant for singles ministry. She has been counselor and president of her own counseling practice, In Spirit and In Truth Counseling Services.

Dr. Corsello holds a doctor of ministry in counseling from Luther Rice Seminary, a master of religious education from Southwestern Baptist Theological Seminary, a master of education in guidance and counseling from Florida Atlantic University, and a bachelor of arts from Florida State University.

Dr. Corsello is listed in *Who's Who in the World*, *Who's Who of American Women*, *Who's Who in Medicine and Healthcare*, *Who's Who in Education*, and *Who's Who in the South and Southwest*. She has published poetry, articles, and self-help books.

She lives with her husband, their two dogs, and their parrot in the Florida Keys, and she has one adult daughter studying to become a medical doctor.

To follow Dr. Lily Corsello, her blog, and the other books and articles she has authored, visit:
www.drlilycorsello.com